Just call it

REDEMPTION

Carl Lawrence

p107 Bich Quong

OAKTARA
WATERFORD, VIRGINIA

Just Call It Redemption

Published in the U.S. by:
OakTara Publishers
P.O. Box 8
Waterford, VA 20197

Visit OakTara at
www.oaktara.com

Cover design by David LaPlaca/debest design co.

ISBN: 978-1-60290-145-2

To

Linda, Shannon,

Sean, Crystal, Levi,

1-5-09

Reagan, and Luke + to

Dick + Linda Johnson,
in grateful appreciation for your years of "LOGOS" friendship — + your examples of how to communicate the character of our Lord Jesus Christ through thick + thin —
~~[illegible]~~ —

In His love,

[signature]

Foreword

There is a strange phenomenon in the United States today relating to Christian books. One can report on some great tragedy or persecution or man's inhumanity to man, and people will read it, or hear it from the pulpit, and before the chords of the last hymn have faded, someone will say, just loud enough for everyone to hear, except the writer/speaker, "Well, I'm sure much of it is exaggeration," or "Well, you can't believe everything he says." However, if the same stories are put in a novel, people believe every word of it.

Be advised that as you read this book, there may be characters you are certain you recognize, or events you think you can identify, but don't sweat it: 'tis only a novel.

One

Henrique Mugabe froze at the harsh crunch of policemen's boots on cinder and a dog beginning to howl. Just then a young boy dashed toward the bamboo forest, but tripped and fell across the rail tracks, crying out as the cinders cut into his naked body.

Instantly, a guard and a policeman were on the boy. The guard held the snapping dog while the policeman beat the bleeding boy's back with the bamboo length of his search mirror. When the boy rolled onto his side to dodge the blows, he wrenched the mirror from the pole. The policeman, now furious, struck him harder.

The boy curled into a fetal position. "Please, don't beat me more!" His cry mingled with the policeman's cursing threats.

The guard moved his dog forward until the animal's bared teeth were inches from the boy's face. "Get out of here, and don't come back!" He picked up the shattered mirror he used to check for men hiding under railcars. "That's for the mirror," he yelled, and kicked the boy one last time in the groin.

The two men walked away, pulling the dog with them. They had done their duty and now they could get a cold drink and relax until the next man or boy tried to get a free ride to look for work.

Mugabe stood erect, straddling one rail of the train track, callused fists clenched at his stocky side. He watched the boy struggle to get up and hobble across the tracks back into the forest, making no eye contact with Mugabe. Sweat ran down Mugabe's wide forehead and around his broad flared nostrils. The taste of salt mingled with anger and fear. Anger, knowing the boy would soon need to try again, desperate, like so many, to smuggle himself into South Africa for a job to keep his family from starving. And fear, that in a few hours he could be the next Mozambican caught and beaten.

Eric Murphy blew an impatient wisp of air through his thousands of dollars' worth of orthodontia while looking at his Accutron, a graduation gift. Chicago's O'Hare Airport always seemed to run late. At least the air-conditioned lobby was a relief from the muggy fall air outside where his father had dropped him off. His line to the ticket counter was not moving. He threw back his shoulders restlessly, adding an inch or so to his athletic frame, chiseled by his years on the university swim team.

In front of him a young father stood with his two children. The girl held her father's hand tightly, pleading, "Daddy, please come home with us?" The man looked straight ahead while the girl persevered, "Mommy really does love you."

People standing nearby carefully looked away.

The boy took his father's other hand. "We'll be good. We won't make you mad."

"Daddy, why can't you live with Mommy and us?" The girl's lips trembled.

"Next," said the ticket agent. The father pushed the children's luggage to the counter, looking thankful to be rescued.

Murphy wondered how many times this scene would be enacted at this airport before this day was over: a father or mother sending their children back to a one-parent home. He thought of the boys he and his buddies had befriended. Those kids had not known what to do with their anger over being abandoned by their fathers. Playing basketball with them, taking them to the lake, couldn't make up for their not having a father, but it was all he and his friends had known to do. Couldn't this father see what he was doing, Murphy fumed.

The father and his two children left for the departure gate. As Murphy handed his ticket to the agent, he pondered the many ways children were abused, and wondered what price this fatherless generation would pay when those children became adults.

It's so easy for me to judge and blame, to get angry for the children—but so hard to love the father, Lord. I need help with this anger. Would you send someone to teach me compassion?

What Murphy didn't know is that the answer to his prayer was on its way.

As the naked boy disappeared into the forest that bordered the railway yard, Mugabe walked with feigned casualness towards the border town depot.

A crowd of people sat in the hot sun, hearing the hum of air conditioners, a painful reminder that the "Whites Only" sign above a door was a line of separation they dared not even attempt to erase. All the men, women, and children, including Mugabe, had one thing in common: Their life was a funeral dirge of legislated and practiced maliciousness, which each of them had patiently endured as though it was their fate.

The waiting room for "Colored" was packed with people. He pushed his way through the door as part of his act of belonging there. He immediately put his hand over his mouth and nose, trying to block the rancid, sweat-filled, stale air, heated by the tin roof absorbing the hot jungle sun.

The crowd shouted, pushed, and shoved, trying to get within reading distance of a large blackboard. The train arrivals and departures were written in chalk. Groans resounded as the attendant erased an arrival or departure time and put in the new. One train was four hours late, one six, another cancelled altogether. He pretended to be angered at the change like the rest, though he knew his train was already in the freight yard. With many others, he made his way outside, hoping for some fresh air.

Having no luggage, except a small package wrapped in a white cloth, he worried he might be watched more carefully by the border police if he stood off by himself. He needed to be surrounded by those who were traveling legally.

He wound his way through the crowd of women balancing on their heads heavy blanket-wrapped loads, with children tied to their backs while dragging another. The men ambled behind, arms empty.

Several hundred people sat on the ground, women feeding their children while men slept or gambled.

Stepping around crying children, Mugabe casually made his way to where a group of young men were sitting in a circle gambling. One opened a suitcase and put a pair of shoes in the middle of the circle. He rolled the dice, and walked away—barefoot.

Mugabe squatted next to the gamblers, as though he belonged; though he hated gambling and what it did to their villages. It was one thing to walk away barefoot; it was another to walk home to a family with no food and no money, both lost in the thoughtless and selfish roll of the dice.

He leaned against the building while carefully holding his precious cargo against his stomach. He could feel the vibration of the air conditioners as the sun continued to remind him of his station in life. The sun burned his bare head, while resentment burned his soul.

After three hundred years the racial separation probably would not change before the next train came in, so he let his mind be filled with the soft body of his wife, Diolinda. They'd only had one night together as husband and wife when they heard about the crackdown on border crossings. Diolinda had urged him to not worry about her, but only himself as he made the dangerous trip to Praetoria while he still could.

As he had walked the fifteen miles to Komatipoert, he had replayed in his mind the first time he had seen her—hoeing in the field, fine practice for being a good wife. It took him several weeks to "accidentally" be in the same place in the market where he knew she would be on a Saturday.

One market day, while she sorted through potatoes, he contrived to be helpful, and blurted her name, "Diolinda," for the first time in her presence. She blushed deeply and continued sorting potatoes. His hand touched hers, as if by accident. Working at not stuttering, Mugabe continued, "You make me feel like our volcano. I look peaceful on the outside, but I'm ready to explode. Soon my love will erupt for all to see."

Both Diolinda and Mugabe had been given away by their parents when children, but what had once been a burden, now became a gift.

They both worked for people with whom they had no family ties, who rejoiced they were to be married. The village supported their budding love and dreams of Bible school, and gave their approval.

There was one thing their society demanded however. Though there would be no "bride price," there was the matter of a *beja* or hoe, which was a symbol of planting and nurturing seed and soil, of prospering and multiplying.

This *beja* had to be a hand-made hoe, never to be used in the fields, but kept in their home. On the wedding day, the groom presented it to the bride, to be hung on the wall of their home. Several village elders helped Mugabe with everything from cutting the perfect branch for the *beja*, to presenting it at the marriage ceremony.

His disappointment over leaving his wife so soon after their marriage, and his fear of being caught riding the rail was temporarily relieved as he thought of the *beja* hanging on the wall of the hut they called home, and of the one night they had spent together.

Making sure he was not being watched, Mugabe carefully undid one button of his shirt. His heart ached as he touched the strips of material that would tie him to the railcar, carefully wrapped round his torso, hidden by his shirt and trousers.

Tears crept into his eyes, remembering that just hours ago, those precious strips of cloth were his wife's woven wedding garment. They were now her wedding gift to him, so that he might use them to accomplish what they were both sure the Lord wanted him to do.

He ran his finger over the wide cloth strips one more time and then carefully buttoned his shirt, making sure no one was watching. He firmly grasped his precious package, wrapped with more of Diolinda's wedding garment. To some it would only be a book, but to Mugabe, his Bible was his most precious possession.

The broken family disappeared from Murphy's sight like a snowflake in a Chicago snowstorm, but not from his mind.

To distract himself, he searched out the array of electronic screens announcing arrivals and departures. His flight would depart in one hour, right on schedule. He accepted as normal, or more explicitly his right, the cool air of the terminal air conditioning, the merchandise kiosks, and the various food stalls that offered varieties of excesses from Italian to Mexican. He made his way to a branch of his favorite haunt to find a book. There were hundreds of choices. What did he feel like reading? It was a four-hour trip to Los Angeles. He needed something to keep his mind occupied. He was in the mood for surrealism. He picked a book, and without looking at the price, handed a clerk a twenty-dollar bill, telling him to keep the change. He made his way to his gate. He had thirty minutes before the plane loaded.

He found a vacant seat and began to read a Stephen King novel.

Next to his Bible, Mugabe's most precious material possession was a wristwatch given to him by a young Canadian just before he was murdered in his village. A watch that actually ran set one apart as being above the common laborer, a recognizable symbol of importance. Mugabe checked the time, and then noticed a uniformed policeman looking directly at him. He quickly pulled his shirtsleeve down. The policeman walked away.

Afraid he had been noticed, Mugabe attempted to be nonchalant by sitting and leaning against the building. As he sweated, the hum of the air conditioner aggravated his sense of injustice over "whites only" considered as having a soul. As he often did when he needed to calm himself, he practiced remembering who he was.

He was pure Shona, proud that no foreign blood flowed through his veins. Shona were bushmen bow hunters who, with poison-tipped arrows, could bring down the fastest animals in Mozambique. However, they could not stop the mosquitoes and the Tsetse flies, which carried the dreaded "sleeping sickness" from tribe to tribe, affecting people and livestock. The disease had taken a heavy toll on his family.

There was also another enemy—the plague colonialism. In 1498, when Vasco de la Gama arrived on the coast of Mozambique on his way to India, the layover was fatal to his people. Nine years later, more Portuguese arrived and took control of the Arab Muslim settlements on the coast. For four and a half centuries, the Portuguese considered Mugabe's people to be animals without souls, bodies to sweat and toil so white men back in their faraway land could live in luxury while worshiping the God who had made man "in his image"—presumably white and elite.

In 1886, another plague hit Mugabe's people: Greed for gold. Mountains of gold, supposedly once part of King Solomon's mines, were discovered in neighboring South Africa. For the Shona, greed was as deadly as a Tsetse fly.

Portugal transported gold from South Africa by train to ports in Mozambique, where it could be shipped throughout the world. The same railcars that brought the gold were used to send laborers back to the mines. It was slavery with a twist. The Portuguese lined their pockets with the largesse from the mines, and a "passport fee" for each Mozambican worker. The fee was taken from the laborer's wages the South African government sent to officials in Mozambique, who then credited the laborers with whatever was left.

By 1892, more than 25,000 of Mugabe's people had left behind their families, their language, and their culture. To men used to working with a hoe, dangerous machinery maimed and killed. Living conditions tore at the soul as well as the body, creating an atmosphere for degeneration. Men had to pay for use of a bed in large dormitories, each bed being used by several men on different shifts.

When not working, they were gambling, drinking, and taking advantage of the "amenities" that mine managers imported to satisfy their lusts. A new urban culture developed around the mines, so that when years later the mines began to close, the depraved culture re-settled in the ghettos of South Africa....

Mugabe awakened with a start as someone stepped on his leg. A boy apologized as an older woman grabbed his hand, scolding him, while leading him past the depot.

The crowds were thinning out. Mugabe jumped up, suddenly feeling vulnerable. He looked at his watch and knew it was time to begin the most dangerous undertaking of his life.

Attempting in vain to concentrate on his book, Murphy finally turned down the corner of the page and gave up. He would finish it on the plane, where noisy little brats would not be tripping over his feet. He looked at his watch. They should be calling his flight in a few moments.

He leaned his head back, closed his eyes, comfortable, anticipating his future.

Murphy's family, like most of his friends, lived in the suburbs, with a two-car garage, both spaces occupied. The economy was fluctuating, but there was no crash on the horizon. Unemployment, though increasing, was manageable.

Murphy belonged to what the wise and sometimes omnipotent social scientists dubbed "Generation X." Some who did not carry the guru mantle called them other names, like "the revenge of the sixties" or "Berkeley's illegitimate children."

Murphy's generation was plagued by word merchants. Struggles in the mainstream of public thought revolved around feminism, abortion, gay rights, and homelessness. Phrases like "drug use among high school students," "the non-absolute of absolute," loss of values," and an active absurdity, "political correctness," filled the airwaves, as well as the editorial pages where the Brahmins waxed eloquent on all the news that was fit to print. These phrases were repeated so often they lost their meaning and became one more linguistic reflex.

The nuclear family was suffering in a nation losing its traditional mooring in the faith and morals of a Judeo-Christian culture. The deterioration was showing itself in the acceptance of one-parent families, child abuse, same-sex partners, co-habitation, and uncontrolled violence, especially among the young. Grandparents were leaving their grandchildren to a latch-key existence as they sold their family homes, the only anchor many families had, to buy a home on wheels and head south. A people once set apart as the world's "light on a hill" was now becoming a candle on a bog in a swamp.

But Murphy wasn't thinking about these things. He, like so many of his generation, for the moment at least, was sound asleep.

Two

Mugabe headed toward the freight yards. He swaggered a bit, softly whistling to appear disinterested in his surroundings.

He was careful not to betray the turmoil in his gut, while straining to make mental notes as to where each empty car was located. There would be no more rehearsals. This time it was success or failure, perhaps life or death.

Taking a deep breath, he cut across several of the rail tracks, heading for a row of empty cars attached to an engine. Steam drifted between the wheels, indicating it was going somewhere, and soon.

He realized he was walking where the naked boy was chased earlier in the day. His fear returned, nearly propelling him around so that he could run into the forest and safety, like the naked boy. He froze, paralyzed, as he heard a familiar sound: the crunch of a policeman's boot on the cinders.

"Hello there, could you tell me the time?"

Mugabe turned, and standing behind him, smiling, was the police officer who had made eye contact earlier in the day. Mugabe lifted his sleeve, looked at the watch, and timorously gave the policeman the time.

The policeman walked up closer. "That's a very nice watch." He took hold of Mugabe's arm. "I've always wanted a watch. Especially one like that, made in America."

Mugabe's heart sank. He regretfully slid the watch off his arm and gave it to the policeman. The policeman, with obvious pleasure, placed it on his own wrist.

Still looking at the watch the policeman spoke, "I'm in charge of the men and the dogs that make sure no one crawls under the freight cars for a free ride."

Mugabe, panicking, took a step towards the forest.

"You're going the wrong way." The policeman pointed to the steaming engine. As he walked away, he looked back at Mugabe and smiled. "I'm going to buy the men a beer. They've had a busy day." So that Mugabe would not misunderstand, he added, "Along with their dogs and mirrors."

Looking at the watch again, he said, "I think I'll buy them a *couple* of beers." He then looked directly at Mugabe and said, "That train leaves in a half hour. You'd better hurry."

Through tears of joy and shame, asking the Lord to forgive him for his fears, Mugabe hurried to the cars. He quickly stripped to the waist, to unwrap layers of strips of cloth. He slid down onto his back, ignoring the cinders. During his many rehearsals under a truck in his village, he had not thought about the cinders cutting through his shirt. He looped one length of cloth over steel rods on the bottom of the freight car, then tied the two ends together, making a sling. He tied three other slings in a row wherever there was a rod. Rolling over, he scooted his body, head first through the tunnel of cradles, and finally hung his feet over the last sling, just in time.

He could hear the cars ahead of him as they began to move. Just as the one he was under jolted, he grabbed his Bible from the ground and firmly tucked it against his chest.

At last Mugabe and his precious book were on their way to Bible school. One day he would return from South Africa to his own people and continue the ministry of the young Canadian missionary—the one who gave his Bible and watch to Mugabe, and his life to Mugabe's people.

Startled awake by movement around him, Murphy saw his flight had almost finished boarding. His book and carry-on in hand, he boarded the plane. He found his seat but couldn't find room to store his carry-on bag. The stewardess told him the overhead bins were full. He would need to stow it under the seat in front of him. A lady was already settled in the aisle seat. She glared as he smiled and nodded towards his window seat. She stood up, ever so reluctantly, and stepped into the aisle so Murphy could slide in his bag. While getting seated, his seatmate rolled her eyes, registering her displeasure at being disturbed. Murphy mumbled an insincere apology.

After a few minutes of squirming, he found a comfortable position. The stewardess gave her safety speech, in case they decided to plow up a bit of land in Nebraska.

Murphy tried to relax. He looked out the window as the plane rolled towards the runway. He tried reading. His attention to his book was interrupted by the pilot's voice apologizing for the delay due to the heavy traffic. His announcement that they hoped to soon be airborne did nothing to encourage Murphy and the other passengers, including his seatmate who hissed some four-letter words.

Murphy returned to his book, knowing this could be a long wait. After all, this was O'Hare. Disgruntled, he set his book on his lap. As he listened to his seatmate cursing her fate that of all the flights available she had to pick this one, guilt wafted over him. It was something he had experienced more often these last few months. Annoyed by his seatmate's testiness, he had to admit his own irritability was only different in the way it was being expressed. The guilt turned to shame.

Sorry, Lord. This is no attitude for a preacher boy on his way to seminary.

Three

The train lurched forward with a painful jolt, sliding Mugabe forward. It was a warning of things to come. He moaned as he realized this was as comfortable as it was going to get. He congratulated himself on the inspiration to place one sandal across his crotch and the other on his chest so he had a place to shift his weight without having the harness cut into his skin. Clasping his crossed arms, he lay his head on them. He counted railway ties passing beneath him until they became a blur.

Mugabe wanted to distract his thinking from his body and its discomfort. Again he practiced remembering his country's history. He thought about his tribe's experiences two centuries before when rounded up by Muslim merchants, torn from their roots and sold to the highest bidder as slaves to be shipped around the world. Complete villages—men, women, and children—became human cargo, stuffed into disease-ridden holds of ships.

Slavery was a disease that permeated every part of society, with Christians being no exception. Long after slave trade was illegal, it still continued, if in a less barbaric fashion. But Mugabe knew society hadn't changed that much. In the eleventh century, Anselm of the Roman Catholic Church officially declared that "children born to slaves should follow the status of the past." Mugabe also knew that Thomas Aquinas, who was later declared a saint, justified slavery as the inescapable consequences of Adam and Eve's original sin.

Foreign missionaries of many denominations sighed while acknowledging slavery as a "barbarous misfortune," confident it no longer existed to any measurable degree. Certainly not in their compounds, as they asked their servants for "more tea, please."

Mugabe stirred in his cradle. He could find no comfort for his body, but his soul found some relief in knowing one man had stepped in and, at least for his people, changed their world. David Livingston used his influence to petition the British government to stop this terrible satanic destruction of an entire race. He pricked the conscience of British legislators and gained the attention of John Wesley. Together they took to the streets of London. Joined by thousands of British, they marched on government offices, and in 1878 slavery was abolished.

Mugabe smiled, remembering one of his heroes, someone he wanted to emulate. This man was born into a family of slave traders rather than slaves. In different centuries, but with equal conviction, they both were converted and became slaves for Jesus Christ.

Though his discomfort was now escalating to pain, Mugabe smiled as he let his hands hang down, careful to not touch the rails flashing by. He began to sing the words of his brother in Christ, John Newton:

"Amazing grace, how sweet the sound,
That saved a wretch like me.
I once was lost, but now am found
Was blind but now I see."

Murphy's plane was finally airborne. His depressing, convicting thoughts were also lifted as he told himself they would be dealt with as part of his seminary training.

Cruising speed was reached, and passengers were invited to move about the cabin if they wished. Then drinks were offered. Those ordered by his seatmate did little to cheer her but did put her to sleep. Murphy put his seat back and tried again to read. After a few more pages he decided that maybe he wasn't a Stephen King fan after all.

Taking earphones from the seat pocket, he flipped through several music channels. Finding what he wanted, he leaned back into his pillow, the lyrics consoling him:

You've got to know when to hold 'em,
Know when to fold 'em, know when to...

Four

Through many dangers, toil and snares…

The words came slow, as Mugabe reached deep into his gut to pull them out.

I have already come…

What is the difference between this and a slave ship, Lord? Let them throw me overboard! But there was only sporadic words, between vomiting and prayers for mercy.

'Twas grace that brought me safe thus far…

His body pulsated with excruciating pain—like lions tearing his flesh. The seconds were like minutes, and the minutes like hours as the strips of cloth rubbed his skin raw. He saw several pieces of cloth dangling. How many more would break before he fell under the rushing train. To die would be relief. No, for what would happen to his new wife? Would the next jolt break his cradle, dropping him to the ground? In hours his body would be torn apart and scattered by wild animals. No one would know what had really happened to him.

He was certain joints were separating, only held together by tearing muscles. He couldn't last much longer. *Come quickly, Lord Jesus.* He let his moans grow, masked by the rattling rails. His body and soul's stress found some relief in the flow of tears.

Accepting his fate, the pain lessened, though still excruciating, and peace settled over him. His body gave up, and the clickety-clack of the train wheels became the rhythm of drums at his funeral procession.

Was the cadence of the drum slowing? The funeral over?

The train slowed down, then stopped. Was this heaven? Opening his eyes, he doubted there were railway tracks in heaven.

It was still dark. His friends back home, who had made this journey before and survived, had told him that once the train stopped, to look for the bright lights. It wasn't that easy.

He nearly passed out from pain as he struggled to pull his legs out of his harness. As he did so, the final cloth that cradled his abdomen broke. His body fell to the ground.

He lay still for a moment before rolling over and crawling out from under the railcar. Sitting up, he immediately vomited. He'd had nothing to eat since the day before. The strain of regurgitating accentuated the damage done to his body. Finally standing, he leaned against the side of the car. Again he vomited, but ignored it as he took stock of himself. Most of the buttons on his shirt were gone and the zipper on his pants was torn apart, exposing his privates.

The sandal he had placed against his abdomen was gone. He looked under the car. It was not there.

My Bible! He reached inside his shirt. It was still there*. Thank you, Lord. We're both here.* Straightening his pants and shirt as best he could, he put his Bible back inside his shirt. How to keep his pants up? Getting on one knee, he tore one of the strips of cloth from under the rail and wrapped it around his pants. He now had a belt, but still only one sandal. He kicked it off and, barefooted, headed for the bright lights of the train depot. It was there Dr. James was to meet him.

Would Dr. James recognize this dirty, barefoot, disheveled man with a bloodstained shirt and a white rag holding up his pants?

He had a couple of hours until daylight arrived and the train from Maputo. He was told the train yard was safe, but the closer you got to the depot, the more careful you had to be. Anybody that looked like a customs agent must be avoided at all costs.

His friends had told him to look for platform four, and act like he was waiting for a passenger. The closer he got to the depot, the more conspicuous he felt. He took his Bible from under his shirt and held it over his exposed crotch. He gave up trying to cover the bloodstains that had been seeping through his shirt.

As the sun rose, the heat felt good on his broken body.

He saw several policemen, but they paid no attention to him. He looked like any one of those who end up at train yards having been mugged or injured in a drunken brawl.

He had accomplished his mission. He had successfully sneaked into South Africa, though it was illegal. He felt more relief than joy. He had made the right decision, hadn't he? What would he be doing if he were back in Mozambique now? Though he had only been home one morning since his marriage, he was certain his wife would have been feeding him breakfast.

His hungry thoughts were interrupted by a voice over a loudspeaker, "Train number 26 from Maputo now arriving on track four."

People moved forward as the train pulled in. Several passenger cars carrying whites went by first, followed by several more for blacks. As the train came to a halt, a small truck pulled up. Men in uniform jumped down and headed for the train.. Fear swept Mugabe's pain aside.

The wait seemed forever as the armed immigration officers went through the train cars carrying black passengers, checking passports and visas. Mugabe had neither of these. The whites had already been checked and were on their way. There were shouts of welcome as loved ones entered the arms of those waiting for them.

Police escorted several passengers off the last car into a waiting truck covered with chicken wire. These were the passengers who had entered illegally or did not have the proper papers.

There were only a few people around when the immigration officers came off the train. As they headed for their truck, one stared through the fence directly at Mugabe. He was now the only person left. The policeman said something to one of the agents who stepped around the fence and walked toward Mugabe.

He froze in place. All this, and now instead of Bible school, two years of forced labor at the mines?

He was almost ready to go quietly, to confess he had no papers, that he was an illegal. Instead, when the agent was only a few feet away, Mugabe heard the voice of Dr. James. "It's alright, Officer, he's with me."

The officer paused for a second, looked at Mugabe, and then at the white man dressed in a light suit. For once apartheid was Mugabe's friend. Not even policemen challenged the authority of a well-dressed, official-looking white man.

The policemen walked away. Dr. James, hiding his sympathy for the tattered man, said, "I'm parked in this direction. Come, we'll get your luggage."

Mugabe held up his Bible, "This is all I have."

Dr. James Graham put his arm on Mugabe's shoulder. Mugabe felt no pain. "Come, brother,' he said with a smile, "Let's go. You look like you've been on a two-week bender with the devil's juice. What did you do—ride underneath that thing?"

Mugabe's smile had returned as he replied, "Well, not this one, but you are close."

Together they walked toward Dr. James's car. Mugabe had arrived and he had all he needed: the arm of a true brother to guide him, and his Bible. He was ready to become a real preacher.

Through many dangers, toils and snares,
I have already come!
'Tis grace hath brought me safe thus far,
And grace will lead me home.

Murphy awakened with a start. A stewardess was smiling at him, requesting he let his tray down so she could serve him lunch, or a reasonable facsimile thereof. He left it untouched.

He put on the earphones again and turned the channel button on his armrest. Having heard enough nasal twang, he stopped the dial at a rather piercing female voice. "Love is like a river, drowning every need…"

Two weeks before, he'd broken up with the love of his life. Or was it the other way round? His male ego wouldn't admit that anyone would want to spurn his affection, let alone be robbed of his company.

Her reason was simple. She wanted to "explore the universe." It was a universe that didn't have room for a seminary student on his way to California.

In reality, love is not so much like a river, but more like a swamp: water going nowhere, stagnating, creating a breeding ground for some disease-carrying bug.

Last week, while attending a movie with his brother, Murphy saw her a few rows in front of them with one of the guys he could never stand, a real dork. What in the world did she ever see in him? It was a horrible movie, immature and irrelevant, just like the dude who was sharing popcorn with his girlfriend. *Oh well, every swamp has a few alligators. That's life.*

His soiree of self-pity was cut short by the announcement that they'd be arriving in Los Angeles in 20 minutes. Looking at his watch, Murphy thought it was about time since they were over two hours late. Being a pessimist, though he called himself a realist, he wondered if the driver from the seminary would wait for him. If not, what would he do?

He could always call Uncle Bjorn. After all, his uncle was the one most responsible for Murphy's going to seminary.

But it was Saturday. As a pastor, Uncle Bjorn might be doing a wedding, or a funeral. He might even be out enjoying himself.

When the plane doors opened, Murphy impatiently waited for his seatmate to rise. Standing up at last, he saw an elderly lady behind him attempting to lift a heavy shoulder bag. Murphy asked if he could help. She smiled, so he put it on his shoulder, saying, "I promise to give it back when we get to the lobby."

"Bless you," she said, making her way down the crowded aisle.

In the lobby, Murphy was handing the bag to her when three children ran towards her with outstretched arms, crying excitedly, "Grandma, Grandma!"

The children's father and mother caught up with them, joining the group hug and laughter. "Grandma" graciously thanked Murphy. *Maybe,* thought Murphy, *there is hope for families after all.*

At the baggage area, Murphy watched, waited, looked at his watch, and waited a little more. He would have no trouble seeing his luggage when it hit the carousel. His mother had put enough red florescent tape around it that even a collector of Picassos would have cringed.

Finally, there it was, glowing and waiting. Murphy grabbed it up.

As he stepped outside, the warm air felt good—not fresh, but inviting. He moved away from the crowd so if anyone were looking for a lost student, he would stand out.

He continued waiting. Finally he took the Stephen King book out of his carry-on and tried to appear nonchalant as he waited. Unable to concentrate, he looked at his watch. It had been almost an hour. Maybe he should try calling his uncle. He looked for a payphone, reaching into his pocket. No change. He tried again to read his book. It didn't work.

What a great beginning. He should have just stayed home. He could be sitting in a theater now eating popcorn and doing a little "Christian cuddling."

He saw a young man walking toward him. It had to be his driver. But it wasn't, and Murphy's irritation increased.

Finally, someone called his name. "Mr. Murphy? I'm Roger. Welcome to Los Angeles." The man stretched out his hand.

"You can call me Murphy. Nice to meet you, Roger."

"Is this all your luggage?"

"That's it."

Murphy picked up one piece and Roger the other, while pointing across the street. "I'm in the parking lot over there. Between your plane being late and the airport traffic, I had to park. The car's not far from here."

Murphy followed Roger, leaving his book on top of a trash bin.

Five

Dr. James could see Mugabe was in pain. They had a 45-minute drive ahead of them.

"When did you last eat?"

Mugabe smiled, and without taking his eyes off the road, replied matter-of-factly, "The night before last."

Dr. James, feigning innocence, said, "But, Mugabe, there is a dining car on the train. Why didn't you eat?"

"I was a little tied up."

They both laughed as two friends sharing a secret.

"I think we need to have my wife fix us some breakfast."

"Food does sound good," Mugabe replied.

As he climbed out of the car, Dr. James wanted to give him a welcoming hug but saw Mugabe wince with pain. "Come on in the house. Gretchen isn't expecting me back this morning. We'll surprise her." He saw Mugabe's reluctance to enter a white man's house through his front door.

"It's only us—your men are hungry and need some breakfast," Dr. James shouted, opening the door.

A tall, graceful, smiling beauty appeared and gave him a peck on the cheek. "Well, this is a surprise; I thought you were going right to school."

"Like women, we can change our plans. Mugabe here has had a long train ride and needs some breakfast."

Dr. James stepped aside, and Gretchen saw Mugabe for the first time. Ignoring his bloody clothes, she smiled, stepped forward, and clasped his hand.

"I've heard much about you from James, many wonderful things from his visit in your country. It's a special blessing to have you in our school and also in our home. I hope, Mugabe, that you will always feel welcome."

This was so unexpected; he didn't know how to reply. Gretchen let go of his hand and turned to her husband. "Why don't you men clean up a bit while I fix breakfast?"

Dr. James took Mugabe into the bathroom. "I think you might want a hot shower."

This would be another new experience for Mugabe. He had taken showers before, but never with hot water.

Dr. James turned on the shower. Handing Mugabe a towel, he said, "Just put your clothes over here. I'll bring you some clean ones for when you get out." From the medicine cabinet he pulled a tube of ointment and a roll of gauze, handing it, along with a pair of scissors, to Mugabe. "After your shower, put this on your wounds. Then we'll eat breakfast."

In the kitchen, Gretchen was cracking eggs. "Oh James, that poor man. He came by the slave express, didn't he?"

"I'm afraid so."

"Well, he must be really hungry; I'd better cook a few more eggs."

"I gave him some ointment for his wounds. I'd better get him some clean clothes."

Gretchen started the bacon. "God is going to use that man, and we must help him all we can."

Dr. James heard her from the next room and popped his head back through the door. "Didn't I tell you he was different, special?"

Mugabe's shower was not a long one. The smell of bacon lured him. Just as Gretchen finished the toast, Mugabe entered the kitchen. She busied herself serving food, averting her eyes from Mugabe. There was no mention of the fact that the pants and shirt of a six-foot one man were not a perfect fit for a man five-foot six.

Mugabe picked up a fork for the first time and ate as delicately as one could when voraciously hungry.

Dr. James opened his Day-Timer and began outlining the day's schedule. "First, we'll meet with Esther." He and Gretchen smiled at each other. "She runs this place, but we don't let her know we know."

Gretchen put her hand on his. "Dear husband, you'll be able to talk to Mugabe for the next two years. I will not be so fortunate. You get what you need to take to the office and let me talk to him. You know, about things women want to know."

Mugabe looked at Dr. James, not sure how to react.

He smiled at Mugabe. "Women not only run the office; they run the home."

Mugabe relaxed, realizing this was something unique to these Americans, though he wasn't sure he wanted to emulate it when he got back home.

Dr. James placed a kiss on Gretchen's chin. "Yes, dear."

Gretchen brought a pitcher of milk to the table. She could see she didn't have to ask if he would like a glass. Filling a glass to the brim, she put it in front of Mugabe. Always the perfect hostess, she knew how to put people at ease. Seating herself across from him, she said, "You have a new wife. Tell me all about her."

Mugabe's broad, contagious smile returned. "Her name is Diolinda. She is like you, very beautiful.And also like you, she is very obedient to her husband, but also loves to make talk."

Gretchen laughed. "How long have you known her? Tell me all about her."

"Her eyes sparkle when she laughs and she loves to laugh. She loves children very much. We will have many sons." He enthusiastically picked up the tempo. "She works at our church. Before I leave, the pastor and my friends helped me build small hut so we have place to hang our wedding hoe and spend our only night together."

"I know of the wedding hoe. It is a wonderful part of your culture." Gretchen reached out her hand. "It must have been very difficult to leave her so soon."

Mugabe took the last sip of milk. "Yes, it was the most difficult thing our Lord ever asked me to do. Our village is dangerous when guerillas come. Our women hide and we must give the rebels what they want. But soon I will be home and protect her."

Attempting to lighten the conversation, Gretchen asked, "Where did you meet?"

Mugabe's face lit up. "At the marketplace, picking out potatoes. I worked in the fields, but she went to school and graduated. This does not happen often in our village to our women. She writes and speaks our native language, as well as Portuguese, and is very good in English. She was taught by the same missionary who introduced me to Mr. Jesus and taught me English. Not as good as my wife, but I am getting better."

Gretchen complimented him on his English. "You say she works for your church. What does she do?"

"One of her jobs is to write letters for people in our village. The officials never write back, but the others do. Some are very funny, some very sad."

"It's too bad you couldn't bring her to school with you."

"Oh, she encouraged me to come to Bible school by myself. She said I could study and learn more." Lowering his head, he said, "I already miss her very much."

Gretchen was about to ask another question when Dr. James returned. "You'll have plenty of time to continue this conversation later. If I don't get Mugabe to the office and register him, we'll face the wrath of Esther."

Mugabe stood, bowed, and thanked Gretchen for the most wonderful breakfast he had ever eaten.

Gretchen laughed. "That's only because you're so young, but thank you. My cooking is not always so appreciated."

Dr. James gave her a kiss, and Mugabe looked away, embarrassed by such a public display of affection.

Dr. James showed Mugabe the campus. "That's the dorm where all of you will stay. Next to it, the classroom, and a dining room that's also a chapel, recreation area, and study room. And this is the Administration building, also known as 'the place where Esther dwells.'

"As we say in America, 'Her bark is worse than her bite.' She happens to be one of the most efficient people in South Africa. She's in charge of balancing our budget, keeping students happy, and being the liaison with the local government and our denominational headquarters. She works miracles every day."

Dr. James opened the door for Mugabe, who hesitated, so James motioned him to follow as he called out, “Esther, we made it.”

A voice shouted back, “Well now, it’s about time.” Suddenly the door was filled with one very large lady, dressed in a bright orange dress, her head tied in a scarf. She stared at Mugabe in his rolled-up pants and borrowed sandals, which fit better than the shirt hanging to his knees.

Dr. James looked Esther in the eye. “Esther, meet our final student, Henrique Mugabe.”

Still staring, she put out her hand, businesslike, as Mugabe tentatively lifted his. “Welcome Mr. Mugabe. We’ve been expecting you.”

“He lost his luggage,” Dr. James said. “Actually he never had any. He came tourist class.”

Esther, who already dominated the room physically, took control of the situation. “Well, I’ll need your passport, your student visa, your personal ID, and your letter of acceptance and financial guarantee for the immigration officers. You know, those not-so-nice men in uniform who come and visit us from time to time.”

The silence was palpable. Mugabe looked at Esther, than at the floor. “I am sorry, ma’am; I don’t have any of those, only this.” He proudly held up his Bible, pulling out a small piece of paper.

She looked at it, then at Mugabe. “All this tells me is that your name is Henrique Mugabe and that you are from Mozambique. I hope your tourist class ticket was round trip because the government is going to be very unhappy about this.”

“Esther,” Dr. James interrupted, “maybe we can go into your office for a second. Mugabe, why don’t you have a chair, and we’ll be right back.”

Oh Lord, did I come this far only to be sent back? He could hear Dr. James’ soft voice, which was suddenly suppressed by one not so soft.

“Dr. James, you bring a student here who has no passport, no visa, nothing but a worthless piece of paper with his name on it and you expect *me* to enroll him as a legal student? You know we have to submit every student’s name, visa number, and a lot of other paperwork to the government *before* we can start classes tomorrow. Like about 22 hours from now. What will happen when they come and see for themselves, and find out we have one student registered that they don't know anything about?"

"I know, I know. But Esther, I also know that the Lord has called Mugabe to be here. I believed that from the first time I met him in Mozambique. So, please, Esther, I have complete confidence in you that if this can be done, you can do it. No one in South Africa is more capable."

Mugabe was ready to head back to the train yard when Dr. James returned, Esther trailing him. She glared at Mugabe; Dr. James winked. As Esther turned to go back in her office, he heard her mumble some numbers before she disappeared through the door.

"Well, that was the hard part. Now I'm going to take you home and let you get some sleep. We'll have dinner at my place tonight and then I'll bring you to the dormitory to sleep so you can be ready to start school tomorrow."

As they pulled in front of the house, Mugabe said, "You said there is an American saying, 'her bark is worse than her bite.'"

Dr. James nodded.

"Well, we have a saying in our country, 'If you shoot an elephant, be sure you run before it falls on you.'"

They both laughed.

Roger and Murphy were silent exiting the airport parking lot. Roger wrestled the gearshift, crawling with leaps and jolts in the stop-and-go traffic. He laughed apologetically, confessing he was still learning to drive a stick shift.

Once they got on the freeway, Murphy relaxed his clenched jaw. After all, it wasn't Roger's fault the plane was late, landing them in the middle of rush-hour traffic. He raised the van window so Roger could turn on the air conditioner.

"Sorry," Roger apologized, "the AC is broken."

Murphy's temper raised a few degrees as he reopened the window.

Feeling Murphy's obvious irritation, and still wrestling with the gearshift, Roger whispered another genuine, “Sorry.”

“No, I’m the one who should be sorry, man. It’s been a long day, but it’s not your fault. After all, this is better than hitch-hiking. Though the thumb might be faster. You just fight that gear shift, and let me sweat the rest.”

For the two hours of the one-hour drive, two strangers thrown together, wrestled alone. Murphy could not know their budding friendship would end in tragedy, and not in a traffic jam.

Six

"Are you awake?" Dr. James gently touched Mugabe's shoulder.

Mugabe stirred, grateful to be released from a dream reliving his train ride.

"Didn't mean to scare you, brother, but it's time to get up."

Mugabe slowly rolled on his side, every muscle crying to be left alone.

"After dinner, I'll take you to the dorm so you can get some sleep."

"Dinner? I just went to bed, didn't I?"

"You need a watch, Mugabe. You slept through lunch. Why don't you stop at the bathroom and freshen up. We'll wait for you in the dining room."

Mugabe followed him down the hall, turning into the room where he'd showered earlier. What was meant by "freshen up"? he wondered. Take another shower? He couldn't change clothes, as these were all he had. He washed his face. It woke him up, and he felt better. He looked at himself once more in the mirror and smiled at how much more "refreshed" he looked than when he'd come in.

Dinner was more food than breakfast, but with fewer questions from Gretchen. As they ate, Mugabe had questions he dared not ask—like why Gretchen ate at the table with them, and why Dr. James cleared the table while Gretchen sat and talked with Mugabe?

After dinner, Dr. James walked him to the dorm and introduced him to his ten new roommates. They were all polite, though their interest in his oversize wardrobe did bring some quizzical second glances.

There were six bunk beds lining the walls with rough open-shelved cabinets separating the beds and a simple table with a bookshelf at the foot of each bed. He made a mental note that this was where they put their books, toothbrushes, and personal belongings and that he would do the same whenever he had his own.

"That's where you take your showers." Dr. James pointed to a door. "Make them short. Our water supply is limited and electricity is expensive. We turn on the electricity that heats the water twice a day—one hour in the morning, two at night so you'll have light to study. I know you men will take responsibility for cleaning the dorm and respecting each other's privacy. If you need anything, you may go to Sister Esther."

He asked if he could pray with them. They readily agreed and gathered in a circle, taking hands. Dr. James prayed for each man by name, to the sounds of "Amen" and "Yes brother, yes Jesus."

"Well, good night, men. God bless you."

Mugabe sat on his bed reading his Bible until the electricity was off. Then he lay on his back, pushing the pillow—a Portuguese invention, he thought—out of the way. Putting his hands behind his head, he stared into the darkness.

Thank you, Lord, for getting me here. It's almost too good to be true. To go to Bible school is worth any sacrifice, but I miss Diolinda. Thank you for her love for me and her love for you. I'm so blessed...but there's something...some disharmony in my soul weighing on me....

Murphy was waiting in front of his dorm for Roger to take him to breakfast. He hadn't had a real meal since leaving Chicago, the day before. While watching for the school's van, a sleek, black Honda pulled up. The tinted window rolled down, and there was Roger behind the wheel. Murphy jumped in.

"I prayed for the school's van and looked what it turned into." Roger said.

"Wow, I'm gonna stick close to you. I could manage one of these."

"Actually it's my mother's," Roger said, "She's out of town again, so I thought I'd take it for a spin."

A few minutes of light banter later, they pulled into the parking lot of The Horseless Carriage.

Roger chose a booth. "This is where I usually sit. Quite a few of the guys from the school come here. This place is pretty student friendly; besides, it's the only decent eatery in the area."

As they sat down, Murphy noticed a waitress sitting in a booth on the other side of the room. She leaned across the table, holding the hand of an elderly white-haired man.

The cashier handed Murphy and Roger menus, smiled, wished them good morning, and informed them their waitress, Ella, would be with them in a few minutes. The cashier nodded in the direction of the two conversationalists, then left to care for a customer at the cash register.

They read the menu, decided what they wanted, and waited. Murphy could smell coffee and was salivating for scrambled eggs, country fried potatoes, and an English muffin.

Still no Ella.

Roger asked Murphy if he was ready for the first day of seminary. "Actually, right now I'm ready for some food, if Ella ever lets go of the old man's hand. At this rate we'll be old before she gets here."

Roger cringed and checked his watch. He assured Murphy they had plenty of time as he unconsciously took his still-empty coffee cup and turned it upside down. Roger tried changing the subject, but Murphy was obsessed with "the waitress and the old man" as his hunger and impatience increased.

Ella finally slid out of the booth. Both she and the old man appeared to be wiping away tears. The other waitress approached Ella and said something, and they both looked in the direction of Murphy and Roger. Ella walked over and, without any explanation, asked them, smiling, if they would like a cup of coffee.

"Yes," Murphy replied, making little attempt to hide his irritation. As Ella went to get the coffee, Murphy blurted to Roger, "Next time I'll wear an old man's wig. Maybe then we'll get some attention."

Roger cringed again as Ella turned and looked at them.

"Sheesh man, she heard you!" Roger said. "I hope she doesn't pour that coffee on our heads."

Murphy was ready to defend himself, but Ella arrived with the coffee. She filled their cups, then with pad and pencil in hand she looked straight at Murphy. "That *old man* has a name. It's Mr. Maxwell. He and his wife came for breakfast every morning for two years. They were always kind, never in a hurry, and they were very much in love. I served their fortieth anniversary breakfast in that very booth."

Roger stared at his cup, while Murphy opened his mouth to say something but Ella never gave him a chance. "Then one day they didn't show up. Two months later he came in by himself. He looked terrible, so sad. His wife had died; he'd lost his home…now he's a church janitor.

She looked directly at Murphy, more with pity than disgust. "Today was his wife's birthday. Last year he came in the day before her birthday with roses so I could have them on their table when they arrived. They often celebrated in that booth. Talking, laughing, holding hands, and always praying together before they left."

She touched the rosebud on her uniform. "This morning he came alone and said, 'I think she'd like you to have this.' I know he's thankful she's with the Lord, and now he wants to be too."

"I'm sorry," Murphy said, now as misty-eyed as Ella and Roger. "Sorry for him, that he's so lonely. Sorry you were exposed to my arrogance, but most of all, sorry for my stupidity." He let out a deep sigh. "Compassion is not my strong suit."

She took a tissue from her pocket and blew her nose in a ladylike way. Throwing her shoulders back, she smiled. "Now, what would you two like for breakfast?"

As they ate, Mr. Maxwell made his way to the cashier. Murphy set his fork down. He had lost his appetite.

Ella brought more coffee. She looked at Murphy's nearly untouched breakfast. "Is something wrong with your food?"

Murphy sighed again. "No, something's wrong with me."

Roger asked for the check.

"This one's on me." Ella said. "I don't preach often to a couple of preacher boys."

Seven

Mugabe was startled awake as the light from the naked bulb on the ceiling cut through the deep sleep that had engulfed him; his wounds cried for attention.

He almost fell onto the floor. It would take awhile to get used to sleeping on a bed raised off the floor.

Slowly, and with considerable pain, he put his feet over the side of the bed. He opened his shirt. The gauze bandages Dr. James had put on were blood red in large spots.

As he stood, his eye caught sight of a neat stack of clothing on the shelf beside his bed. He self-consciously looked at the oversized clothes he had slept in and felt more like a refugee than a student. Then he noticed a tube of ointment and box of gauze bandages next to the clothes with a note on top with his name. The note told him how to care for his wounds. It was unsigned, but he was quite certain where it came from. It was the same kind of medication Dr. James used on his wounds the day before.

Slowly he went through the stack. There were two shirts and pants, underwear, two pairs of socks, handkerchiefs, a brightly colored pair of shorts for soccer or work, and a towel. Beside the pile sat a new pair of shoes.

He took the towel, ointment, and gauze and headed for the shower. As he turned, he noticed that on top of the little table at the bottom of his bed were pencils, a tablet, toothpaste, and a toothbrush.

Tears came to his eyes. *Lord, I don't deserve this. I am a man of unbelief. Please forgive me.*

Though an undefined heaviness was still there, the joy of having new clothes overflowed as he walked to the shower, repeating again and again the words of the Lord: *"For I know the thoughts that I think toward you…thoughts of peace and not of evil, to give you a future and a hope."* He put his new clothes and shoes on. "A perfect fit. How did they know?" Then he remembered the numbers Esther had murmured as she'd left him standing outside her office.

Dr. James joined the students in the dormitory the next morning. "We have a building project before we can begin our studies. We need a classroom. I want to read something to you from Ephesians." He opened his Bible. *"You are no longer strangers and foreigners, but fellow citizens with the saints and members of the household of God...* Even though you and I come from different nations and tribes, we are now fellow citizens and members of God's family. Listen: *Having been built on the foundation of the apostles and prophets, Jesus Christ Himself being the chief cornerstone, in whom the whole building, being fitted together, grows into a holy temple in the Lord, in whom you also are being built together for a dwelling place of God in the Spirit.* So, *fellow citizens of God's household..."* He smiled. "Any ideas for building a classroom?"

Taken by surprise, no one spoke.

Then Mugabe's eyes lit up, remembering the thoughts that had flooded his mind during his arduous train ride. "What about building a slave's roundhouse?"

Dr. James looked puzzled.

"At the outskirt of many villages are small roundhouses for kidnapped slaves."

"Yes." His fellow students nodded. "Slave houses have no windows and the door is so low you have to kneel or stoop very low to get in. We have not been kidnapped, but we have been bought by Jesus. We have come here ready and willing to be servants. So, why not do our learning in a slave house as a reminder of who we are?"

"We could build it with our own hands," someone added, holding out his hands. "It would be ours."

"Yes!" other voices chimed in eagerly. "We want to be slaves for Jesus."

"Not slaves, but servants. Hopefully those days are coming to an end." Dr. James interjected. "Remember Jesus said, *'No longer do I call you slaves…but if you keep my commands I call you friends.'* Yes, let's build a roundhouse for our classroom—a good place to learn our Master's commands."

Soon they were outside, in a clearing, where someone drew a circle on the ground with a stick. With little talk and much work they began stomping the ground inside the circle, pounding it into a firm floor. Those who had machetes began to cut grass. Others dug dirt with shovels, piling it in small mounds. This was not a new experience for them. Their ancestors had built their homes this way for more generations than they could count, but never with men from different tribes working together. And never with a white man working alongside them.

Buckets of water were poured on each mound, grass was added, and the mud was mixed with their hoes, making a thick mortar to pat into place around the circumference of the marked circle. As the sun beat down on their sweating bodies and the drying mud, the wall took shape. They stood back and admired the work of their hands: a circular wall about four feet tall with a narrow three foot opening for a door. They stood in a circle and gave thanks to God for men and nature being able to work together.

For several days skeptical villagers watched as the wall was allowed to cure and the dedicated student servants worked as a team cutting tree branches for making a large cone shaped frame, trimming off the foliage. When the frame was lifted and set on the wall, the foliage was carefully woven in to create a roof.

Just as darkness began to fall, the last branch was firmly fixed in place and twelve voices shouted, "It is finished!"

Darkness claimed the jungle again as the villagers dispersed and twelve young men thoughtfully walked to the dormitory. Pride and humility mingled with joy over having completed their goal of transforming a symbol of slavery into a place to willingly learn to be their Master's servants. "It is good," they said to each other, grinning, before lying down to rest from their finished labor.

The next morning, as light pushed back the darkness, the men entered their new classroom on their knees, placed their mats on the floor, and settled in, cross-legged, to begin their studies.

A naked 100-watt bulb hanging on a cord from the ceiling and a thankful heart illuminated Dr. Nichols' face as he began to pray. "Master, we've entered these servant quarters to kneel at your feet. You have called us from several nations and tribes to be your own possession. We humbly accept your calling to be your servants. You have called us out of darkness into your marvelous light. Master, teach us to serve you by serving one another."

Dr. James placed a basin in front of him, wrapped a towel around his waist, opened his Bible and laid it on the floor in front of him, and began to read: *"Jesus rose...laid aside His garments, took a towel and girded himself...like the lowest of slaves of his day."*

He reached for a pitcher of water and poured some into the basin, while continuing to read: *"And Jesus...poured the water into the basin and began to wash the disciples' feet and to wipe them with the towel with which he was girded."*

Slowly Dr. James rose to his knees, moved the basin to the front of the student next to him, washed the student's feet, dried them with the towel, and moved the basin to the front of the next person. Dr. James sat down. The one whose feet had just been washed rose to his knees and washed the next student's feet. The washing of each other's feet, one by one, continued until all were cleansed.

Silently, Dr. James took the basin, the pitcher, and the wet towel and set it at his side. He thumbed through his Bible again and laid it in front of Him. "*And Jesus took bread, blessed and broke it and gave it to his disciples.*"

Dr. James reached behind him, took a piece of unleavened bread that his wife had made for the occasion, held it up, and broke it. Again he rose to his knees, kneeled before the person next to him, broke off a small piece of bread and lifted it to the student's mouth. *"This is the body of our Lord Jesus Christ. Take, eat. Do this in remembrance of him."*

The act was repeated as the unleavened bread went around the circle, each student receiving and giving a piece of bread and speaking the same words Dr. James had spoken.

When completed, Dr. James took what was left of the bread, set it beside him, and reached for a wooden chalice filled with wine. As with the bread, he knelt before the student on his right. His hands trembled as he held the chalice to the student's mouth, quietly saying, *"This is the blood of our Lord Jesus Christ; take drink, in remembrance of him."*

That student served the wine to the next until everyone had kneeled to be served and to serve.

"We are not slaves to an earthly master," Dr. James intoned, "nor are we slaves any longer to the ruler of darkness, but we *are* servants to a Heavenly Master. As he himself said, "I have given you an example, that you should do as I have done. A servant is not greater than his master, nor is he who is sent greater than he who sent him.'"

Dr. James sat up straight. "Together, we have begun a two-year apprenticeship in spiritual warfare. We are called not only to be servants, but soldiers in a continent filled with apartheid, slavery, immeasurable hate, racism, corruption, and villages controlled by witch doctors and demons. We are soldiers in a fallen world—a battleground between good and evil, between right and wrong. It is a battle between the fallen angel and his followers, and the Risen Savior and his disciples."

Dr. James tapped himself on the chest as he explained, "The real world, and the real battleground is here in our heart." He picked up his Bible. "Turn with me to Ephesians, chapter 6, verse 12: *For we do not wrestle against flesh and blood, but against principalities, against powers, against the rulers of the darkness of this age, against spiritual hosts of wickedness in heavenly places.* This battle is taking place right now, right here."

As he again tapped his heart with his fist, the students joined him, saying, "…in our heart."

"If I was in my country and spoke of witch doctors and demons, I'd probably be accused of living in the dark ages when people believed in demons under every stone. 'Why waste our time talking about myths of the Bible—about devils and angels?' someone would say."

Dr. James paused and looked up. "Well, we may have a twentieth-century light bulb in our catacomb-like meeting place, but nothing else has changed. The saints in the West may not believe in the powers of darkness, but you know we *are* in the middle of a great spiritual battle."

The roundhouse echoed with "Yes, yes, I've seen them…villages controlled by witch doctors."

"And so have I," Dr. James quietly replied. "Those in the West may not believe in Satan, witches, or evil spirits, but I will tell you who does. Our Lord Jesus Christ—and Africa."

Dr. James held up his Bible and began to read again from Ephesians: "*Therefore take up the whole armor of God, that you may be able to stand against the wiles of the devil.*"

Again the students repeated his words.

Dr. James continued. "This struggle is not against flesh and blood; this spiritual warfare is not man against man. It is not a political struggle…"

Each statement was greeted with shouts of "Amen" and "Yes Lord!"

Dr. James' voice rose with each proclamation: "It is not a social struggle…nor economic. It is not a struggle between human beings, but a struggle *within* human beings." He waited until the students quieted. "Understanding we are at war, we must prepare like soldiers in training. We are going to study and pray and together put on the full armor of God that Paul talks about. In two years, when you leave here, you will leave as a soldier ready to not only fight the enemy, but pursue him wherever he might hide, and destroy him, all in the power and name of our commander, our Lord Jesus Christ."

One by one, on their knees, they followed Dr. James out of their classroom into what they now recognized as not only their place of service, but the battleground.

Murphy passed up the elevator, choosing to use stairs to reach his classroom on the fourth floor of one of the newer buildings on the campus of Mt. Hattin University. He entered a sunny room that smelled of fresh paint. Several windows faced a taller, newer addition to the campus. In the front of the room was a new-looking desk with a leather upholstered chair. A large gleaming chalkboard hung beneath a pull-down screen used for overheads. A lectern stood in front of the desk, in easy reach of a switch connected to the overhead projector, which sat with two computers on a long table at the back of the room. Facing the lectern were 22 traditional classroom chairs, too new to have yet been carved with initials. As Murphy sat down, he was grateful for the cool breeze from vents that kept the room a comfortable 72 degrees.

Murphy was one of 23 young men chosen to participate in a 24-month program, consisting of five hours a day of theology and three hours a week of Greek, as well as an internship in a local church. The goal was training to be ministers of the Gospel of Jesus Christ. One student came thousands of miles, from Calcutta. Another had grown up six miles from the school. Twenty others came from cities and towns as far east as Chicago.

Murphy settled into the last empty chair. All eyes turned to the door as Dr. David Nichols entered. He was a tall, handsome man of 55, immaculately dressed in a dark suit, red tie, and white shirt. His thick hair was graying, but his body and countenance suggested he enjoyed physical and spiritual labor as much as a young man. Dr. Nichols was responsible for overseeing this new program, which had been in the planning stages for several years. He had taught at Mt. Hattin for 24 years and had a reputation as an affable but no-nonsense man with a single dedication: to mentor young men in preparation for the ministry.

Dr. Nichols silently surveyed the men in the room. "This day of beginnings has been a long time in coming. There are several beginnings for every man. The first, when he is born into the world. The second, when he is born into the Kingdom. And third, when he discovers the purpose for which he was born. When we discover whatever task God has assigned us to accomplish, there remains the question: when to begin? If we start too soon we may not have the necessary experience, education, or equipment for the task. If we wait too long, a once-in-a-lifetime moment may pass forever, leaving us stumbling through life full of regret, wondering what might have been."

Dr. Nichols stopped and looked into the face of each of his students. "There is no doubt in my mind that you are in the right place, at the right time, to fulfill the mission Jesus Christ has given you. So, gentlemen, when times of doubt flood your soul, remind yourself that the Lord called you, and tell the devil to get lost. So, sure of our calling as Jesus' disciples, let us begin."

The students visibly relaxed in their seats.

"I'd like to set down a few principles to guide us as we travel together for the next two years down this spiritual road. First, I want you to understand that I am a theological fundamentalist. As a fundamentalist I believe all the Bible is God's Word to man. I emphasize that point because there are many in important positions in the Church today who deny the resurrection of Christ, rejecting the proof texts of Scripture. This is a vital point in that much of the misuse of Scripture today can be laid directly at the feet of the teachers and graduates of some of our most prestigious seminaries. We do not intend for that to happen here. That's why you've come here to Mt. Hattin.

"Next, I warn you in advance that I will teach what I believe the Scriptures teach and those views may sometimes differ from those you hold. However, you will have every right to disagree. All I ask is that you come to me privately, or at an appointed time in class to give your rebuttal—based on your exegesis of the same verses. You may be right, and I promise you I will not be afraid to admit it to the class. If you challenge me in the spirit of love, I promise that your rebuttal will not take one point off your grade. None of this 'I am right and you are wrong, and if you don't agree—take a walk' stuff.

"Finally, in your application to Mt. Hattin, you all read the Apostles' Creed and signed on to its theology as our starting point. We consider this Creed to define Critical Truth of Scripture. After all, one wouldn't meet with an electronics engineer to discuss that discipline and begin by saying, 'I do not believe in Ohm's law or resonant frequency,' and expect to have anything to discuss. Such is the case with the Apostles' Creed.

"I would also like you to leave your political beliefs at the door. However, there are some spiritual issues that have been hijacked by politicians, that we will discuss, but as theologians and not as politicians. At the end of two years, you will still not know my political affiliation. As for my theology, I am a Calvinist/Arminian/pre-post-ami-millennialist/Charismatic. That does not mean that I believe nothing, but rather that theologians have rather inflated egos and I like to know I am right at least some of the time," he said with a smile.

Dr. Nichols picked up his Bible, and while thumbing through it, said, "John, chapter 5. This is the story of the healing at the pool of Bethesda. How many of you are familiar with it?"

All twenty-two men raised their hands.

"Good. Today, being our first class together, I would like to build a filter through which much of our learning will pass during the next two years. *Bethesda* means house of mercy. Five portals surrounded a large pool of water that was, according to tradition, stirred at various times by an angel. Lying under the portals, surrounding the pool was a large number of sick people suffering from paralysis, blindness, festering wounds and other debilitating diseases. They not only shared pain and suffering, but the belief that when the angel came and stirred the water the first one to get into the pool would be healed. We'll discuss this and other aspects of this incident at some length in a later class, but today I want to concentrate on two people: *a sick man* and *a stranger*. Not a stranger to us, but to them.

"The sick man had been paralyzed for thirty-eight years. It doesn't tell us whether or not those years were all spent under one of the porticos. It does say he had no one to put him in the pool, indicating he had no family. Many of the others had someone to help them to the pool, but not him.

"It is here at the pool that our lesson begins. The sick man lay on his bed—a simple mat. A man appeared, a stranger to all at the pool. He stopped, and fixed his gaze on the sick man. Though surrounded by many blind, lame, withered bodies, he seemed to keep his gaze on one as he carefully navigated his way towards this particular unkempt man on a filthy mat.

"The stranger's shadow fell over the sick man who slowly looked up at him, and with undisguised contempt broke the silence. 'What's the matter, haven't you ever seen a cripple?' He lowered his voice.

'You're blocking the sun.' He pulled his robe over one of his shrunken legs. He was about to speak, then stopped, asking himself, 'Who is this guy? I've never seen him before…he looks different...why doesn't he say something?'

"The uncomfortable silence was broken when this stranger, eyes full of unfamiliar compassion, gently asked him a question: 'Do you want to get well?'

Dr. Nichols held up a Greek lexicon. "That word *well* actually means whole, referring not just to his body but to his spirit as well. What the stranger said is important, and so is what he didn't say. 'Keep the faith, man. One of these days you'll make it to the pool. In the meantime, let me make you a little more comfortable. Maybe I can help you turn over.' Or, 'Your sleeping mat has about had it. I know some ladies at the synagogue who supply fresh mats. I'll have them drop off a new one for you. They also arrange chariot delivery of free meals at noon. I'm on my way, my friend, to the harvest festival to celebrate this year's bountiful harvest the Lord has given us. While there I'll talk to one of the officials who works closely with the Roman government agencies. They may be able to help you.'"

Dr. Nichols shook his head. "No, that is not what he said. He simply asked the sick man, "Tell me my friend. Do you really want to get well…do you want to be made whole?'

"I think what happened may have been something like this. The sick man sneers and replies, 'What kind of a stupid question is that? Of course I want to get well. Do you think I enjoy lying here like this, waiting, yet knowing it will never be any better?' His voice softens with longing. 'No matter how hard I try, these skinny, emaciated legs won't hold up an old man like me.' He looks at his legs, then into the face of the stranger. 'You see, it's not my fault. Yes I really do want to get well.'

"I can imagine Jesus looking down at the sick man, his gaze eliciting excitement and conviction. Haven't we all experienced this at one time or another when Jesus asks, 'Don't you kind of enjoy sympathy? Do you really want to be a healthy man and work for a living, feed a family, deal with the problems of survival that supposedly well men have to face?'

"I can imagine the sick man looking away, hoping yet fearing he will be left alone. The stranger breaks the silence. 'My friend, pick up your bed and walk.'

"'What?' The sick man sits up, pointing to his shrunken leg. 'You expect me to stand, and then pick up my bed and walk. Even if by some miracle my legs were healed, I don't have the strength to pick up my bed.' He looks in the face of the stranger, pleading for pity. 'Whoever you are, believe me, I really do want to get up and walk, just like you, so I too can go to the temple with my offering. I really do…I…' His voice trails off as, helpless, he reaches towards the stranger. The stranger steps back as if to say, 'I've done my part, now you do yours. Trust me. I *have* made you whole.'

"Hesitantly, the sick man puts the palms of both hands on the ground, and for the first time in 38 years, slowly attempts to get up. His eyes widen as his legs move. Looking at the stranger, and then at his legs, he mutters in awe, 'I can stand; I am healed.'

"As those around him look on in disbelief, a great smile crosses his face. He laughs and does a little jig, raising his hands high. Soon he's shouting, 'I can walk, praise Yahweh, I can walk, I am healed!'

"The stranger touches his shoulder, then points to the filthy bed still laying on the ground.

"'But what if I get sick again? I will need a place to lay…maybe I better…' He bends over, picks up his bed, puts it on his shoulder, and smiles at the stranger. 'You're right. I'm not planning to come back.'"

The students sat still, not sure how to react. Dr. Nichols picked up his open Bible and held it out to them. "Of all of our Lord's miracles, I find this one the most convicting. I am reminded of an old comic strip, long before your time. The characters would get into all kinds of troubles of their own making, sit around, and curse their luck. Finally one would recognize the truth: 'We have found the enemy and he is us.'

"I like to paraphrase it: 'We have found the sick man and he is us.' Us, being the Church. What happened at Bethesda is happening today. It is vital for you young men to understand, because you are the Church, and in two years you will be in positions of leadership in the body. The body of Christ has many cripples. The Church is hurting—

and often paralyzed. Jesus is asking: Do we want to be whole?

"What about those in the pews who, if not like the man at Bethesda, are like the woman who for twelve years had an issue of blood? She tried every new fad, spent all her money searching for a cure, attended every seminar, and read every book that promised healing. But the tell-tale symptoms continued to drain her.

"The sick may be elders, deacons, the hardest workers in the body, but their secret sickness still haunts them. They sing loud, pray with seeming vigor, and always say the right things at testimonial meetings. But they live under the shadow of some out-of-control moral issue: drugs, drinking, lust, pornography, perhaps sudden outbursts of anger that isolate them from the people they love and those who love them. Like the sick man at the pool of Bethesda, they see themselves as victims, wallowing in self-pity or anger, not realizing that self-victimization is self-induced, self-perpetuating, and in the end self-destructive. Sometimes, convinced their theology is unimpeachable, the proud are blind, rejecting any who dare to challenge their comfort zone.

"Sickness is not always caused by sin. Reading from John 9. Jesus had just healed a blind man, and he was asked by the disciples, *'Rabbi, who sinned, this man or his parents, that he was born blind?'* Jesus answered, *'Neither this man or his parents sinned, but that the works of God should be revealed in him.'*

"However, in the case of this sick man at Bethesda, his sickness was caused by his sin. We read further on, in John 5:14: *Afterward Jesus found him in the temple, and said to him, 'See you have been made well. Sin no more, lest a worse thing come upon you.'*

"There is no indication what that sin might have been, but he represents the body, whose head is Christ, the Church. Yes, there is sin in the body of Christ, in what we call the 'kingdom of heaven.'"

Dr. Nichols' eyes glistened. "There are few things in this world that I would die for. My family, yes, but also for what we call the Body of believers. I love the Church. Sitting in the pews are caring, loving people and because of that love I will praise the Church when I feel it is appropriate; but I will also criticize it when that too is appropriate.

"We must remember that our Lord Jesus Christ did not come to earth to cast aside the Jewish religion, but rather to save it from its arrogant leadership. We, you and I, are not called to cause harm to the body of believers, but to lead people to rediscover the glory of being made whole. That is your personal assignment. This is your moment to begin. Time is up but I want you to read this portion of Scripture, meditate on it, talk about it, and next week, we'll discuss the character of the Stranger."

Dr. Nichols closed his Bible and cocked his head. "The question still rings in the air. 'Do you want to be well?' See you next week."

Eight

Mugabe's wounds had healed, but two months away from Diolinda still left him aching. He feared for his wife, for he heard reports of rebel activity in Mozambique. One BBC report told of bands of teenagers roaming the countryside, raping and looting. He prayed for her each day, then attacked his studies with fresh fervor, not wanting to waste any day he was away from Diolinda. He applied himself to his studies, memorizing and reciting Scriptures, discussing the lessons with the other students as they hoed the gardens and milked the goats. But when the lights were out and all was quiet, the undefined heaviness haunted him. No matter how hard he worked or how well he did on exams or preaching assignments, something did not feel right.

Is it some unconfessed sin? Is it fear, Lord? What is it?

One morning, Dr. James told him after breakfast; it was his day to give his testimony to the class. It was a moment he had been dreading. Speaking to a church full of strangers was not as frightening as speaking to his peers, but he had no choice. It was a mandatory assignment. He drew courage remembering two other students had done it, and they both survived.

Two hours later, shaking, he began:

"My name is Henrique Mugabe. I am from Cancanabe in Mozambique. I am 25, almost 26 years of age."

He gripped the podium, blushing slightly, as he lifted his head and voice. "I have been married to my *minha vida,* the love of my life, Diolinda, for two months and eleven days." Everyone laughed. There were congratulations, while several made sounds that needed no translation as Mugabe added, "And four hours and sixteen minutes."

Clearing his throat, he continued: "I am the son of a chief. But like most chiefs in my country, my father had more children than he had pots of food. As was the custom in such a case, I was sent to live with an uncle who had more pots than children. My uncle and relatives had one thing in common with all the Shona people. We shared the god, *mwari.*

"One day, a very tall white man came to our village. He was not old...maybe like an older brother." Mugabe smiled, "...with yellow hair. Unlike other white men I've seen, he was not very well fed, but he had a gentle smile, and none of the arrogance of those who had made us slaves. Word spread of a stranger in our village. Men stood in the doorways of their huts, admonishing the women and children to stay inside.

"The stranger smiled, and called out '*Masakati*—Hello,' for all to hear. He then spoke a greeting in Portuguese, but still no one responded. My heart seemed about to explode out of my chest, but I did not know why. It was not fear, just an excitement as strange to me as this stranger in our insignificant African village.

"The chief and his 'angry son,' as he was not so affectionately called, came out of their hut and boldly marched, carrying a machete, toward the stranger. Some of the braver men cautiously fell in behind him. The stranger stood at attention, like a soldier greeting his general. Our chief carried himself with dignity, but his son is hot-headed with a tongue as vicious as a viper, a mamba.

"The chief greeted the stranger and welcomed him to his village. The stranger bowed, returning the greeting in our own language. The chief smiled at the stranger's way of doing to our language what the chief's son wanted to do to the stranger."

Mugabe's listeners chuckled.

"The women and children came out of their huts and stood behind their men. Everyone relaxed when the chief suggested they use Portuguese, a language they each understood. Meanwhile, the chief's son stared, demon-like, gripping his machete, at the stranger.

"The stranger said he was from Canada. Then he spread his arms out, as though to encompass all of us and said he had come to tell the chief's people about Jesus Christ. His eyes took us all in. I felt loved...by a stranger! His boldness shocked us. Before, when white strangers came, they said it was to teach us how to grow more food or to bring us medicine.

"The chief said, 'My friend, we have seen many like you before. Though they did come to teach us to grow more food, it was only so that they could put it on a ship, take it across much water, and give to their own people to make them fat, while we starved.'

"Several of the other men gestured and grunted, confirming what the chief had said. The son raised his machete and moved around his father, coming closer to the stranger. Their faces were only inches apart as the son shouted vehemently, '*Iwe! Hamba!*' then in English, 'Hey you, go way, go way!' raising his machete. 'Look at us.' He spit out the words, 'Do we look like we live in your Christian paradise? No!' slapping his gut with his free hand. 'We starve while you be in Maputo eating food this machete and these hands gathered so you can come and take away.' Putting his face against the stranger's, the son said, 'Unless, of course, you say more stupid things and I cut your gut open and bury you.'

"The stranger reached toward the shoulder of the son, who arrogantly jerked back in surprise. 'You may kill me,' the stranger said, 'but first you must go through Jesus. I belong to the Lord Jesus Christ. If he gives you permission,' he said, lifting his shirt and exposing his belly, 'you may kill me. But if Jesus says no, you cannot touch me.'

"The crowd gasped as the son aimed his machete at the stranger's belly. Everyone backed off and children clung to their mothers' skirts, certain they would see a killing. The chief watched as the two young men stood face-to-face. He knew his son was a coward, and if he harmed the stranger, it would be in the dark with no one else around.

"The son shouted at his father, 'If you do not kill this devil, then I will!'

"The chief spoke so quietly, we couldn't hear his words. The son turned angrily and walked away, pushing and cursing as he went. Everyone knew he had murdered before. The chief apologized. 'Please excuse my son; he gets very angry at times.'

"'I understand. I sometimes get angry myself,' the stranger said.

"'Perhaps,' replied the chief, 'but my son's anger is out of control.' The chief then led the stranger to his own hut, saying he wanted them to talk. We had never seen our chief do this before.

"*Who is this stranger so unafraid of death? And who is Jesus*

Christ, his master? I wondered.

"As the stranger went with the chief—he looked directly into my eyes and nodded. I nodded back, not knowing why. Others were also asking, 'Who is this stranger? He must be important if the chief took him to his own hut.'

"I returned to my uncle's home where I lived. I felt very strange inside, like I already knew this stranger from somewhere. But from when and where, I could not imagine. For several months the stranger came to our village. Sometimes he brought medicines, sometimes food, but always kindness and words about his friend, Jesus. The chief always welcomed him as an old friend and took him inside, so we didn't see much of him.

"At each visit we all pretended to go about our business, while waiting for the chief's angry son to storm once again out of his father's house, cursing, swinging his machete, heading to the *muroyi*—the witch doctor who lives in the forest. Though we were glad to see him go, we were all aware what this son was capable of, especially under the influence of the *muroyi.*

"One day, as I was hoeing corn in my uncle's field, one of my cousins came running and said the chief wanted me. I knew that the stranger was visiting him, so my mind raced with possibilities. When the chief invited me, I shyly stepped inside. The chief and the stranger were each sitting on a rug, cross-legged. I was introduced to the stranger. Our eyes met for a moment. The same feeling I had when he walked by me that first time returned. I had no idea what it meant, but yet there was no fear.

"The stranger extended his hand as must be the custom in his country, to people that you want to befriend. But, I thought, surely not to a person as unimportant as me, covered with dust from the cornfield and sweat from the sun.

"The chief stroked his chin as though he was deep in thought, then said, 'Mugabe, our good friend here has agreed to come to our village and teach the young boys to read, to write, and to figure out numbers. We want our young men to be educated, to show the world we are not a 'higher type of animal' but are men, made in the image of God, and not simply beasts of burden.' Looking at me, he continued, 'He needs someone to help him.'

"Before I had time to think on this, the chief stood. 'I have agreed. He has asked for you.' I stood up, too, as he continued, 'You may have the small hut near the creek where we now store some of our tools. I would like you to take him there, and get it ready so class may start tomorrow.' He then dismissed us with a nod.

"That was the day my life was changed." Choking up, Mugabe looked at Dr. James and apologized. "I am going very long. We will graduate before I finish."

Dr. James asked him to continue.

"In the months that followed, the stranger taught me so I could teach others. He gave me a Book to study. I spent hours reading it. When the stranger taught, I had many questions for him from the Book he gave me." Mugabe glanced at Dr. James again. "I have found in that Book that not all is joy and happiness. Not every story ends as we would like it to.

"One day one of the villagers began calling the stranger *Mahondra,* instead of 'white man' or 'stranger.' In our language *Mahondra* is a word of honor. It is one who has a 'great lion's spirit.' Not just any lion, but one that protects the people from predators. After we heard the chief say, "Mahondra, I trust you are not eating our students alive,' he was known by all as 'Mahondra.'

"Mahondra moved to our village, living in the classroom. Our village became well known as a place where a 'lion spirit' dwelt. For two years I read my Book in the light of the sun, and late at night by the light of a candle. I could not get enough. The stories of Jesus made me weep.

"Mahondra took me to other villages, so I could read from my Book to the people. One Sunday morning, walking back to our village, we sat on the bank of a creek to eat wild pecans. Mahondra took my Book, thumbed through it, and pointed to the part I'd read to the people that morning. It was the story of Nicodemus. Mahondra asked, 'Mugabe, did you understand what you were reading this morning?'

"I told him I had read it many times, but confessed I was not sure what it really meant. Mahondra began to explain it to me and a short time later, there by the side of a stream, I not only knew what it meant,

I knew Jesus Christ—not just as a wise, wonderful, compassionate man, but as my Savior."

The room was very quiet as Mugabe continued. "We went back to my village, though I am not sure I remember it very well. I was too excited. I went to my hut and began to tell my cousins what had happened to me. I was very surprised. I thought they would rejoice with me, but they got very angry. They shouted at me, and yelled, 'You are no longer one of us. You have betrayed us. You are no longer a Shona; you are now one of them.' They kicked me as they angrily left the house. I was alone. But then I realized I wasn't really and I knew in my heart that I would never be alone again."

Mugabe's glowing face sobered. "One morning, just as the sun was coming up, we were awakened by a horrible scream, like a wild animal. Had a lion invaded our village and dragged off some of our children? That sometimes happened. Had the guerillas come and raped some of our women? That, too, sometimes happened. People came running out of their huts.

"The woman who brought breakfast to Mahondra was screaming in terror. I ran to the classroom. I was the first to arrive. There on the floor, was our Lion Spirit, Mahondra. He lay in a pool of blood. His throat had been cut. He was nearly beheaded. Our teacher was gone. And so was the chief's son.

"Even though the socialists allow no missionaries, Mahondra was buried in a Maputo church cemetery because we held him in high honor. As his body was carried away, the chief had tears in his eyes. We had never seen this before. 'Via Mahondra,' he cried, 'you have loved us until the end.'

"It was more than a farewell; it was a blessing. Our chief had believed Mahondra's stories of the greatest chief that ever lived and trusted him as Savior."

Mugabe looked drained as he concluded. "One day I will return to my people, and I will read to them and teach from my Book." He tearfully opened his Bible and read from the flyleaf: "To my young brother, Mugabe, I give this Book. There is no other like it in the world. Hunger and thirst for its words of life, and then teach and feed your people."

Dr. Nichols' gentleness and obvious intellectual acumen interlaced with firmness of purpose created a stimulating, yet welcoming atmosphere.

From behind the lectern, he said, "As I told you in our indoctrination I have randomly programmed your names into the computer and on some Wednesday or Thursday morning it will sound-off with a few bars of the *Hallelujah Chorus* and one of your names will appear. At that point you and I will exchange places and you'll give your testimony of how God drew you to Jesus. John Wesley told his students that every preacher must be ready at all times to preach, pray, and/or die. I'm sure you come in here all prayed up, you're too young to die, so the options are limited."

The students moaned, then laughed as Murphy dropped his arms to his side like a dead man.

Dr. Nichols smiled before giving his let's-get-serious look, causing them to sit up straight, getting the message. "We were looking at John 5. The story of the man healed at the pool of Bethesda. We centered on two people: the sick man and a stranger. Tell me, who is like the sick man?"

Several replied, "We are."

"That's right. We have found the sick man and he is us, or in a broader sense he is the Church. So, now as we continue, if the sick man represents the Church, which includes all of us, then who is the stranger?"

They replied, almost in unison: "Jesus."

"Yes, Jesus Christ, the one who came to reveal God to us and to seek us out. Scripture does not say how many sick men were lying within the porticos, but notice that none seemed to recognize Jesus. He could have stretched out his arms and healed them all. But he went to one man. This same stranger, when he saw Peter and Andrew, called out, '*Follow me and I'll make you fishers of men.*' He did the same with John and James.

"When Jesus said to Nathaniel, '*I saw you under the fig tree,*' Nathaniel was compelled to follow him. Matthew, a rich tax collector hated by all, was called by this stranger, '*Follow me.*' And he did.

"Let me illustrate. A close friend of mine, a missionary to China, was raised on a dirt farm in Northeastern Montana. As a child he had a fascination with China. It didn't come from newspapers or television. His only frame of reference, other than a feeling inside, was when he dug post holes for fences. Then his dad would say, 'Son, you dig any deeper and you're going to end up in China.' He dug deep but never hit China. The interest continued through high school and Bible school. At 26, he and his wife landed in China as missionaries. He would tell us, moved by his strong sense of calling, 'I realize God planted China in me before he planted me in China.'

"These encounters share a point. This may be a point with which you disagree and I respect that, but it's a belief I've long held. Christianity is not man reaching out to God, but God reaching out to man. Some recognize him, but others see him only as a stranger and miss the significance of what he has come to be.

"Jesus tried to call, to summon, the religious leaders of His day—even as they plotted to kill the One who should not have been a stranger to them. Jesus' love for them compelled him to plead, *'You know me and where I was born and raised, but I am the representative of one you don't know, and He is Truth. I know him because I was with him, and he sent me to you.'*

"Two important points: God sent Jesus to find them, but what they wanted of their Deliverer was so different from what he came to offer, they did not recognize him." Dr. Nichols slowly shook his head, articulating his deep concern. "This problem continues in the Church today. They did not recognize him because they, and we as well, mentally construct in our minds the kind of Jesus we want. If he is not what we want or imagine, we don't recognize him. He is a stranger.

"I am not talking about those who deny the virgin birth, his crucifixion, his resurrection, and yes, his celibacy. They deny basic critical truths and the inspiration of God's Word. These are not sheep lost for a period until he brings them back to the fold. No, these are wolves in sheep's clothing and that is not what I am talking about."

Dr. Nichols pulled a sheet of paper from his Bible. "I have here a growing list of the false Christs that some evangelical Christians have created that require little of us. When Jesus was led into the wilderness to be tempted, he was tempted to be false to His calling. Jesus remains a stranger to those expecting him to have the very self-promoting weaknesses the Tempter advocated. '*If you are the Son of God, command these stones to become bread!'* Use your authority for personal gain and satisfaction. Give the people health and wealth. *'If you are the Son of God, jump off the pinnacle; angels will catch you.'* Do whatever *you* want; your God will back you up. You're eternally secure. Build your own kingdom. Be what the people want and they'll never forget you. Make a name for yourself. Don't be a stranger.'

"Men, many a minister has succumbed to one of the suggestions of the Tempter, failing the test. Be on your guard. Ministers have served well for years, and then, even in retirement, have fallen prey to the temptation to want to be remembered, to be important, to receive glory that should go to the Lord God. Jesus stood fast. He did only what the Father told him, and gave all the glory to him. He did not become a self-serving or revolutionary or political or socialist Christ. Many have created in their mind an imaginary Christ who says, 'I want all of you to be happy and wealthy...and free of any boundaries'—ignoring the necessity of repentance, redemption, and transformation."

Dr. Nichols seemed to be talking to himself, his head bowed. "Our Western culture is running amok on relativism and individualism; following a therapeutic approach to life that believes a screwed-up life is someone else's fault. We live in an age of talking heads, where the prophets have been replaced by pundits and comedians and we bow down to a god made in our own image."

Dr. Nichols looked at his students and shook his head. "My point is this: Christianity is not man reaching out to God, but God coming to earth as a stranger, reaching out to man. He remains a stranger if we are looking for a Jesus whose main job is to do what we want, rather than a Savior who came to do the Father's will. That is the Christ. Will you bow your heads as I read something from an anonymous poet?

"When Jesus came to our campus,
We simply passed Him by.
We never hurt a hair of Him... We only let Him die.

We had grown more tender,
We would not give Him pain.
But we went to our dorms,
And left Him alone in the rain.
The streets of the campus were empty,
Without a soul to see
That Jesus crouched against a wall,
Wet, cold, crying for Calvary.

"May you recognize him and always respond with a wholehearted 'Yes!' when he who was a stranger asks you if you want to be whole."

Nine

After three months at Bible school, Mugabe was getting used to the routine: breakfast, three hours of class, lunch, three hours of work in the fields, dinner, and study. Today, instead of hoeing, he helped dig post holes for a fence to keep the cows and goats out of the newly planted corn.

Finishing the last hole, they put their tools away, wiped sweat from faces with their handkerchiefs, and dragged their tired bodies into the dormitory. Each one was eager for a shower and a short rest before the evening meal of last year's corn.

Mugabe saw an envelope, lying on his bed. He knew it would be another immigration form to be filled out, with a note from Esther saying she could not hold the immigration officials off much longer. He dreaded being admonished again to fill it out and deliver it to her office before class tomorrow morning. He knew exactly what information was wanted: name, approximate date of birth, tribal name of his clan, date of entry into South Africa—and the section he had to leave blank, his visa and student permit number and date of issue. His country was tightly controlled by socialists, who insisted on a self-imposed isolation, other than their economic relationship with South Africa. Only a limited number of people were granted visas or permits to leave Mozambique, and only to work in the mines—never as students.

However, on picking up the envelope, he realized it was different. He turned it over. It was addressed to him, but this one had a stamp from Mozambique. Since his country had no diplomatic relations with South Africa, mail exchange was very rare.

This was his first letter from Diolinda. He held it to his lips and kissed it, giving thanks. It smelled of her fragrance on their wedding night. Reluctantly, he set the letter down. He wanted to be clean and to read the letter somewhere in private.

After a quick shower, his adrenaline pumping, he took the letter to a quiet place inside a small circle of trees. Settling himself on the ground, he was finally ready to absorb the precious pages.

My dear husband,
I am missing you very much. I think of you before I sleep at night and first thing when I awake. I pretend you are in the field working before the sun comes up, and I make your breakfast. As I eat alone I offer praise to our Lord that one day you will return to me and our home.

The drought continues, and we are blessed to have grass by the stream to boil and eat. We planted corn, and to make it grow, we hauled water from the stream. But the stream is drying up.

Each day I herd Pastor Jonathan's three cows to find feed for them. We must search far from the village. The cows give very little milk. Hardly enough for the children.

I have learned to make pots from mud and even fire them. You will be proud of me. Pastor says I have a talent. He sells them for me.

We have had several visits from the rebels. I do not know if they are Renamo or Frelimo, but they come with guns and take our food. In one village they raped two girls. They are but children themselves.

But, my dear husband, we are not complaining. The Holy Spirit continues to rain down on our small congregation and we are being blessed in spite of the drought.

Pastor keeps telling people that when Mugabe gets back from Bible school we will start new churches in our province. He has great plans because he has a "great young man to fulfill them." That is you, my husband.

I hope and pray this letter reaches you, my husband, because there is something I want you to know. Many days I could not keep food in my stomach.

I know we have "the finest health system in all of Africa" under President Marchel's scientific socialism—about as fine as "the finest school system in all Africa," which has had no classes since you left. So I saw one of the government's barefoot doctors. He told me it was not the boiled grass that was making me throw up, but little Henrique Mugabe that is beginning to grow in my belly.

Yes, I have not only made you a husband, but in six months I will make you a father. Please do not worry. I feel sure it will be the son you desire. I love you my husband.

Your wife, and mother of your son,
Diolinda

Mugabe sat stunned. The tears flowed as he kept repeating, "I'm going to have a son." A bird landed on a branch above him. It was the first living creature to hear Mugabe's joyful news.

The clang of the dinner bell announced supper. He wanted to cherish this good news all by himself for awhile longer. Shona men did not show their emotions in public, and he wanted to be a good Shona father.

Mugabe tried to act normal as he ate his supper. Fortunately no one asked about the letter. He didn't want to talk for fear he would not be able to contain his joy and awe. He ate as fast as he could without gaining attention and then excused himself, unable to sit still.

Finally, study time and evening devotions were over. Time for lights out and privacy, at last. He thought of his son, in the belly of the person he loved most in this world. He wondered whether he would have enough love to share for both of them when he returned home. He smiled; of course God would give him enough love.

He lay on his back, hands behind his head. This was his favorite position to think and to pray. *What name should we give our son?* His mind ran through Scripture. He thought of several names from the Old and New Testament. One kept coming back to him. As though the Lord was prompting him, he said the name to himself: Levi, a gift of Jehovah. If the name didn't fit his son, they could call him Matthew.

Mahondra had taught much about the Levites—sinners called to serve God. Levites ministered to the Lord in the Tabernacle and Temple. They were priests and servants and musicians. *I need to learn to play the guitar,* Mugabe thought.

The Levites lived in cities of refugee, a place where people in trouble could find safety.

He began to visualize how he and his son, Levi, working together, could serve all of Mozambique, not just his village. Not just Shonas, but all the tribes and nations. They would build churches to be places of refuge from witch doctors, demon worship, and cruel government measures. Together, as he had with Via Mahondra, they would go from village to village, leading the Lord's people in worship in their tin-roofed tabernacles, encouraging, building up, not destroying like the rebels, but being revolutionaries, effecting change as soldiers of the Lord Jesus Christ. Yes, he had found God's name for his son!

Exhaustion overtook him. He would make his announcement at breakfast. "His name shall be called Levi," he whispered, falling asleep.

Murphy had imagined working with his uncle, Pastor Bjorn, ever since bonding with him at a family reunion the summer before his senior year of high school. There were 37 relatives camping at the lake in Michigan that year. The older generation always enjoyed reminiscing over the past, sharing their lutefisk and lefse. The younger generation preferred creating a past to remember—swimming, boating, fishing, and barbecuing hot dogs and hamburgers.

On a quiet Sunday afternoon, Murphy found a secluded spot on the lake's shore to think. What direction did he want his life to take? He knew he would attend the University of Michigan, in his father's footsteps, but did he also want to follow his father into the financial business? He skimmed a stone across the lake, counting the number of times it skipped. He tossed another, watching the ripples spread.

Uncle Bjorn appeared beside him, unexpectedly, and joined him under the shade of a tree. Murphy threw another stone. "Want to talk?" his uncle asked.

Murphy threw another stone before answering. "I'm thinking we all make ripples in the world, and then we disappear." As stones were tossed and skipped, casual and leading questions were asked and thoughtful, philosophical answers were also tossed back and forth. God was not seen, but the trees, the deep lake, the pure sky, and their growing respect for each other proclaimed his presence.

In Murphy's mind, that afternoon with his uncle was when he came of age. He no longer felt a child, but a living stone with great potential for making ripples, maybe even waves.

At the distant sound of approaching campers, Pastor Bjorn stood, put his hands on Murphy's head and shakily prayed, "My son, may God use you in the service of our Lord Jesus Christ."

The blessing, the warmth of his uncle's hands on his head stayed with Murphy wherever he went, whatever he did, guiding him—or haunting him—at university frat parties or in the back seat of a parked car.

Today, after several weeks of seminary preparation, Murphy was to begin his internship. Though he and his uncle never mentioned their lakeside counseling session, the unspoken memory was a third person in the room as they faced each other across the pastor's desk.

Pastor Bjorn had added some gray to his thick wavy hair since that peaceful day at the campground, but everything else was the same. Well, maybe a few more wrinkles, but they only added to his wise appearance. His blue eyes reflected his gentle spirit and twinkled with his Norwegian humor.

Murphy hoped he looked that good at sixty-three.

Of those sixty-three years, thirty-two of them were spent shepherding a church that started in a rented VFW hall, only blocks away from where they now sat. Over the years the church had grown from three families to nearly a thousand people worshiping in the two Sunday morning services. Pastor Bjorn's messages were often delivered with tears of compassion or joy, as he identified with his flock's sorrows and joys. His flock saw him as a shepherd servant and teacher who expounded God's Word with unwavering conviction.

Finishing their coffee, Bjorn repeated his Norwegian mantra. "God made coffee to awaken our prayer muscles." After praying together, Bjorn gave his new intern his first assignment: Find the janitor who would round up an unused desk for the new "associate"—a term Pastor Bjorn preferred. Some members of the staff, seminary graduates themselves, considered Murphy an intern, not an associate pastor, but Bjorn's will prevailed.

Murphy found the door marked *Janitor* and knocked, waiting for a response. He knocked a second time, then remembered his uncle telling him to wait in the janitor's office if he wasn't there. He was sure to return soon. Murphy opened the unlocked door, walked in, and the door closed behind him.

The office was furnished with an overflowing bookcase, a large leather chair, and a well-used welcoming smaller chair. Murphy saw the usual pencils and pads on the desk, along with a Bible and a picture that captured his attention.

Murphy was so drawn to it that he picked it up for a close look. The picture itself was not more than four by six inches. Jesus' dark, bearded, bigger-than-life face was suspended between a half-shadowed cratered moon and a cloud-covered watery earth. The light of the world revealed tears, overflowing Jesus' grief-filled eyes. The wide black velvet frame blended with the dark star-studded cosmos background. Staring directly into the face of Jesus, Murphy was so mesmerized he didn't hear the door open behind him.

"Good morning. You must be Pastor Murphy."

Murphy, startled, quickly set the picture on the desk and sheepishly turned around. He was being greeted with the cordial smile and outstretched hand of the janitor—Ella's favorite customer, Mr. Maxwell.

Murphy's initial discomfort around Mr. Maxwell dissipated after a few awkward references to their mutual friend, Ella, the keeper of all secrets at The Horseless Carriage. Murphy took the easy chair, as Mr. Maxwell sat on the corner of his desk, moving the unique picture of Jesus that had captured Murphy's interest.

"You like my picture?"

"Yes, yes I do," Murphy replied.

Mr. Maxwell picked it up, handling it as though it were something very precious, then placed it on the desk where they could both look at it. He flicked a piece of lint off the velvet frame.

"My son gave it to me." He stared at the picture. "My only son."

He turned to Murphy and slowly said, "I'll see him again one day, but under more blessed circumstances."

Murphy, knowing only that the son was dead, replied, "I'm sorry. You must miss him very much."

"Yes. Also my wife. As you know, she died not long ago."

Murphy nodded and bowed his head.

Maxwell's face lit up. "Ella is a wonderful friend. She has a gift to know when to speak and when to be quiet. I'm sure she did not give you all the details."

"No, no she didn't," he said, to assure Mr. Maxwell his secrets were safe with Ella.

Maxwell picked up the picture again and Murphy saw suffering in the lingering gaze. Murphy leaned forward, catching Maxwell's eye and said, "I'd like to hear more about him, any time you'd like to tell me."

Mr. Maxwell needed no additional encouragement. Settling into his chair, he leaned back. "I was known in Toronto as a very good architect, admired for my expertise in stacking one story above another, none of which ever collapsed." He smiled.

Then his brow wrinkled as he looked at the picture once again. "I was much better at building offices than I was at building relationships with my wife and son. I was a religious man. I was born high church and would die high church. And I did just that. Not physically, but spiritually. But, I get ahead of myself."

He focused on the floor, as if what he was saying was still painful. "You've heard that acorns don't fall far from the tree. Well, that was my son. He never missed a chance to assist the bishop in some liturgical duty. My son carried out his responsibilities not as a spiritual experience so much as to please his father. It was something he worked very hard at, but he never quite succeeded. Everyone knew I hoped to have a bishop in the family one day. In the meantime, my son and I filled just about every position available to a young person or a layman.

"I was also generous with my architectural fees, probably being appreciated for that more than anything else. The church didn't own my mind, but it did possess my ego. I expected points from God when I read the liturgy. I memorized and repeated morning and evening prayers that had been uttered by kings and princes before me, and with about as much effect on my life.

"Gradually, everything fell apart. My son had gone off to college and gotten involved with what the good bishop called 'born-again theological misfits.' To make matters worse, he spent his Christmas break trying to get his father 'saved.'"

Mr. Maxwell's tone shifted from sarcasm to sadness. "The bishop told everyone who would listen that if Mr. Maxwell's son continued to follow the path of those religious fanatics, he would never become a bishop, let alone be invited to participate in Sunday services, which he had faithfully attended his whole life.

"My son not only refused to recant his 'pagan' beliefs, he came home at Easter even surer of his new beliefs. My wife listened to what he had to say, thoughtfully, then took up what I saw as my son's cudgel against me. She had the nerve to ask me if I thought I possessed all truth! She was too gentle and obedient to tell me she thought I was wrong in this case, but she did say, 'I love you, but...even though none of your buildings have collapsed, your relationship with your son has. You know, dear, maybe our son is not all wrong.'

"So sure that I was right, I railed at her, 'How could a son betray a father like this? How could my own son fall for all that born-again garbage?' Thinking he was now turning my wife against me, I made like the Pope, speaking ex-cathedra to his Cardinals, and declared, 'As long as our son continues to turn his back on our church, and his father and mother, he is not welcome in our home!'" Maxwell closed his eyes as the memory flooded his spirit with fresh grief. "I remember shouting, 'Not now, not ever. And what's more, we will treat him as an infidel. He's no longer our son!'

"I stormed out the door, leaving my wife crying in the kitchen. The bishop was appeased and my reputation increased in the church. I communicated my declaration to my son with an infallible sounding epistle, sent to him where he had moved in with a friend. Actually, I thought he would come home, apologize, and all would be well. He didn't. We heard from people less attached to our church that he went to Alberta to attend Bible school. I never inquired how he could pay for it. I never inquired about anything. The break was complete.

"For the first time in my life, I began to grieve over what this was doing to my wife. I loved her more than I realized. I saw her beautiful, happy countenance fade with sadness. She often said she was too tired to go to worship services. More and more I was isolated from those I loved and who had loved me and was controlled by those who loved themselves.

"Unfortunately, my grief was too short-lived to stop me from devastating my wife. When she thought I was occupied, I heard her on the phone, talking to our son. I went into the kitchen and heard her say she had to go, as she hung up the phone. 'Who are you talking to?' I said, my anger barely suppressed. For the first time in our marriage, she spoke with deep bitterness. '*Our* son, *our only* son—or have you forgotten?'

"She then told me he was leaving the country and wanted to drop off a gift. He was on his way to the mission field." Maxwell choked up, unable to speak. After composing himself and wiping his eyes, he continued. "I forbid her to answer the door. She went to her room weeping while I waited, watching from behind a curtain. A car pulled up and my son rang the doorbell several times. Finally, giving up, he left on our doorstep this picture, wrapped in brown paper and string."

"He slowly returned to his car, looking back toward the house. I wanted to run out and enfold him in my arms like the father did for his prodigal son. But I was no father, and my son was no prodigal. I stood firm for my faith. The car was gone and so was my son. It was the last time I saw him. I still have the paper and string this picture was wrapped in." He opened one of the drawers in his desk and took it out to show me.

Mr. Maxwell sighed, as he and Murphy both wiped their eyes. "Well, I guess I'd better get you a desk so you'll have someplace to put your paper clips."

Murphy followed Mr. Maxwell out the door, suspecting he was being led by someone who had much to teach him.

Ten

Mugabe joined his fellow students at the breakfast table and filled his bowl with the fresh maize they had watered with their sweat. He smiled as someone asked the question that had become a humorous morning ritual.

"Well, Mugabe, how many more days?"

"Three months tomorrow if I have it figured right." Three months and Mugabe would be a father. Diolinda and his son were never far from his thoughts. When he went to bed, he thought of Levi and the things they would do together one day. But he also occasionally had haunting dreams of young roaming rebels coming to his village, attacking his wife and son.

In the morning, relieved the evil had only been a dream, he fed his hunger and thirst for righteousness by drinking deeply in his Bible studies.

Dr. James was so impressed with Mugabe's growing grasp of the Scriptures he had asked him, on several occasions, to teach the class.

Each day Mugabe thanked the Lord for the opportunities and blessings. This temporarily shook off the dream, and the heaviness that came every time Esther pushed him for official paperwork.

As Mugabe ate breakfast, his thoughts turned to the evangelistic concert that the school had been preparing for. A team of American college students was going to give an evening sacred concert. They were from California, where all the movie stars lived. There was talk that some of the musicians might even know Michael Jackson or U2. In preparation for the big event, they were given a two-week course on using free literature for witnessing to those who came forward at the end of the concert to accept Christ as their Savior.

Finishing breakfast, they made their way to the area site. They watched in awe as two Americans unloaded gigantic boxed speakers from their truck. "They'll be heard all the way to Capetown!"

Several of the bolder students asked if they could help. One of the Americans smiled, jumped off the stage, and motioned for them to follow. An American, using sign language, slowly enunciated, "Help...lift...speaker...out...box."

In perfect South African English, the students told each other, "He wants us to help him lift the speakers. They need to stay upright as we remove them from the crates."

The American didn't even blush, oblivious to his unintentional insult. "Wonderful—you speak English. Why don't you stick around and be my interpreter so your guys can help me set up?"

Sarcasm prevailed over grace as the students ribbed each other. "Sure, man, we'll be glad to help, won't we fellas?" "Cool man," and "We are very glad to have you here, man, and we will be honored to help you get ready for this concert tonight."

The American student finally caught on. He dropped the sign language and spoke to them as equals. Two hours later, working together, the students had the stage ready.

Never before had the students or the village seen such an array of equipment. What was it all for? They would find out when the sun went down, and the generator truck revved up and the lights and sounds filled the countryside, drawing the curious near.

As the students stood in front of the stage, surveying their morning and afternoon work and complimenting themselves on what they had accomplished, a large van pulled up near the side of the stage. Yelling young people surrounded the van, anticipating seeing the American performers, "Michael Jackson's friends!"

With all the equipment, the stage looked more like a site for a satellite launching than a worship band. There was a complex and shiny drum set, a synthesizer, and three guitars, each attached to long looped cords trailing to the off-stage generator. As the sound engineer set up his soundboards, the crowd grew and pushed forward, watching and listening as each musician did a sound check. The cacophony of instruments tuning brought more gawkers.

Hundreds of neighbors joined the many who had already staked out their place on the ground for watching the big event.

One of the American team, a tall blonde, sat down with her guitar and called out, "Hey, we better go eat and get changed. We can all go in one van."

Leaving the stage, the engineer said to the Bible school students, "I understand you're going to watch this stage while we're gone. Don't let anyone on the stage. This equipment's very expensive."

After the van of Americans drove off, the Bible school students circled the stage, laughing, as one said, "OK, my fellow warriors, grab your spears and bows and arrows and guard the white-man's bounty."

As darkness fell, the stage became a dark silhouette hiding the mass of technology assembled to amplify a message to hundreds of people gathering on a grassy knoll. Many came directly from work, by bus or walking, dragging their children with them. They would eat later. This was a special event they would talk about for months.

The Bible students wanted to grasp every opportunity to evangelize their own people. To others, it was something to break the monotony, a time to relax after a day in the mines or meaningless menial tasks. Tonight would be an exciting event.

Only a few white Afrikaans stood on the sidelines. They would have their own concert the next evening at their church, free from the mosquitoes and the smell of sweat.

The American team returned. One guitarist climbed on stage, picked up his guitar, and pointed at the young people in the front, emitting stuttering sounds like a gun. No one laughed.

The silhouettes of the worship team members could be seen as they took their places on the stage. Dr. James and Gretchen took their seats on the ground, with the Bible school students. A less cynical or judgmental pair could not be found in Africa, but they had seen this kind of event before. They prayed this one would be different.

A spotlight lit a microphone on the dark stage. A young African pastor went to the microphone and shouted in English, "From America, not to entertain, but to bless you in Jesus' name, please welcome The Young Prophets!"

Applause and lights burst forth simultaneously, capturing attention for the six performers, two with flowing dresses and tresses, and four young men who could have walked out of the magazine ads the youth of South Africa labeled "cool."

With the sound of a thousand elephants running through the forest, the guitars wailed as the Young Prophets sang, "Jesus, Jesus, Jesus." The crowd responded as they were directed, clapping and swaying.

Mugabe sat quietly, hoping to sense the Spirit's presence. Gretchen and Dr. James winced when one of the girls was spotlighted for a solo interlude on her conga drums. *Don't play your violin when Itzhak Perlman is sitting in the front row,* Gretchen thought. *Don't try to imitate Africans when, in Africa, they come out of the womb tapping their feet.*

Dr. James silently groaned. He leaned over and whispered into Gretchen's ear, "Can you believe these are grad students in Cross-cultural Communications?"

The drum player gave her testimony about how God led her from a promiscuous lifestyle to where she was now. Many did not know the word *promiscuous*, but the young guys could imagine. After an hour concert, one of the young men stepped forward and gave an abbreviated message that was interpreted into local dialects. Fortunately, as is often the case, the African pastor gave his own message in the native language.

The Bible students stood in front of the audience and held up their free booklets on how to become a Christian. Each had a picture of Jesus, an American Jesus, on the cover.

People did come forward. This is what the team would talk about when they went home. However, many were illiterate, but believed if they had a book to read, people would think they were literate, even if the book were held upside down. Others came, took the book, then moved closer to the stage to get closer to the Americans who were still playing and singing. Finally, as they strummed their instruments, the African pastor prayed that all those who came for the literature would receive Jesus Christ as Savior.

Gretchen and James held hands, weeping and praying, "Jesus, please don't let our frustration get in your way. If just one person is saved tonight, all this will be worthwhile. Father, we don't question the sincerity of these young people. Thank you that they are doing as they feel directed. We don't want to dictate how you fulfill your Great Commission, but this has not worked before."

The evening ended as it began. The musicians unplugged their guitars and went to the van. Soon the only Americans left were the engineers. The students helped them pack the instruments and load the rental truck. Many of the children from the villages watched until their mothers led them away.

Gretchen asked her husband, "Is this a case of the method overwhelming the message?"

Dr. James sighed. "I fear it is, but we must not judge."

Attempting to lighten the conversation, Gretchen chuckled. "Do you think the musicians caught on when the translator shook the leader's hand and thanked 'Docker' for coming to minister to them? Did they realize the pastor thought the label on his shirt was his name, and not the designer's?"

Mugabe joined them. "We have a story in my country. It is probably what you called one day in our class, an apokafrill."

"You mean apocryphal?" Dr. James asked.

"Yes," Mugabe replied, "something like that. But I remember your definition: 'a story of doubtful authenticity' but useful in making an important theological point."

"As usual, you learned your lesson well, Mugabe."

Mugabe then asked, with some hesitation, if he could tell them his apocryphal story. He thought it would make an important theological and cultural point.

"In my country there was a chief whose son thought his father was too old-fashioned. The son was eager to adopt modern ways. He had visited the city and seen many kinds of magic boxes that he wanted to bring to his village. He told the villagers of boxes with a shining red eye, boxes that made meat so hard that worms could not get into it, boxes that cooked meat and boiled water without fire. He told of a box with moving pictures from around the world.

"When the chief died, the son took all that the village had that could be sold to the city in order to buy several magic boxes. The boxes were delivered to the village by truck. As it drove away, the chief's son was eager to prove how smart and modern he was. So he lined the magic boxes up in front of the village. He pushed buttons, but nothing happened. He pushed the buttons again and again, wanting to prove their power and his wisdom. But no magic happened.

"A young warrior standing behind the boxes shouted that he knew what was wrong. 'There are long, black snakes coiled in the back—snakes with flat gold fangs!' And he hacked them all to pieces with his machete. All the magic boxes that man can make are worthless if they are never plugged into a source of power."

There might have been a smile in heaven when just at that moment the generator shut down and the stage went as dark as it had been the night before.

Dr. Nichols was about to make a point when the computer chimed that deadly sound dreaded by some and heard by all. Who was that technological monster sentencing now to at least 20 minutes of mental torture? Murphy thought Dr. Nichols seemed to enjoy that moment of suspense.

"Ah yes, we have a candidate for the coveted *Spurgeon Award*." Dr. Nichols leaned toward the screen. "And it is....." As he looked around the room, his eyes rested on the second row back, left side of the room. The other students gazed in the same direction in relief. Dr. Nichols removed his lecture notes and Bible from the lectern and headed back to exchange seats with the candidate, speaking as he went, "Michael Aristas, may we exchange places?"

A few applauded, which Mike knew was motivated by their relief rather than admiration. Those sitting beside Mike gave some good-natured suggestions: "Atta boy, Mike, let's hear some hellfire and brimstone."

"Don't forget; have three points."

"No fair speaking in the original language."

"Yeah, ya gotta use your Midwest twang."

The bravado of his walk to the lectern did not fool those who knew the shy, close-cropped seminarian. He tightly grasped the chest-high lectern to still his trembling hands.

"My name is Mike...I think." He moistened his lips with his tongue, staring at his Bible on the lectern. Taking a deep breath, he looked out at his fellow students and Dr. Nichols and saw only encouragement and anticipation on their faces. That, and the silence of the students, gave him the mettle to continue. "Right now, I wish I was back in Kansas."

There were encouraging and relaxed chuckles from the students.

"As long as I can remember, I've been a people pleaser. Confrontation made me sick to my stomach. In uncomfortable situations, I became whatever was expected of me. I was a good actor...or deceiver. I was surprised to discover in my Bible dictionary that the words *hypocrite* and *actor* were synonyms," Mike said as a side remark.

"So, I guess I was a natural hypocrite, and proof that practice makes perfect. I knew what role to play and when. I was one character with my friends, and, at home with my family, quite a different character. But I played my most convincing role in church. In Kansas, church is Sunday morning, Sunday evening, Wednesday evening, and many times in between. I had a knack for appearing serious and earnest so people thought I really believed the church stuff, and in a way I did. But my friends knew it had no effect on my everyday life.

"In college I joined a fraternity. It was our second Friday night, and we were now big-time university students. We needed to celebrate our newfound freedoms, as well as our manhood. One of the guys had a friend who was old enough to buy us some whiskey. Everyone chipped in some money. We were a few bucks short. One guy sighed. 'Well, it looks like we have to settle for a six pack of Coke.' This was my moment to walk on stage. The last thing I wanted was a drink of whiskey. I had never touched it in my life and didn't want to start now. I knew it was wrong. But, the show must go on. I stood and reached into my pocket. My mother had slipped me some money as I'd left home. I took out my $20 bill. Like some great actor on the stage of Old Vic's theatre, I lowered my voice and delivered lines that haunted me for the next four years: 'My fellow Americans, we must sacrifice so that we might all participate properly in this great rite of passage from being mere boys to men.'

"With an eloquent gesture I dropped the $20 bill onto the pile of mostly $1 bills and quarters and half dollars. There were even a few pennies. There were whoops of conviviality. I accepted it from the footlights as another great performance. An hour later, we sat in a circle on the floor. After all, this was a ritual. We held out our water glasses as one of our frat buddies poured out generous libations. My first smell of whiskey almost made me puke, but the smell of acceptance was sweet. An hour or two later, or was it days, the whiskey was gone and so were we. Some guys had gone to bed, but some never left the bathroom.

"This began the second act. By day I was the student who never missed a class, kept up a B average, and wrote home to say I love you. I was always polite. I even attended a weekly Bible study on campus, and of course, a local church where I was once again known as that 'wonderful young man we'd love to have as our son.'"

Mike left out the lurid details, but told how the Friday night parties became coed. He knew premarital sex was wrong, so he simply "fooled around." But over time his earlier views on fornication slowly drowned in whiskey. What he called an "undress rehearsal" with a girl could have led to love, except the girl would not talk to him again. The classes, the parties, the trips home, the lies, and the performances had a long run.

Now 22, he could drink legally. The curtain had come down and his stage of life was dark. He often went to local bars and drank alone. One night he ran into a woman whose husband was away on a long business trip. He accepted her invitation and went home with her.

They continued their bedroom scenes for several weeks, until one night, she called in a panic. Her husband had just called from the airport and was on his way home. Mike went for a drive and ended up at the same bar where they had met. To his surprise, there she was, snuggled up against the weekend bartender. She saw him but showed no sign of recognition.

Mike took another deep breath. "I have to tell you the next couple of months were rough. It's hard to act when your ego has been crushed. I kept forgetting my lines. I just wanted to be alone. Forget church. The last thing I wanted to face was a communion table. My hypocrisy had become an acid eating at my soul.

"I graduated and got a job in a bank. I felt relief that Act Three could be a new beginning. The only problem was, the real me dogged me from the teller's cage, to the restaurant where I ate alone at night, to my barren studio apartment. Even Monday Night Football drew me back to bad old days."

Mike's stance changed. His eyes had often lowered in shame as he spoke, but now he stood straight, as if ready to face an accuser. "Then one day something happened. A guy from my high school, who'd gone to college in Texas, was killed when his car hit a tree. Like me, he had been the paragon of an all-American-boy. He was like me in a lot of ways, but brighter and a much better actor. He was very active in church, loved by the gray heads and the airheads alike, and everyone in between."

"I went home for his funeral. The church was packed. Several of his frat brothers were invited by the family to speak. That was a mistake. One by one, his innocent frat brothers got up and told hilarious jokes about their deceased brother—stories the family knew nothing about. Some bordered on the profane, others simply on the ribald. None fit the description of a Junior High church leader. The folks were in a state of shock. Were the boys pulling a frat gag on them…at a *funeral?*

"As the funeral continued, that hope had a funeral of its own. Their last hope got up to speak. His story was not only the last, but the worst. I could almost hear him driving nails into the coffin. The pastor, in his formal robe, rose, fully aware of the families' and friends' consternation. Staring at the frat brothers sternly, he said, 'I knew this young man all his life, and as his pastor I have been given the authority to declare spiritual truth.'

"The frat brothers looked at each other, foreheads wrinkling in bewilderment over incurring the wrath of the preacher.

"The pastor moved to the family. With a gracious smile, he pointed upward and said, 'I know that your precious Donald is at this very moment in heaven with his God. I know that because I baptized him as an infant in the name of the Father, Son, and Holy Ghost at the baptismal fount right there. Donald was 13 years old when he came to this very altar, and as a confirmed child of God, received his first communion.'

"The next thing I knew, people were lining up to walk by the casket. Fortunately, I was seated near the back. I made a quick exit out the door. There was no way I was going to look at that body. On the way to the car I knew why. I was afraid I would see myself in that casket. I had to get out of there. Instead of going back to work, I found a secluded park. My mind and heart were racing with fear. I kept saying to myself, 'That could have been me. That could have been me.' Many were the nights I could have killed myself while driving in a drunken stupor. My frat brothers could have told the same stories about me.

"I reminded myself that I, too, had been sprinkled with Holy Water when I was only a few weeks old. Not just dedicated, but baptized. I, too, had memorized all the questions in the catechism, giving all the right answers to my pastor. I remember when he called my folks to proudly announce that their son, Mike, had passed all the requirements and that in two Sundays, all the communicants would be served their first Holy Communion. Family and friends came to celebrate what I thought was the best fire insurance policy available. My mom prepared a feast. Of course I didn't have to rehearse. I knew the script by heart, but I also knew I was the biggest phony on the planet. My life was written in large handwriting across the sky on my confirmation day: 'Playing tonight at the theatre of life, the great stage actor Michael Aristas in the new drama, *God is My Buddy*.'

"When I got home from the funeral, it was dark. I went inside, but was too restless to stay. Well, *afraid* might be a better word. I went to a bar and had a couple of beers. I tried to forget what I had heard and seen. I bought a couple of six-packs and called a couple of friends. I got within three blocks of their apartment, then made a U-turn.

"Fifteen minutes later, I was back at the same spot where I had spent the afternoon, only now the park was dark—no streetlights. I knew I was taking a chance on getting mugged.

"I'm still not sure what happened, but I woke up hours later on a country road. Both my car and I had run out of gas. I got out of the car, leaned against the hood, and puked. I started walking down the road. I don't how long I walked, or even where I was. I saw a glow of light on low clouds up ahead and headed for them. After walking a mile or more, a few slivers of light began forming on the horizon. I knew I was walking east. Morning couldn't be far away. I still had a little money left, so I planned to buy some gas and get home, take a hot shower before going to work, then act as if I'd had a normal night.

"But, suddenly, I felt someone walking behind me. I could almost feel his breath on the back of my head. I walked faster. 'Mike, why are you here?' I turned. There was no one there. I started to run, but then realized I was no longer running from me, but from God.

"I know this sounds weird, but I remembered the words of one of the Christian guys at school. He said he'd been raised in a good Christian home, and knew Scripture, but he never really knew Jesus—never grasped the truth that Jesus Christ had died for his sins. When he did, he was able to stop running. I thought how wonderful it would be to have nothing to hide, to be free of guilt, not having to play act through life. But I still got drunk that night.

"Well, here I was, drunk again—and out of gas. Just then an old man came by in his pickup. He took me to get gas and drove me back to my car. Just as he was ready to leave, he looked around. He noted the isolation and desolation, and told me he hadn't seen anyone on this road for a long time. Then he looked at me and asked, 'Why are you out here in this wilderness? Young man, you are lost.'

"I don't know what kind of expression came across my face, but he said, 'Well that's none of my business, now is it?' and took off down the road, leaving me in a swirl of dust. I swear it really happened.

"When I got home, I called work and told them I was sick and couldn't come in. I wasn't lying. I was and had been sick for a very long time, and it was time to get well. I called a former friend of mine from high school; he was the son of a pastor. I asked for his help. He listened and helped me pray through, and that's why I'm here today.

"Two weeks later, I went forward in his church to publicly confess my faith in Jesus Christ. Two weeks after that, at a Sunday morning service, his father dipped me under water three times, in the name of the Father, the Son, and the Holy Ghost. He used a term I'd never heard: believer's baptism. This time when I was baptized, I did believe. No acting out a role. I was a new character—for real!"

Eleven

The calendar in Mugabe's head had only a month and a half left. Heading in from the cornfield, Mugabe stopped as he heard someone call his name.

Gretchen walked toward him with a bright smile, holding up a letter. "I have something for you, and guess where it's from? A place called Mozambique."

Mugabe's mind raced. *Has something happened? Is Diolinda sick? Had something happened to Levi?*

Gretchen interrupted his thoughts, teasing, "Now who in the world do you know that would be writing you from Mozambique?" She handed Mugabe the letter.

"Thank you. I will save it until I freshen up, as you call it. Then I will read it."

After showering and dressing, he went to what he called his library, a place of private retreat in the small circle of trees where he had last read a letter from his wife.

Sitting down, he studied the envelope. He wondered why she had typed it instead of writing it. Was someone else writing about her? No, he told himself, she was the only one in the village who could type. Enough of this, he told himself, as he opened the envelope and pulled out a typewritten page.

My dear husband,
I am typing this letter because I just finished some official correspondence for the village chief.

Mugabe relaxed for the first time since Gretchen brought the letter. He leaned back against a tree and continued reading.

As I sit here typing, our son, Levi, is playing another game of soccer. The midwife was here this week and said that he should be ready to kick the ball into the net for a goal in about seven more weeks.

Mugabe sat up and imagined how her slim body must look with a soccer player in her belly.

Please do not worry about me, my husband. I am feeling quite well. Pastor Jonathan no longer lets me herd the cows, and I do not need to hoe. See, God works all things together for good. Without water, the corn and beans, and weeds, show little sign of rising up to meet the sun.

Since our fasting is involuntary, I am praying there will be enough nourishment from my own breasts for our little Levi. But remember, my dear husband, God will take care of us. The three of us. There is no place in our lives for fear. Remember what he did in the village of Chipaja where you lived as a child.

O-w-w! Another soccer practice has begun again.

There are not enough words on this typewriter to express my love for you, but when you come home we will speak to each other in another language as we lie together holding our beautiful little Levi between us.

Mugabe smiled as he saw how she signed it: *Your loving soccer field.*

Relieved, he leaned back against the tree. As always, the heaviness that never seemed to leave him acted as a damper on the joy he might have felt. He felt shame for his lack of faith, guilt that he was not with her during these difficult times, frustration that he still had no official papers that would allow him to go home for a quick visit.

Attempting to change his mood, he replayed in his mind the miracle of Chipaja. No matter how desperate things might get, it was a memory that always massaged his soul and relieved the pressure on his heart and mind.

He let his mind return to a day when the people of Chipaja were in their huts, trying to escape from the relentless sun that made the land a burning oven. There had been no rain for months. They carried water from the river and carefully applied it to the roots of the corn and beans. If the river dried up, they would all starve to death.

Suddenly, drought was not the only enemy. A sound like an approaching rainstorm could be heard in the distance, but people pointed to the sky in fear, screaming. A black cloud was coming directly toward their village, darkening the noonday sun. The villagers frantically grabbed their children and ran to their huts. They worked furiously, sealing doors and windows as best they could. The sound like thunder suddenly ceased, and was replaced by a chomping sound. The locusts had arrived.

In desperation, the villagers yelled and screamed at the grasshoppers as they attempted to beat the insects to death. Those who had nothing with which to beat the invaders stomped them with their feet. Everyone knew it was hopeless, but they were driven by fear of starvation.

Mugabe remembered it was a Sunday morning. He and some other young boys ran to the church and yelled at those kneeling and praying to come and help kill the invaders.

Mugabe recalled how angry he had been with the pastor when the pastor had quietly said, "This is the Sabbath; we are having prayers. The grasshoppers belong to God, and so does our corn, beans, and everything else that we or they can eat." The pastor stood at the church door admonishing the people, but some from inside the church had had enough prayer and were running to join the rest of the village in their attempt to protect their fields.

Mugabe recalled that only six people remained in the church, along with the pastor. They stayed on their knees, praying that God's will be done on earth.

Darkness descended. The locusts were gone, having devoured every green thing in sight.

The village chief shouted to those inside the church: "I will never darken the door of this place again. You refused to help us. I swear you wretches will starve to death before we give you one handful of the beans and corn we start planting tomorrow. When harvest comes, no one will let you put your shriveled hands into their cooking pots." Everyone knew the chief didn't really mean it, but someone had to be blamed for this catastrophe.

Help from the six men and the pastor praying in the church would have made no difference in protecting the fields from the devourers. But they believed their prayers could.

Early the next morning, the pastor, his six farmer friends who lived just over the knoll from the village, left the church and headed home. Some of the villagers shouted obscenities at them. Some children threw small stones.

As the pastor and six men continued their walk, they saw the same things the other villagers had seen: every scrap of vegetation had disappeared. It looked like a desert. This land would produce no food until it rained. The children would starve. The people would pack their meager belongings and begin a trek to where, they did not know. Many would die on the way. It was a cycle of history repeated again and again.

A little boy ran up, tugged at the pastor's arm, and whispered something in his ear. The pastor and the six farmers then picked up the tempo as they continued to walk up the knoll to their farms. The villagers, sensing something was happening, followed the trekkers. As they reached the top of the knoll, the pastor, the six farmers, and the two ladies fell on their knees.

The villagers ran to the top of the knoll, stopped, and gasped in disbelief as they looked down the other side. Though some of the fields had been stripped of all vegetation, the six plots owned by the six farmers remained untouched by the grasshoppers.

What happened?

An old leper limped across to the pastor. He told how he saw in those six fields a host of black crows, filling up on grasshoppers.

The village chief stared in disbelief. The pastor put his arm around him and said, "My good chief, they were God's crows. The same God that will soon send us rain, and we will stand here and see the fields with their rich harvest of beans and corn. When the harvest of those fields you see down there is complete, everyone in the village will be welcome to put their hand into our cooking pots."

Mugabe knew this story to be true. He had been there. There may have been some small exaggerations as it had been told and retold, but when the harvest came and the villagers put their hands into the six farmers' pots, one could not exaggerate how good it felt to an empty belly.

There had been no doubt in young Mugabe's mind that God worked miracles.

Oh Lord, forgive me. Increase my faith.

"Are miracles for this age, or did they end with the Apostles?" Dr. Nichols asked. He then presented both theological points of view. It seemed to Murphy that those who believed miracles ended with the New Testament Church were in the majority.

Rajan, the student from Calcutta, India, spoke up for the first time in class. "I have a question , but it requires a story, and like most stories from my country, it is rather long."

Dr. Nichols assured him that they had plenty of time, and encouraged him to proceed.

In his melodious English, Rajan began: "You must understand this is a true story." He did not smile.

Dr. Nichols indicated that they understood.

"Pastor Veejay was in charge of twenty congregations. Some were forty or fifty miles away. A few of the churches were connected by roads, but most only by walking trails. He visited them as often as he could, but he was also responsible for the church in his own village.

"An American evangelist was traveling through India spreading a teaching that God wants every believer to be wealthy, and happy, and that if you weren't both, you weren't accepting all God wants you to have. People were being told there should be oxen in their pasture, and food in their storehouse. One just needed more faith. He called it something like, 'name it and claim it.' Pastor Veejay felt he should intercept this false doctrine with teaching of truth about the Kingdom of God.

"He wanted to call the pastors of the twenty churches together for a time of teaching and prayer, even though their region was having a serious drought. Each morning, his wife had to stand in line for hours just to get enough maize for one day for his family. They had not had meat for almost a month. Feeding twenty-two pastors and their wives seemed impossible, and the other pastors had no more food then they had. After much prayer, Veejay and his wife agreed that God was still in the business of—" Rajan paused—"miracles. They agreed that what was impossible for them was not impossible for their Lord.

"His wife said, 'We women will be the Marthas and you men be the Apostles. We'll prepare whatever food the Lord provides while you seek the Lord in prayer and study.' She then went to the dwindling river to search for grass.

"The pastors and wives arrived. Veejay's wife gathered wood for fires and borrowed cooking pots. The only thing lacking was food. The first night of the conference they ate a soup of the grass she had gathered by the river. They fasted and prayed the next morning. In the afternoon Pastor Veejay taught his disciples the Scriptures that contradicted the gospel the foreign evangelist was preaching. As he was speaking, his wife slipped in to the church and whispered something into his ear. He asked to be excused for a few moments, then followed his wife outside. It seemed there was a visitor to their village, a broad-shouldered, red-headed man, who appeared to be a missionary. After they greeted each other, the man pointed to his truck and said, 'I have your supplies. Where would you like me to unload them?'

"Veejay said, 'We haven't ordered anything—certainly not anything that needs a truck.' The man pulled back a tarp, exposing vegetables, fruit, and grain. Veejay was confused, but the man insisted he'd been ordered to deliver it to the conference for pastors and their wives.

"By this time, everyone had joined them and was staring at the food. They had not seen so much food in one place in months. Everyone quickly helped unload the truck. As the last basket was removed, the man got into the truck, smiled a 'God bless you!' and disappeared down the road.

"One of the pastors said to Veejay, 'That was wonderful of your friend to bring us all this food.'

"'I've never seen that man before in my life,' Veejay said, bewildered. He knelt where the truck had been parked and gave thanks to God. Then he rose in awe and asked, 'Have you noticed there is no sign that a truck was even here? There are no tracks in the dust!'

"They had a three-hour praise meeting, then the women prepared a feast."

Rajan's eyes scanned the room. "I know this to be a true story. This did not happen two thousand years ago, but less than two years ago. So, my brothers, how do you explain such a thing?"

Dr. Nichols also looked across the room, waiting for the class to respond.

Someone near the back of the room said, "I would ask them what they ate for dinner the night before."

"We know what they ate," Rajan responded, looking his brother in the eye. "A small bowl of boiled grass. That was all they had."

"Did they eat that grass or did they smoke it?" Oscar, the class clown, chuckled.

Murphy had not seen Dr. Nichols angry before, but he gave Oscar a look that could wilt a fig tree, then turned to Rajan and apologized, not only for Oscar but for the rest of the class as well.

Rajan asked, "Sir, may I have one last word?"

"Yes, please do."

Rajan spoke quietly but with great conviction. "My brothers, if miracles such as this only happened during another time, then much of the world is living in that other time and I must tell you I like their time better than yours." As Rajan left the room, he was heard muttering, "Lord, have mercy on us. So much for the head, so little for the heart."

Twelve

The Grahams always looked forward to their weekly quiet dinner alone. The rest of the week dinner was with the students in the cafeteria, but on Fridays, Gretchen tried to surprise her husband with an American meal, or at least as close to American as she could find in the local market. It was a ritual everyone knew and respected as being important to them.

He smelled the night's surprise when he walked into the house. "Um-m." He inhaled. "Love you, and love those pork chops!"

She hugged him, then gently pushed him toward the bathroom. "Your first and second loves are ready, so get washed up."

She brought the pork chops to the table and removed her apron. James pulled out her chair. That, too, was part of the Friday night ritual. They held hands across the table as they gave heartfelt thanks. But before they could take a bite, there was a knock at the door. They looked at each other in surprise at being interrupted on a Friday night.

Dr. James opened the door. Mugabe, eyes glazed, a letter in his hand, was slumped against the wall. Dr. James helped him to a chair at the kitchen table. "We were just sitting down to eat. Would you care to join us?"

Gretchen set a plate in front of Mugabe. "What's wrong? You look like you've seen the angel of death."

"Yes!" Mugabe groaned, turning anguish-filled eyes on Dr. James as he thrust the letter at him.

Dr. James began to skim the letter. "It's from Pastor Jonathan?"

Mugabe nodded.

Dr. James shook his head in disbelief as he reread the letter from the beginning. "No, this can't be." He knelt beside Mugabe and held him tightly as Mugabe's shoulders heaved. "Oh Mugabe, my brother Mugabe, I'm so sorry."

Gretchen reached for the letter, but James pulled it back. "No, you don't want to read it."

"Why?" Gretchen cried out, "What terrible thing has happened? Please tell me."

James rose and took Gretchen in his arms, whispering as they embraced. "My dear, Mugabe's wife was raped by a young rebel. She will survive, but the baby is dead."

Gretchen gasped, nearly fainting. "No!" He led her to her chair.

"I must go to my wife," Mugabe cried, starting to rise. "I must go weep with her."

Dr. James gripped Mugabe's shoulder firmly. "Mugabe, the letter says she pleads for you to not come home early."

"I need her. She needs me!"

"She feels she has failed you."

"No," Mugabe moaned. "No, I failed her. I must go; she's my wife."

"Of course, Mugabe." Gretchen's tears flowed in sympathy.

But Dr. James gripped his wife's shoulder and his friend's, his eyes pleading to be understood. "Diolinda wants you finish your studies to become a pastor. She doesn't want what has happened to stop you. She's begging you to respect her heart's desire, Mugabe. Can you hear me? She knows what will happen if you get caught. Do you understand?"

"But she's all alone! I must go." Mugabe groaned.

Gretchen asked James for the letter. As she carefully read it, she began to understand Diolinda's fear—as well as her griefs. She gave her husband an understanding, sad smile as she put the letter down. "Mugabe," she said, "may I tell you something about a woman's heart. When a woman and man love each other as you two do, a woman finds wholeness in giving to her husband. Diolinda is grieving over the loss of the child she carried close to her heart, but she also grieves over your grief for your son.

"Her body was so full of promise. That promise cannot be delivered now, and I know she's weeping over that. Mugabe, the only thing she has left to give you is a very sacrificial gift—she wants to give you this chance to become a pastor. Accepting her sacrifice will help her heal. Can you understand that?"

He put his head in his hands, sobbing, "My Diolinda, it's too much.

I'm not worthy of such sacrifice."

James took Gretchen aside and whispered, "I'll stay with him. Will you go to the dorm and tell the men what happened? Mugabe must not weep alone."

Gretchen left to bear the tragic news to Mugabe's fellow students.

Dr. James knelt down to look up into Mugabe's face. "I understand your longing to comfort and care for your wife. But if you're sent to the mines for two years, you'll only add to her grief. God has not abandoned her; she will not be alone."

When Gretchen returned, darkness fell and seemed to fill the house…and their hearts.

James and Gretchen knew there was a time to speak and a time to be silent. This was the time for silence. So they simply held on to Mugabe and silently prayed. The Friday night feast sat untouched.

Finally, Dr. James asked Mugabe if he wanted him to walk him to the dorm.

"No, I must walk alone. I must weep alone."

Dr. James put his arm around Mugabe and walked him to the door.

Gretchen handed him a flashlight. "You'll need a light."

After James saw Mugabe out and closed the door, he took Gretchen in his arms. "Lord, the way is so dark. We all need your light," he prayed.

Mugabe entered the darkened dorm. Without undressing, he lay on his back, silently weeping. He had no salve for his wounded heart.

Then he felt a hand on his shoulder, his arm. Another hand, and another. One by one his brothers anointed him. Mugabe did not have to weep alone.

The computer had performed its task again. Roger knew the routine.

He exchanged places with Dr. Nichols.

Roger was a night owl while Murphy was a morning person. Consequently, their breakfasts at The Horseless Carriage didn't often coincide. The connection formed during their trip from the airport and the first couple weeks of class was now intermittent. Roger lived at home, and Murphy spent most of his social time with the dorm students.

As Roger stood to speak, Murphy made a mental note to ask Roger to join him and some of the guys to hang out on Saturday night. Murphy and some of his buddies went to a pizza joint fifteen miles down the freeway so they could have beer with their pizza without running into anyone they knew from school.

Roger was well liked but not known well. Tall, well-groomed, with a body chiseled from long bouts on the tennis court, Roger's designer clothes looked like they belonged on him. He gave a quick, wry smile as he stood before the class. "As you know, I'm Roger. I live with my parents, six blocks from here. I'm an only child. Some of you might have heard of my mother, Kelly Benton-Walker, one of the wealthy Benton girls who married my dad, James Walker, now wealthy also."

Murphy caught another wry smile.

"In case you are unfamiliar with the Bentons, my grandfather was a well-known radio preacher. My mother is a Christian motivational speaker. She gives spiritual advice on being beautiful on the inside, and sells all kinds of lotions, creams, and herbs to keep one beautiful on the outside as well. My father is her husband."

The implications of the remark were not lost on Murphy.

Roger went on. "He's a financial consultant, but usually accompanies my mother on her weekend church soirees all over the country. He holds seminars for the men on how to invest wisely. He practices being wealthy, on both the inside and the outside."

Everyone laughed.

"My father was a first-string basketball player at UCLA. That was in the days when a six-foot-three guard got on the floor to do more than wipe up the sweat when a real player fell down. He tried to transfer his success to me. I stopped growing at six feet one, but he still had illusions of grandeur and of my number being retired and hung from the ceiling."

Murphy felt sad for Roger. Here was obviously very angry. Yes, he'd ask Roger to join him this weekend.

"I went to UCLA," Roger said, "where I graduated with a degree in business. I happened to like tennis. When I first came down the stairs wearing my tennis attire, my father acted like I'd come sliding down the banister in ballet tights and pirouetted across the living room. My mother knew when to bury her face in the morning paper, though I doubt that she read anything more than *Dear Abby*."

No one laughed. Roger's pain was too obvious. Those who knew him outside of class didn't think he even knew how to be sarcastic, though they had noticed he often seemed lonely and frustrated about being unable to please his father or mother.

"My parents are active in a wealthy church several miles down the road, at least when they're not 'ministering' elsewhere. The pastor prays for them every Sunday to be 'greatly used of the Lord.' Of course, the fact that they mail in their tithe, whether they are there or not, keeps them on the prayer list."

Murphy began to feel very uncomfortable. This didn't sound like Roger. *I've never heard him be so bitter.*

"I was a cheerleader in high school. I didn't mind it. My dad hated it. My mother ignored it."

"My mother, who by the way is a beautiful woman, is also a fitness freak. She spends hours keeping herself beautiful on the outside. My dad gets bugged that she spends so much time on herself. But they never fight. Christians don't fight; they just destroy each other with silence. Like when my dad noticed my mother had a new herbal product that was—now don't laugh—to put on your butt to keep it tight." Roger grabbed his to make the point.

Everyone but Murphy started laughing.

Roger never smiled as he continued. "It gets better. My dad told her he understood. He said it was the same way with his business. 'It's important to keep close track of your investments so they don't sag at either end.'"

The room echoed with laughter.

Roger's face turned red. He was angry. "You wouldn't think it was so funny if you had to live in a house where no one spoke to each other for a month. At any rate, I've said enough. After all, the only question Dr. Nichols asked us to answer when the computer puked out our names was to tell why we were here, preparing to be a pastor.

"The answer: Well, I thought my folks, being religious as they are, would be proud of having a pastor for a son, but I'm like the woman we studied in class...you know, the woman with the bleeding problem. She had it for years, spent everything she had, but no one could help her. She was an outcast, living a lonely, separated life, thought of as untouchable. Then one day she sees Jesus. She touches his garment and is healed. I like that story. It never worked for me, though. But, as my mother says, 'Hope springs eternal.' I'm sure that's a new herbal product she's pushing."

Murphy gave Roger a forced smile, as if he'd heard a joke. But he realized neither of them was in a joking mood.

To everyone's surprise, Roger signaled Dr. Nichols he was through. Dr. Nichols thanked Roger as he returned to his seat, commending him for his honesty.

When class was dismissed, Murphy turned around to invite Roger to hang out, but Roger had already left the room. Murphy had his phone number, so he could call him later.

Before Murphy knew it, the weekend was over. He had thought of calling Roger several times, but something always came up and he put it off. There were a few guilt pangs on Saturday night as Murphy and his buddies downed their pizza and beer companionably.

On Monday morning, Murphy was hoping Roger would be in class early so there would be time to ask him about next Saturday.

But Roger wasn't there early—or late. Murphy began to feel uneasy. Several people noted he was missing. His chair remained empty. Murphy's apprehension increased. This wasn't like Roger.

The door opened and Murphy prayed that Roger, with his wry

smile, would walk through. But it was Dr. Nichols. Instead of giving his usual greeting and casual questions about their weekend, he walked straight to the lectern. His sober face and moist eyes alerted the class that something was up.

Dr. Nichols cleared his throat. "I've just come from the President's office. He informed me that Roger's mother and father returned from out of town last night. When they drove into their driveway and the garage door opened, they saw in their headlights, Roger hanging from the rafters. He had taken his life."

Dr. Nichols choked up, unable to go on. No one spoke or moved. Murphy's mind riveted on the fact that he had put Roger off all weekend, and now it was too late.

Rajan got up and ran to the door. The class could hear why before the door closed behind him—he didn't make it to the men's room.

Dr. Nichols took an envelope out of his folder. "He left us a note. His father gave it to the President. It hasn't been opened."

Dr. Nichols opened it, slowly read it, and shook his head but could not speak. Quiet weeping was heard from around the room, along with murmured prayers. Murphy stayed frozen, afraid to think.

Dr. Nichols regained his composure and read aloud the note:

> *My Fellow Preacher Boys (now minus one)*
> *Forgive me, my brothers. I sit here in the dark surrounded by my demons, and I can't fight them alone. They will win. I'm too tired to pray another prayer or to lift my hand to touch his garment one more time. Forgive me for being a coward.*
> *Roger*

Dr. Nichols folded the note and placed it in his inside suitcoat pocket. He picked up his folder and walked toward the door. "I think we all need some time to be alone. I'll see you tomorrow morning."

One by one, the students left. Only Murphy remained. He moved into the seat that Roger would never again occupy. He put his elbows on the desk, cupping his head in his hands, and cried, "Roger, Roger, please forgive me. I betrayed you. I could have stopped you, but no—I had places to go, friends to meet. Now it's too late. I could have called you to see if you wanted to hang out...." The irony of his words was a kick in the gut. He wept convulsively, shoulders shaking as he lay his head on the desk, crying out, "Forgive me, God. I let him do this, and he died alone...all alone."

Thirteen

For weeks after the rape of his wife and death of his son, Mugabe's emotions zigzagged like a Richter scale measuring aftershocks of "the big one." One minute he wanted to tie himself under a railcar back to Mozambique to care for his wife and avenge his son's death, the next he was on his knees crying out for forgiveness for wanting to take revenge. He couldn't concentrate on his studies. Mugabe had written to Diolinda immediately, assuring her she was not at fault for what happened, and that he loved her more than ever. He tried to encourage her by saying they would start their family as soon as he finished school, but he had not yet heard anything from her. He battled with fear for his wife and anger over her being violated. He asked himself again and again, shouldn't he go home?

When Dr. James asked him to stay after class, one day, Mugabe expected to be told he might as well go home, since his mind was always there.

"Mugabe," Dr. James said, "all the other students look to you for leadership, and help in their understanding of the Bible. They learn as much from you in the dorm at night as they do in my classroom, for which I praise the Lord. You're the one they ask for help when they don't understand my English, or my illustrations. You're the one who puts the lessons in cultural context so they can relate to them."

"I'm sorry that I interfere with your teaching," Mugabe said. "Maybe it would be better if I were not here any longer."

"No, Mugabe, this is a good thing, not bad! When your class moves into its second year, we will have a new first year class—eleven more students joining us."

Mugabe wondered why Dr. James was telling him this.

"Though you will still attend my classes," Dr. James said, "I would like you to help teach the new students."

"Me?" Mugabe pointed at himself.

"Yes, you."

Mugabe tried to absorb what he had heard.

"I want you to think it over. There's no hurry. Just let me know if you're willing to take on the responsibility."

Teaching would not lessen his vision to return to Mozambique and preach the gospel. Teaching experience would better qualify him to plant new churches. But look what had happened to his wife while he was preparing to minister to his country, Mugabe debated as he walked towards his private retreat among the trees. Why should he return to Mozambique, where rebels were free, like hyenas, to rape his wife? And rape the economy, the culture, their minds, their very souls! He picked up a stone and dashed it against a tree. *My country will never be any better,* he thought, *but Diolinda is there. Wait! What if God worked a miracle and made a way for Diolinda to come to South Africa?*

He immediately started out for Dr. James's home to tell him he had settled his mind. He would stay another year and pray that God would make a way for Diolinda to join him. They could start their family here.

On his way, a fellow student came running with a letter, excited at bearing good news. "It's from Mozambique!"

Mugabe's heart leapt as he recognized the handwriting. He held the envelope to his lips, rushing back to his private retreat.

His anger and fear completely melted into shame and relief as he read: *My darling husband.* Tears filled his eyes. It was the same greeting she had used before the tragedy.

> *All is well. The life-giving rains have finally come. For so long we were parched and unclean. Now the river runs with water and all is being cleansed. Mothers watch their children play in the water, smiling again, as they gather at the river to wash clothes and bathe. Fathers rise early each morning, looking for signs of newly planted seeds beginning their upward search for the sun.*
>
> *When a man's field remains barren, even when there is rain, there can be no harvest. Often that man would not want to keep land that was useless, but find new land that would give him a crop.*

Mugabe almost missed the message in her poetic prose, but suddenly it hit him. Diolinda was telling him she was barren. There could never be a Levi.

A week after Roger's death the chapel's seating overflowed to standing room only for his memorial service. His once-proud parents held on to each other as they stood and Roger's mother introduced to the crowd his classmates—all twenty-one, by name—sitting in the first two rows. Then, speaking directly to them, she said, "You've made us realize there was a Roger that we as his parents really never knew."

The aging basketball star who had expected his son to follow in his steps wiped his eyes and addressed the gathering, "These young men here changed our lives. We would not have made it through these terrible days without them." He struggled to continue. "My wife and I have never witnessed this kind of Christianity before. Their love and compassion filled our home and our hearts. They had nothing to sell; they were only there to bring the love of Christ. They wept with us, prayed, and shared stories about Roger. Their presence made us realize how much we missed, and are going to miss, by not having spent more of our time with Roger."

Both mother and father, who had never before been at a loss for words or advice, were now totally broken. They hung their heads.

At last, looking upward, Roger's father said, "I'm sorry, son, that we did not love well—you, or each other." Turning to his wife, he placed a kiss on the top of her head. She buried her head in his shoulders, and her weeping eulogy fell on the room like a quiet rain.

After the tears stopped flowing, she was able to smile at them and, with a tender voice Roger had seldom been privileged to hear, she pleaded, "Don't leave us now. Keep coming over and maybe someday we'll be able to laugh together."

As the service drew to an end, the class crowded forward, placing their hands on top of the casket. One classmate began singing the refrain that always seemed to touch Roger, and one by one each of them joined in.

Draw me close to you. Never let me go . . .

A week later, twenty-one somber young men slowly made their way into the classroom. There was none of the usual banter that ordinarily began their day of classes. No one exchanged glances as they quietly sat down at their desks. An ominous silence pervaded as each watched as one more seat was taken. The tension increased. Three empty seats remained. They watched the door without lifting their heads.

Rajan came in, followed by Murphy, who slipped into his place. The moment they had all dreaded had arrived. The reality of loss sunk in. Roger's seat remained empty.

The silence was broken as Dr. Nichols walked in, went to the lectern, nodded, and looked down at some papers he was shuffling. He was acutely aware of their vulnerability. He knew their tears had run the gauntlet of emotions—from anger towards Roger to guilt over what they might possibly have done to prevent the tragedy. Understanding their grief, he searched for healing words.

He looked up at them as he slowly began: "Well, men...it's been almost four months since we first broke bread together. On that same day we began our two-year journey as our Lord ended his—with washing each other's feet. Since then we walked together in the furnace. Only our beloved Lord knew back then that he was preparing us to drink of the bitter cup of grief he also had to drink."

Dr. Nichols wiped his eyes with his handkerchief and, with trembling voice, said, "I want you to know how tremendously proud I am of you. As you gathered around Roger's mother and dad, you demonstrated, not just to each other, but to this whole campus that you know how to weep with those who weep, and to mourn with those who mourn. You were used in their lives to transform a situation that the Enemy meant for evil, but God meant for good.

"You have passed through a crisis which has shown you that the Lord has indeed called you to fight for Him the good fight. It wasn't a perfectly fought battle, but forgetting what is past, we push towards the goal—the upward call of God in Christ Jesus! Our struggle, our pull, is not against flesh and blood, but against spiritual forces of wickedness in the heavenly places. Paul warned us about the enemy Roger faced and the enemy you have been facing the last few days. There's no escaping being drawn into the lifetime battle of spiritual warfare. Roger lost his last battle, but our Lord has won for us the final victory.

"Men, life will go on; life must go on—and so will the battles. But we must never forget what has been won, nor the lessons learned in each battle."

Fourteen

The Sunday morning service was about to begin. Wooden pews were feeling the burden of three hundred people hoping to be unburdened. Mugabe, the guest speaker for the morning, joined in as people began shouting to the Lord, dancing as the music seemed to enter the tips of their toes, travel through their bodies, and burst from their raised fingertips like geysers.

The cracked voices of the old waiting to die and the syncopated cadence of the young waiting to live blended in jubilant harmony, their voices accompanied by the rhythmic sound of the hollowed gourds and acoustic guitars.

The Spirit swept over the sanctuary in waves, rising and receding in cries for mercy, in admonitions, in prayers for healing, in joyous surges of song. The waves spread and dissipated, leaving peaceful hearts prepared to feast on a fresh word from God.

The pastor, seated next to Mugabe on the elevated stage, turned to Mugabe and nodded. It was time to preach.

Mugabe had spoken at this church before, but he was a different man from the last time he stood at this pulpit. He was still the most respected student and preacher at the Bible school, but he was a vessel that had been broken and was in the process of being re-formed. His theology was moving from his head to his heart. He was learning the meaning of "crucible."

"My brothers and sisters," Mugabe began, "much has happened in my life since I was last with you. God has led me through fire that I hope and pray will make me more usable as His vessel. When I was here before, I received generous encouragement from you. Unconsciously, I started to think I was special, that I would be given an honored place among my brothers in the Bible school. I was thinking too much like the disciples James and John, hoping to sit on Jesus' right or left." He paused. "I learned that my wife was going to make me a father. I was thrilled and immediately dreamed of how my son and I would do great things together. I was so proud of myself, enjoying God's blessing, and telling him what we would accomplish together. I wasn't listening and didn't hear if my Lord Jesus said something like, 'My son, be careful, you don't know what you are asking. Can you drink the cup that I must drink?' Had I heard, I probably would have thought my spiritual progress in the past months indicated that, yes, I could.

"I thought I was ready for any cup God put in my hand. Before I realized how wrong I was, God handed me the cup. Sorrow poured in through a letter from my pastor in Mozambique. He told me that my wife (who was soon to deliver our first child, who we already called Levi) had been raped by rebels. She survived, but our son did not. The first swallow of this bitter cup was a shock, but the second was even harder to swallow. Though my wife will recover, she is unable to give birth to another child. Thinking of only myself, I cried out, 'Lord, now I will never be a father. There will never be a Levi to carry the Mugabe name and the work we were going to do for you together. This is too much to bear—too much to drink.'"

Shattered dreams were a common experience for this crowd of listeners. He had their attention, especially of a distinguished, well-dressed, gray-haired gentleman in the front row.

Mugabe continued. "The hardest to swallow was that my dear wife pleaded with me not to return home. She needed time to heal, she said, and she didn't want to be the cause of my not becoming a pastor. I resisted this cup, unable to swallow.

"Dr. James and his wife urged me to accept her wishes, for her sake. I finally agreed, but my heart kept weeping—for Diolinda, for Levi, for myself. Night after night I cried out to God for help. Should I not be with my wife? I wanted to run and jump on a train home. Every time I was ready to break, day or night, my brothers were right there beside me, holding on to me, encouraging me, praying with me on our knees. There was no escaping them." Mugabe smiled at the memory of their faithfulness.

"In the many dark hours that I lay awake in bed, I repeatedly tried to swallow the bitterness. It was too much. I literally threw up. I could not drink the cup.

"You see, this was not a cup of communion, sweetened by repentance. We drink that cup sometimes without even thinking. Nor was this a cup of remembrance of Jesus' sorrows. It was my personal cup of sorrow, passed to me by the hands of my Lord. This cup was filled with bitterness fermenting from hate, betrayal, fear, and the desire for revenge. Had I not felt totally abandoned by the Lord, I would have passed the cup back to him."

Mugabe stopped for a moment, shaking his head over the memory of the despair. "I knew the Father asked Jesus to drink his bitter cup for my sake, so I wanted to drink mine for his sake. One small sip was all I could handle.

"I cried out, 'Jesus, I can't do it. It's too bitter.' I fell on my face beside my bed. I knew I was surrounded by my brothers, but there had been many nights of little sleep for them as they prayed with me. I did not blame them for sleeping now. I know there are things one has to do alone, in the darkness of one's soul. The words of Isaiah came to me: *'I have trod the winepress alone.'* These words burned into my soul. I cried out that if this cup cannot pass away unless I drink it, then drink it I shall.

"My heroics were nearly ended as I once again lifted the cup and tried to drink. It was even more bitter, for I was nearing the dregs. 'Father, I can't do it. Please take this cup.'

"I thought of an olive press, its purpose similar to that of the winepress. A new resolve came over me. A press has a job to do. It is cranked and cranked, putting more and more pressure on the olives. Skin is ripped open, flesh torn, seeds crushed, until finally there are a few drops of holy oil. My soul had been ripped and torn by grief and sorrow, but now my soul was crushed by the knowledge of my foolish pride and arrogance.

"Then I heard my Lord's words, *'Father, forgive him, for he did not know...'* But now *I* know; I have no more excuse. I drank of the bitterness of the cup of sorrow, but my Lord mercifully swallowed the dregs. I am not able to drink the cup he drank, but I tasted. If Job and Abraham and Moses and David all had to drink from the bitter cup of sorrow, so must we. However, no one but our Lord has been able to drink it all. But as he swallowed the last awful dregs, he could joyously cry, *'It is finished!'* He emptied his cup and he drinks the dregs of ours."

The distinguished gentleman in the front row joined the many voices crying out "Amen!" and "Thank you, Jesus!"

"He then handed me another cup," Mugabe shouted, to regain their attention. "I grasped it. I could feel cold tears of condensation running down the sides. I took it to my lips. The sweetness washed away the bitterness. I drank it down without stopping. When it was empty, I wiped it with my fingers, licking the last drop. No dreg in this cup, for this was the cup of joy."

Mugabe was exhausted with the reliving of his own Gethsemane. His eyes locked with those of the distinguished gentleman. Both of their faces glowed through their tears.

"My brothers and sisters," Mugabe said, "I am here to tell you that Jesus filled my cup with joy after he and I drank the cup of sorrow together. Jesus emptied his cup and downed the dregs of mine. What is our Lord doing? He just calls it redemption."

Sleep eluded Murphy night after night as he wrestled with guilt over Roger's suicide. Pastor Bjorn was concerned about the dark circles under his eyes, even though Murphy assured him he was "fine." Pastor spoke to Maxwell and suggested he might spend some time with Murphy, suspecting the two could actually be a comfort to one another.

Soon after that, Maxwell almost collided with Murphy, as they each rounded a corner. "Murphy, just the man I hoped to run into. I was at The Horseless Carriage this morning. Ella said she hadn't seen you for weeks. She wondered how you were doing. Said she spent so much time waiting on 'old men,' she was wishing for a 'preacher boy' to break the monotony."

Before Murphy could reply, Mr. Maxwell continued: "I told her we'd come for breakfast tomorrow morning, 6:00 sharp. Ella said she'd even buy."

Murphy watched Mr. Maxwell disappear with his mop and pail into the men's room.

After another sleepless night, Murphy arrived at The Horseless Carriage right on time. He saw Ella standing beside Maxwell's booth, pouring his coffee and talking, as usual.

Ella grinned upon seeing Murphy, insisted on a hug, and gestured for him to sit. "See, Mr. Maxwell, I told you he couldn't resist a free meal."

They drank their coffee and engaged in polite chit-chat, then placed their order. When Maxwell toyed with his cup, Murphy knew time for small talk was ending.

"So," Maxwell began, "would talking help?"

Murphy stared at the booth where he and Roger had sat the day Ella taught him a thing or two about Mr. Maxwell. Fighting back tears, he said, "Roger and I sat there, and I mocked you and Ella. Roger was so embarrassed and I didn't care. I ignored his hints that I should show a little compassion. Ella had to blast me before I got it. Instead of grousing, I could have used the time to get to know Roger. I could have learned from him. I knew he was lonely, but I was so caught up in myself, I...I failed as a friend."

Mr. Maxwell touched his hand; just like Ella had touched Maxwell's that first day.

"Mr. Maxwell, you told me about rejecting your son. You felt you failed as a father, didn't you?" Murphy's eyes pleaded for help. "How did you ever forgive yourself?"

"It's a long story, and I'm still working it out. Redemption can be a slow process."

"Well what happened after your son gave you the picture? You never saw him again?"

Maxwell flinched.

"I'm sorry," Murphy said. "I didn't mean to hurt you."

"No, it's alright. Our Lord calls us to share each other's pain and comfort each other, in the same way we've been comforted."

"Were you comforted? Did your son forgive you? Did you forgive him? What about your wife? Did you forgive each other?"

"Whoa! That's a lot of questions. Maybe I best start where I left off. When I hardened my heart against my son, I had to harden it against my wife as well because she kept in contact with him by letter. I wouldn't let her talk to me about him. As far as I was concerned, he was dead.

"But one day she collapsed in tears, holding out a letter so pathetically I couldn't *not* read it. It was from his mission board, telling us he was dead. I dropped the letter, ran to the bathroom, and vomited. I had to get out of there. I rushed out the door, leaving my wife alone. I jumped in the car and drove and drove. I ended up at the church my son attended before leaving the country. It was a Wednesday night, but the parking lot was full and I could hear music from outside.

"God was inside waiting for me. I felt him drawing me through the music. The preacher, about the age my son would have been today, talked about God's mercy, compassion, and his willingness to forgive sinners. That was me, a sinner. I never expected to need forgiveness, but suddenly that was all that mattered. I didn't have to be asked twice if I wanted prayer. A nice young man sitting next to me offered to pray for me. It seemed like God answered even before he prayed. He hugged me. I wasn't the hugging kind, but I hugged him back, thanked him, and hurried out, eager to get home and ask my wife to forgive me.

"I had hurt her terribly. I'd not only robbed her of her son, but of her husband. As we held each other, crying, she assured me she forgave me. I said something then that surprised us both. I asked if there was something the Lord wanted her to tell me. She hesitated. But at my new birth God rekindled the love we had the day our son was born, and we were no longer strangers living in the same house.

"'This has been terribly painful for both of us,' she said. 'We're both learning much about broken hearts. There's another broken heart whose forgiveness we need to seek. Imagine what this did to the heart of Jesus.'"

Maxwell leaned back in his booth as he continued. "Our lives changed at that moment. The Lord Jesus Christ became the heart of our marriage. We gauged our actions and emotions by what they did to him. When we worshipped with people who loved Jesus, we knew it brought him joy. When we, as husband and wife, began praying together, it probably brought even more joy to him than to us. And that's saying a lot.

"I retired soon after that and we moved down here for warmth and a fresh start, thinking the worst was over. We had a good year. Then my wife was diagnosed with cancer. We had one more year for me to care for her as she had cared for me. Then she died."

Maxwell reached in his top pocket, pulled out his Gideon Bible, and thumbed through it. "After the Lord showed us his heart, we had a new hunger for his Word. I was surprised one day to find a description of how I now felt. It was in the Beatitudes. *Blessed are those who hunger and thirst after righteousness, for they shall be filled."*

Mr. Maxwell stopped thumbing. "One night I was making my way through Joel's prophecy when I read a phrase that jumped out at me: *I will restore to you the years that the locusts have eaten."*

Maxwell's face lit up. "I was certain this was written just for me. God pulled me from behind the living room curtain. The shame I'd felt for years was gone. I knew he was promising to restore to me what arrogance, anger, guilt, and remorse had devoured and destroyed.

"You and I, young man...we share a common grief." Their eyes locked. "We aren't going to get another chance with those who are gone. But our Lord offers us the gift of forgiveness and hope. It's redemption. Murphy, my friend, it's time to let the locusts know they've had their last meal at our expense."

Ella placed their breakfast on the table. "Preacher boy, you're looking puny. Something been eating at you? Down your breakfast now!"

That night, Murphy slept.

Fifteen

Mugabe knew, and believed, even if he didn't feel, that God would not have allowed so much harm to come to his beloved wife and him without a plan to bring good out of it. But what that good was, he had no idea.

Not too long after Mugabe's opportunity to preach in a local church, the Lord spoke to him. It was as if Jesus was putting his arms around his servant and saying, "Mugabe, you always were a gifted speaker. You articulated well your love for me and reasons why everyone should. You've been like a lawyer, pleading on my behalf. But now, my son, I want you to be my witness. Before, you eloquently argued the case from books, precedents, case studies, and interpretations. But now, you are my wounded servant, standing in the witness box, speaking the truth, the whole truth. Mugabe, my son, you are no longer only an advocate. I'm calling you to be a witness now, and give testimony."

Peace almost filled Mugabe. It was a privilege to suffer if it would make him a more useful servant and witness. But what about the still gaping disqualification in his life that convicted him and ate away at his peace? The nights of troubled sleep continued.

Then one night he was jolted awake as the student next to him shook his shoulder, begging, "Wake up, Mugabe. You're having another nightmare."

Mugabe sat up in bed, confused, as the student rolled back on his own bed and told him this had been his third nightmare that night.

"Go to sleep, man, you're keeping everybody awake."

"Yeah," several other students muttered.

Mugabe fell limply on his bed. He was now wide awake. That had been more than a nightmare. He knew what he had to do, and in the morning he would do it.

He hardly closed his eyes the rest of the night.

At dawn, as the dorm came to life, he dressed and said, "Please, tell Dr. James I've got to go to town. I'll explain when I get back."

Mugabe quickly left as the other students stared at him. This would be a major topic of conversation at the breakfast table.

Arriving in town, Mugabe sat on the ground in front of the ostentatious building and read his Bible. It was an hour before the office was to open, but people were already queuing up in front of the locked doors. Mugabe closed his Bible and got in line. He wanted to be one of the first to get in. The seconds slowly ticked away in his mind, all 3600 of them, before a guard finally opened the door.

Mugabe headed for the window marked "Information." Only two people were in that line. A matronly woman came to the window, removed the closed sign, and gave a stern nod to the first person in line. He handed her some documents. She examined them for a moment and, without speaking, pointed, to the next line. She nodded at the second person. He handed her a sheaf of papers. She curtly sent him to window six.

It was Mugabe's turn. He smiled. She wasn't impressed. He opened his Bible, took out his Bible school ID card, and handed it to her. She looked at him quizzically. "As you see, my name is Henrique Mugabe. I am from Mozambique, and I am here illegally. That is the only identification that I have."

"This is all?"

"Yes, that's it." Unloading the heavy burden of his heart, he said, "You see, I have been here ten months now. I came in under the—"

She raised her hand to cut him off and turned to a desk directly behind her, passing the ID card to another woman. She looked at Mugabe to verify the photo was of him, then took it to an office door marked "Supervisor."

Several people had lined up behind Mugabe. He was motioned to step to one side to wait. He watched as a guard was called to take a man from the next line down a long hall.

Oh Lord, is this what you meant for me to do? Am I doing the right thing? I could be in class right now. Was that just a dream I had last night? I know this isn't.

He was startled by hearing his name called. The woman at the desk who had taken his ID card stood at a window. She handed him a form. The bold title read, "Illegal Entry."

"Go to that counter," she said, pointing, "and fill these out. Then bring them back to me."

With hand shaking and heart pumping, Mugabe wrote his name, the date he'd entered the country, means of entry, his address in Mozambique, and why he was here. Finished, he reread it, and got in line again, waiting his turn. He was in no hurry.

The woman who had given him the papers noticed Mugabe standing behind several people and motioned him forward. She examined the form and motioned to one of the guards near the door while pointing to Mugabe.

The guard led Mugabe by the arm down the hallway toward the closed door. Mugabe again wondered if he was making a terrible mistake.

As the door shut behind him, he saw bars on the window and several rows of backless benches. The guard motioned him to sit down. The room was full. All the benches were taken. He walked toward a vacant spot on the floor, near a wall. On his right, an older man glared, claiming his territory. Mugabe got the message.

A young man on his left moved over to give Mugabe room to sit. He was almost knocked down by the odor from the open urinal in one corner and the sweat produced by thirty or more occupants cramped together. Looking around, he realized they were considered criminals, already convicted and sentenced. They were on their way to the mines.

Mugabe whispered to the young man who had moved for him, "Is everyone here an illegal?"

"Yeah," answered the young man, "they're here from Tanzania, Mozambique, Malawi, and who knows where." He paused. "What about you? Let me guess—Mozambique?"

Mugabe nodded.

"So you got caught."

"Not exactly," Mugabe said. "But I did come in illegally, under a train—"

"Under a train?" the young man interrupted, "You mean you're one of those guys who tied himself under a train?"

"Yes."

"Man, you must have been desperate for work to do that." He smiled. "Or do you have a girlfriend here?"

"Neither," Mugabe replied. He raised his Bible. "I came to learn more about Jesus and his Word."

"You mean you rode under a train, chancing ending up here, in this room, just so you could read that stuff?"

"That's right," Mugabe said.

Both were silent, then Mugabe asked, "What is this room?"

"This 'room,' if you can call it that, is a holding cell where we sit and smell other people's piss and sweat until they call our name. Then they take us to another room that smells a little better, but is more dangerous, where a Judas Judge will sentence us to two years of hard labor for illegal entry."

Mugabe looked in the direction of two frightened boys in their early teens, obviously brothers, clinging to each other. "What about them?"

The young man shook his head. "I hate to think about it. I was about their age the first time I was caught. They'll be sent to the mines. But it's the dorms that will get them. They stink, like this room, with bunk beds used by someone else on each shift. The beds are never empty; they only need half as many dorms that way. Two hundred men to a dorm. No women, just a lot of perverts." He dropped his voice. "I was there for a year, the first time."

Mugabe looked at him in disbelief. "You mean…"

"We were considered 'toy-boys.' That's why I don't believe in God, but I do believe in the devil! I still have nightmares, and if I ever run into one of those men, I promise you I will put a knife in his gut and listen to him scream as I did when they did worse things to me."

Mugabe silently prayed.

A policeman entered from a room at the other end of the cell and called out several names. The two shaking boys were among those who reluctantly followed the guard out the door.

The young man spit on the floor. "They can't win. If someone doesn't kill them, they'll come out with sweat disease and die anyway; it just may take longer."

He stood and motioned Mugabe toward where the young boys had been sitting. "There's some room on the bench. Let's move up there, away from the pee can. So, how did you get caught? Somebody snitch on you?"

Mugabe held his Bible on his lap. "I gave myself up."

"You gave yourself up? Is that the kind of stupidity they teach you at Bible school?"

Mugabe replied with a half smile. "Actually, it is, but they don't call it stupidity."

The young man and two others leaned over to listen as he related how he came in under a train, about the heaviness he felt, and about the Lord telling him in a dream to turn himself in and confess he was here illegally.

"You're saying God told you to turn yourself in and you did it, all because you felt, what did you call it, a 'heaviness'?"

One of the other men listening laughed. "That 'heaviness' must have been one huge boulder that fell on your head."

Mugabe had just opened his Bible to read to them when the cell door opened. Everyone on his bench was called, except Mugabe.

The young man stood, looked at Mugabe, and with a twisted smile, said, "Well, at least I can write my grandmother that I met someone else who believes in God." He touched Mugabe's Bible, the smile gone. "I wish I could believe." Squeezing Mugabe's shoulder and fighting back tears, he said, "Pray that I get out alive." He turned and walked toward the open cell door. He didn't look back.

Mugabe prayed as he waited to be called. His stomach told him it was well past lunchtime. There were only four other people in the cell now. Two more were called, leaving Mugabe and two older men, who both glared at Mugabe, forbidding conversation.

The cell door opened, again, and the guard called out the names of the two older men.

Mugabe was the only one left. Was that good news or bad news? Was he going to have to spend the night here? He sat alone for what seemed an eternity as he prayed and continued to read his Bible.

The cell door at the far end, the one that led to the judge's chamber, did not open again. The door Mugabe came in opened instead.

A guard asked, "Are you Mugabe?"

Mugabe's strength drained from him as he got up. The guard motioned for him to follow. He led him up the same hallway he had come down hours earlier.

Back in the room where it all started, there were fewer people waiting in lines. The guard led him back to the woman who had taken his ID.

Seeing Mugabe, she laid out two official looking documents on the counter. "You're a political refugee. You will have to excuse us, but we had to cut your picture off your Bible school ID card." She almost smiled. "But you can easily get a new one from them."

Her "official face" melted. "Mr. Mugabe, you are free to live here, *legally*, for two years, then you must request an extension if you wish to stay longer. However, you cannot work, but only go to school. If you wish, you may request papers for your wife to join you. If you leave the country, this document is null and void, and if you return to South Africa you must go through the proper channels. These papers will not let you get into any other country other than your own."

Mugabe legs were shaking. He gazed in wonder at the heading on the document. *Political Refugee*. He had never heard of such a thing. He stuttered, "Thank you, thank you very much."

She smiled, returned to her desk, sat down, and went back to work as though nothing had happened. Mugabe, hands shaking, collected his papers and put them in his Bible. As he turned to leave, he heard a deep, resonant voice behind him.

"Mr. Mugabe."

There, standing across the room in front of the open door marked "Supervisor" was the distinguished, gray-haired, meticulously dressed gentlemen who had sat in the front row of the church where Mugabe had delivered his message on that Sunday morning.

He looked at Mugabe and smiled. "Brother, just call it redemption."

He turned and closed his door behind him as Mugabe made his way outside in dazed amazement. A policeman politely opened the door for him as he left the building. He stood still, breathing in the fresh air.

Mugabe was no longer an illegal. The heaviness was gone. He was a free man.

Real: We were with FEBC on Okinawa 1974. & flew to Guam to meet Vietnamese staff & process them to USA, CA

"Since spiritual warfare is taking place in an invisible realm, we are often unaware of our Lord's victories on our behalf."

Dr. Nichol's opening statement took Murphy back to thinking about Roger, wondering what was taking place in the spiritual realm when Roger gave up.

"I recently met a lovely Vietnamese lady," Dr. Nichols continued, "who, along with her husband, has a ministry to Viet Nam and to local Vietnamese families as well. I've asked her to share a particular story she told me that illustrates God having events in our life under control even when it appears He has abandoned us to our own devices. Will you welcome Bich Quong?"

"We were in just as much need of a miracle as the Hebrews when they were slaves in Egypt," Bich began. "The communists in North Viet Nam were determined to take over South Viet Nam. I assume you are all familiar with America's role—hoping to help deliver us and how that turned out. My pastor husband was drafted into the South Vietnamese army, but by the grace of God, he was assigned to be a chaplain."

Murphy soon realized her native dress was worn mainly to set the scene for her story. Listening to her beautifully spoken English, he could have easily forgotten she was Vietnamese.

"We had been regular listeners to the Christian programming of Far East Broadcasting Co., beamed to Vietnam by shortwave from Manila in the Philippines. We corresponded with FEBC and in time we were asked to set up a recording studio to make programs for Manila, which we did. Eventually we were asked to move to Manila in order to do live broadcasts. There was no way my husband could leave the country since he was in the army, but he encouraged me to take our young daughter, Nga, and go. At this time, FEBC was able to get me a multiple-entry visa, so Nga and I went. We lived on the FEBC missionary compound. I did Bible programs and news broadcasts to supplement the taped programs done in the Saigon recording studio by my husband, my sister, and several others.

"I went back to Saigon to visit my family several times. We began to realize the war was lost. America was withdrawing her troops and the Viet Cong was closing in on Saigon. We discovered the Viet Cong had a liquidation list and we were on it because of our association with an American organization. Each of us on the FEBC staff were marked to die.

"When the American home office learned this, they immediately sent one of the missionaries from Manila, Mr. Wayne, to go to Saigon and find some way to rescue us. This was not an easy assignment. Vietnamese from the countryside were flooding towards the coast looking for a way to escape the Vietcong. Hundreds of sampans, some seaworthy and some not, were, for a price, taking panicking refugees out to sea. Mr. Wayne hired a boat, but timing for the escape was tricky. Mr. Wayne told us to listen to the daily newscast for a code word, *green*, to be used the day before the boat was ready to leave.

"Because I already had a multiple-entry visa, I was allowed to purchase a plane ticket to Manila, but Nga (and of course the rest of the staff) was refused an exit permit. I could not leave my daughter behind. I tried again to get permission for her to leave and was refused. The FEBC Manila missionaries were praying for a miracle for all of us.

"I tried again for her exit permit, without success. There was only one more day before our flight. I made one last attempt. Standing in the long line, I could finally see the official who would be making the decisions this day. To my dismay, I recognized the man as someone whose advances I had once spurned. He had never forgiven me. But I had no other option. I had to trust God to let me find favor in this man's eyes. To my astonishment, he stamped Nga's application APPROVED without even looking up. It appeared God had blinded him to seeing who I was.

"When Nga and I arrived in Manila, we were all a little like Rhoda when Peter's friends had gathered to pray for Peter's release from prison. When he showed up at the door they were in shock. When Nga and I walked off the plane, oh how our friends in Manila laughed and cried at God's deliverance.

"But the rest of the Saigon staff and their families, thirteen in all, including my husband and sister were still in imminent danger.

"One night, in Manila, we received word that the arranged-for ship had cleared the Mekong Delta. We were thrilled that we were getting our own Red Sea miracle, even if God was using a boat.

"But the next day we heard that the ship had been apprehended and everyone on board had been incarcerated. Our joy turned to mourning. We were helpless.

"Two nights later, I was awakened in the middle of the night by Mr. Wayne pounding on the door.

"'Good news!" he said. "I just got a call from the Red Cross at Clark Air Base and they said there are thirteen Vietnamese here who say they belong to FEBC. They asked me to come and clear this up."

"We were amazed! How could this be? How did they get here? How did they get out of prison? So many questions! But Mr. Wayne couldn't leave the mission compound until curfew lifted in another four hours. He and his family and the friends Nga and I were living with were so excited with the news we couldn't go back to bed. Mr. Wayne telephoned the home office here in Californian and we all sang over the phone Praise the Name of Jesus. Somehow, He was the Deliverer. No Moses for us, but our Lord Jesus.

"Even after celebrating over the phone, we couldn't contain our joy, so the eight of us started around the compound, one house at a time. We threw rocks on the tin roofs of the two-story buildings until someone came to a window. We started singing and they just knew without being told the reason for our joy. At every house the grinning listener grabbed something to wear and ran out the door, crying out, "Praise the Lord!"—until the last house, where the staid British missionary's words were, 'Jolly good!'" Jolly good, indeed!

"We were all so thrilled at God's deliverance, but we had no idea how it had been possible. When the curfew lifted, Mr. Wayne took Nga and me to Clark and we heard the story firsthand.

"My husband, Captain Quong, was the one trying to drive the car, crammed with thirteen people, when it was time to catch the boat to freedom. The coded message had been received. They were alert, prepared, ready to go, but the car wouldn't start! Again and again he tried, praying with every attempt. How could God let that happen? The timing was so crucial. They couldn't go to the dock too early and be seen loitering. They couldn't get there too late and cause other refugees delay—or miss the boat.

"Finally, after much lost time, the engine turned over and they were off. But when they got to the dock they saw the boat chugging away. It was too late. They dared not linger, but went back immediately to the studio—to face their fate...So how *did* they escape?

"Back at the recording studio, where most of them also lived, they mourned the loss of their chance to escape. They prayed for strength for what lay ahead. They waited for the Vietcong to pound on the door. Even though they were full of dread, they still needed to eat. My sister, Mai, left on her bicycle to get food.

"The sound of gunfire and mortars drew closer. Then they heard the dreaded pounding on the door. Upon opening it, imagine their amazement when they saw a black limousine with a large American flag hanging from the bumper staff.

"'Get in, get in,' the American ambassador's driver, urged, opening the car's doors. 'Quick!' All twelve stumbled into the vehicle and the doors were slammed shut.

"'There's one missing,' my husband called to the driver, but there was no time left.

"The limousine weaved through the noisy streets crowded with bicycles, cars and carts, people going every direction. Everyone in the car was silent. Mai was being left behind.

"Then, there she was! In the street, on her bicycle. Pulling up beside her, they opened the door and yelled. She left the bicycle—and food—in the street, and jumped in the car. The limousine plowed through the sea of people, American flag fluttering in the breeze, while those inside the car prayed for those being moved aside and left behind. An airport gate was opened for them, and the limousine, sent by the American ambassador, an FEBC listener, drove right onto the tarmac. A plane loaded with an anxious press corps stood on the runway, engines running, and door open. In minutes they were in the air.

"When the car wouldn't start, and then they missed the boat, it appeared that God had abandoned us. But what if they had made it to the boat on time? They would have still been in prison!

"You are young. As future preachers you probably think that God is expecting you to do great things for Him, but when you are older and look back on your life I suspect you will discover what I have—God is the one who expects to do great things for you. We simply put our feet in the water, acting on faith and trust and God does the powerful thing, the things we cannot bring to pass.

"We were appointed to die by those who considered us the enemy. But the angel of death passed over us. God didn't choose to part the waters for us, but He flew us across the Sea! First to the Philippines and then to America. The enemy was thwarted once again, and God continues to give us opportunities to serve Him."

Murphy thought again of Roger and his assumption that God had abandoned him. If only he had not taken his own life. Surely God would have in time provided a way for Roger to cross over his sea of despair.

Lord, help me to never give up too soon.

Sixteen

It had been a month since Mugabe had written to Diolinda, assuring her that her inability to bear children didn't affect his love for her, except to make him treasure her all the more. He no longer struggled with thoughts of revenge, now conscious of being forgiven himself. He had a new understanding of redemption as he enjoyed the freedom of being out from under the heaviness of being an illegal. Yet he couldn't be at ease in his spirit until he heard from Diolinda again.

She was always in his thoughts. She was there when he awoke in the middle of the night, when he was hoeing in the afternoon sun, when he was eating or studying.

At the same time he was learning much from Dr. James' teaching, which felt personally delivered to him by the Holy Spirit. During communion, washing of his brother's feet, praying in his private place of retreat, Jesus was there. But coming down from the mountaintop, he was met with his own heart's cry, "Why can I not help her heal?"

Finally, the heartache found release the same way it began—a letter from Pastor Jonathan.

Rushing to his private place of worship and prayer, he tore open the envelope.

Dear Brother,
I am concerned about Diolinda. She seems to have separated herself from the village. She rarely smiles. Most of her time is spent hoeing in the field. She looks almost emaciated. She comes in from the field and disappears into her hut. No one sees her until the next morning as she walks with her hoe back to the field. Our great fear is that one day she will keep on walking into the forest, leaving only her hoe behind. My brother, it is time. I think you should come to her. She needs you.

Mugabe's heart leaped. Forgiveness, redemption, and Diolinda became one. He looked up and shouted, "Yes Lord, it is time!"

During the three-hour passenger train ride back to Komatipoert, so different from his illegal entry, Mugabe was overwhelmed with memories of ways God had provided for him.

He remembered his first day at school, when Esther was mumbling numbers to herself as she stormed into her office. He realized now those were his clothes sizes, and that is why he had clothes that fit him the next morning. She was also the one behind his finding medication on his bed the time he was afraid he had pneumonia.

He relived those moments at the train depot when he and Dr. James said good-bye. While standing among the jostling crowds of people, Dr. James had asked him what time it was. They laughed as Mugabe, still from force of habit, absently lifted his shirtsleeve and looked at his bare arm. Dr. James placed his watch on Mugabe's arm.

He chuckled, remembering the astonished stares of people watching a weeping black man and a white man unashamedly embracing each other.

His stomach then ached as he thought about his fear of how Diolinda would receive him. Would she be hurt by his leaving Bible school? Dr. James had assured him he was ready for the ministry and gave his blessing to his returning home. He even provided the ticket.

As he walked the fifteen miles from Komatipoert, word of his coming reached his village before he did. Many villagers came to walk the last mile with him. When Pastor Jonathan reached him and they talked face-to-face, Mugabe discovered Diolinda had never received his last letter. No wonder her heart was breaking.

Jonathan walked Mugabe to his hut, and then sent everyone on their way. Mugabe entered, crying the name of his beloved, and closed the door. He was home.

Mr. Maxwell turned around and welcomed Murphy to his office.

Murphy went to his chair, and sank into it with a depressed sigh.

"I've lost something, but I don't know what to do about it."

"Well what did you lose?" Maxwell asked with a sympathetic chuckle.

"Joy, excitement about being a Christian." Murphy sighed again. "I'm taking great classes on theology, and hermeneutics. I've got godly mentors—Dr. Nichols, Pastor, and you. But it's not working. The fire's gone, the passion I had when I first became a Christian, when I decided to come to seminary. I don't know how to get it back."

"I know what you're talking about, and maybe this will help." Mr. Maxwell opened his Bible, looked at the picture on his desk of Jesus, breathed a quick prayer and said, "Look at Luke 15, verse 8. *Or what woman, having ten silver coins, if she loses one coin does not light a lamp, sweep the house and search carefully until she finds it?* So, preacher boy, what's the message here? It seems quite obvious, doesn't it? When something important is lost, one searches until it's found. If you've already seen the light, just say so."

"No, I'm intrigued. Carry on, Augustine."

Mr. Maxwell leaned back in his chair, "Who is 'woman'?"

"Well, the Church is the Bride, so I guess I could be 'woman.'"

"So, let's just assume so for now," Maxwell said, "what about the 'coin'?"

"Weren't the coins the woman's dowry? I think Edersheim said, though, that if her husband divorced her, she kept her dowry. What we call a 'prenuptial agreement.'"

"Yes," Maxwell said, "the dowry in this parable was in the form of ten coins attached to a headband. However, the parable says she lost one coin. What might the coin represent? What is lost that I, you, the body of believers, bring into our new born-again relationship with Jesus Christ? Something that is ours, and by Law, no one can take it away?"

"You're not talking about salvation?" Murphy frowned.

"Now don't get nervous. I'm not talking about salvation, but something that one brings into the relationship with the Lord, when two become one. Want a clue? Think Revelation 2? Our Lord told the church at Ephesus they were good, moral people. Like those who don't drink and don't chew and don't hang out with those who do. But the Lord says he has something against them.

"You know what it is. It's exactly what you were talking about when you came in here. They lost their first love for Jesus. This woman lost her first love, her contribution to the relationship. Perhaps the zeal, the passion shared during the honeymoon had cooled considerably. The relationship had lost its zing.

"I'm certain she didn't set out to lose it. It's interesting to note where she lost it. She didn't lose it out doing the town, she lost it where you would least expect her to: in her own home, where you would think the relationship would be nurtured instead of lost.

"So, what are we talking about here? Perhaps she lost her first love through benign neglect while living a sloppy Christian lifestyle. I can imagine how it went. One day, she was on her way to lead a Bible study when she saw herself in the mirror and realized something was missing. She told herself she'd check it out when she got home.

"While at the Bible study, she held her head straight so no one else would notice the headband wasn't just right. Finally, the Bible study ended. She hurried home and headed for the mirror. Her heart pounded as she counted. There were only nine there. One had been lost. But where? Today was the first time she left the house; it must be at home somewhere."

"She made herself a cup of tea as she strategized. She could move the coins so the empty spot wouldn't be noticed. She could buy another coin, a counterfeit. She could go to the Christian bookstore and buy that latest book, *How to Feel Good Even When You Don't* or *Jesus Wants You to Be Happy*.

"That one was on cassettes so she could listen to it while driving to teach her Bible class," Murphy added.

"I see you get the point."

"Yes, the coin represents her first love, and she has lost it, like me. But let's get to the part about finding it again."

"OK It says here, 'she lights a lamp.' Now, Brother Murphy, I'm not going to insult your intelligence. We both know what that means, though we keep looking for a version we like better than what we have."

"Yeah, we've discussed this before." Murphy sighed. "If the one we're reading isn't satisfying our hunger for His Word, it probably means we're really not hungering and thirsting for His Word."

Mr. Maxwell was obviously pleased Murphy remembered. "I'm beginning to believe we Christians want a Bible we can put under our pillow at night and learn through osmosis."

Murphy sat up. "Seriously, lighting a lamp or letting God's Word do the searching, is pretty convicting. It reminds me of a story from a missionary I heard at our church back home. Did I tell you about this young Russian guy, Alexander Ogorodinikov?"

Mr. Maxwell leaned back in his chair. "No, but I'm in no hurry if you're not."

Murphy picked up the invitation. "It was a journalist/missionary from Toronto; I think his name was Estabrooks. He told about this university student in Moscow who came to Christ, then insisted on testifying of his newfound faith to his fellow students. He was so zealous with, I think we could call it his first love, only he didn't lose it. His zeal took him out of the University and landed him in a prison camp in Siberia.

"Estabrooks told how he and a group of Canadian Human Rights pastors were in Moscow, just before Glasnost. President Reagan was about to come to Moscow to meet with Gorbachev. Reagan had specifically asked to privately interview some dissidents. The Russian Government brought Ogorodinikov back to Moscow for that purpose.

"Because Estabrooks was with a Human Rights group, officials in Moscow allowed him to interview Ogorodinikov as sort of a warm-up for his interview by Reagan. I remember Estabrooks choked up as he told Ogorodinikov's story. It was wintertime, and Ogorodinikov nearly froze to death. He was put in a slimy, smelly isolation cell, but worst of all, his Bible was taken away. He told the prison official he wouldn't eat until they brought his Bible back.

"As Estabrooks told it, the prison officials could have let Ogorodinikov freeze to death and buried him in an unmarked grave. Instead, they force-fed him to keep him alive. They stuck a tube down his esophagus, filled a soccer ball with boiling hot sugar water, taped it to the tube, and jumped on it forcing the scalding liquid into his stomach. But, eventually, they gave him his Bible, only to take it away again as soon as he healed. He went on a hunger strike again. They gave him the scalding treatment again, but apparently his insides lost all feeling. So the guards had to find another way to entertain themselves. They stuck needles in his arms and fed him intravenously. They toyed with him, giving him his Bible, then taking it away, and he'd go on another hunger strike.

"We were all teary when Estabrooks repeated what Ogorodinikov said about his days of fasting and torture. 'Sometimes the hours were so long. Oh brother, sometimes the minutes were so long. Oh my brother, sometimes the seconds were so long.' Then Estabrooks said Ogorodinikov's face literally lit up and he cried out, 'But they gave me my Bible back!' and he raised it high, grasping it tightly.

"You know how many days he held out, fasting, in order to hold God's Word in his hand? Over his years in prison, a total of 659 days!"

Murphy shook his head in awe. "But you know what? After Reagan interviewed him, Ogorodinikov was released in the name of Glasnost."

Greatly moved, Mr. Maxwell murmured, "You shall know the truth, God's Word, and the truth shall make you free."

The two men sat quietly, heads bowed, taking in the significance of what Ogorodinikov represented and how they, personally, would respond to such a challenge.

Murphy broke the silence as he looked up. "Well, we can't stop here. I'm ready for the rest of the parable, if you are."

"Yes," Mr. Maxwell replied, "but we have to remember that when our first love is lost, we have to let the light of the Word expose every nook and cranny of our life. She sweeps the floor. Those floors were either packed dirt or cow dung. My understanding is people did not have comfortable chairs to sit in. So, to eat, visit, sleep, they reclined on the floor. To make it more comfortable, they spread straw over the floor."

"There's something interesting about straw: It has no power to reproduce. The seed has been removed. It's used as filler for an aching stomach when there's no real food. Straw would muffle the ping of a coin hitting the ground, so you wouldn't know when it fell. But most significant, straw was often mixed with mud, with man's hands, to make idols."

Mr. Maxwell paused while Murphy took notes. "So what are our idols? What substitutes for God have we created for ourselves? Today's idols often become tomorrow's bonfires, like today's Bible translation becomes tomorrow's relic.

"I recall the words of G. K Chesterton who said something like, 'When we cease to worship the true God, the danger is not that we worship nothing, but we worship anything.' What is an idol? It's anything that replaces the commands of God when we think He doesn't understand us or our needs. What we don't like to hear is that those needs are self-centered, self-inflated, and self-deceived. Idols are what give us an inflated idea of our position and ourselves. The main problem is that they cover up our consciousness of the loss of our first love."

Murphy said, "That reminds me of something in Corinthians about fire revealing what our foundation is made of—imperishable gold and silver, or wood or straw."

"And don't forget in the end, straw, our idols, are thrown on the dung heap to be burned." Mr. Maxwell added, "Little wonder one American poet wrote, 'We are the hollow men, the stuffed men, headpieces filled with straw.'"

Looking at his watch, Mr. Maxwell continued, "Now we are running out of time. Two more things to do while looking for the lost first love: the passage in Luke reads, 'She swept the house and searched diligently.'"

Murphy interrupted, "In Greek, *diligent* means 'to move forward hastily, energetically, painstakingly, without looking back.'" He then added with a smile, "See, I have learned something at school."

"Ah…" Maxwell continued, "I can see that lady sitting on the floor with the light shining, picking up each piece of straw as she searches diligently, saying to herself, 'I'm not doing anything else until I find that lost coin. I'll not teach any Bible studies, I'll not attempt to disciple anyone until I find what I've lost.'

"Now, quickly, because I've got to get upstairs and clean up after the Ladies Missionary Luncheon. 'And when she found it she called her friends and neighbors together saying, "Rejoice with me, for I have found the piece that I had lost."'

"She's compelled to tell everyone how she lost her first love but that now she has found it. She tells her Bible classes and anyone else who will listen. She tries to keep from dancing in the aisles during the worship time. But let's not stop there. What do we call, 'losing our first love?' Read on, don't miss this: 'Likewise I say to you, there is joy in the presence of the angels of God over one sinner who repents.'"

"You know," Murphy said, "to lose one's first love is sin. Why call it anything else? I thought I was the only one hurting over my loss, but not true. It hurts the Lord Jesus."

Murphy closed his notebook and Mr. Maxwell his Bible. Without saying another word to each other, they left the room.

Murphy got back to his office and dug out a book he had just finished reading. He had read something that had offended him, but now it took on relevance:

> Visit a church on Sunday morning, and you would be likely to find a congregation comfortably relating to a deity who fits nicely within the precise doctrinal positions of their social stream, or who lends support to many wonderful causes, or who conforms to individual spiritual experiences. But you will most likely not find much awe or reverence, or sense of power and mystery. Not much "wow, what do you think God is going to do for us this morning?" The New Testament warns us: offer to God an acceptable worship with reverence and awe, both of which have been replaced by the yawn of familiarity.

Murphy went to his knees. *Lord, use Your light to expose whatever is dimming the first love I brought to our two becoming one.*

Seventeen

The sweat ran down Mugabe's face as he hoed the beans his wife had faithfully planted and nurtured. They were showing promise of adding some variety to the maize and millet daily diet, often-savorless, though much better than the boiled grass that Diolinda and the other villagers had subsisted on for too long.

Hoeing the fields was a task Mugabe enjoyed. It was one of the few things he did that had measurable results. It also gave him time to think and to pray about Diolinda's and his future ministry.

Since returning to his country and his own people, he had spent much time thinking about the past, the present, and the future. He found the present and future especially disconcerting. His country seemed to be heading backward instead of forward.

Before the white man came with their guns and much learning, the leaders of the villages met under a tree and solved the problems of their communities. That was closer to a democracy than what the white man had forced upon them, Mugabe thought.

The Portuguese had built towering buildings of pink tile, explaining, not very patiently, that showy buildings are what made cities great.

The white man then dressed the natives in western clothing and pretended to give them governing responsibilities. This created a stratum of black society much less equal than the white man but more equal than other black men. This new class pompously strutted into the foreigner's building, pretending to lead, but in reality, being led by the white men.

Now the Portuguese were gone, but Portuguese-appointed natives met in secret, determined to rule like their predecessors, by edict, not by consensus. Mugabe thought to himself that the rape of a people is even more vulgar when it involves incest, when they are violated by their own people. Mugabe sometimes became so discouraged that he thought the unthinkable: *Maybe life under the Portuguese was not so bad after all. What are we today? A nation of soldiers and rebels, whose young men terrorize an entire nation.*

Mugabe did not differentiate between Frelimo and Renamo, the two forces fighting for control of Mozambique. Regardless whether you were shot by a weapon manufactured in the Soviet Union or Sweden, they both tore at the flesh and heart and soul of a nation. The politics of those who raped one's wife and killed one's son made no difference if they both had sold their souls to the devil.

Mugabe's land was now a nation of 15 million people with empty guts, empty pockets, and empty lives.

While hoeing one day, he got carried away with these angry thoughts, muttering, then airing rather vehemently his grievances. It was loud enough that a slender boy walking by stopped to stare at him. Mugabe knew that what he was saying about his country's leaders should not be uttered in public, especially not in the presence of a ragged, shoeless boy who could get a free meal by telling government officials what he had heard.

More embarrassed than frightened, Mugabe attacked the weeds, real and imagined, with renewed vehemence as he said to the young boy, "These stupid weeds, you cut them down in the morning, and they're back at night. I shout at them every day, but they just arrogantly laugh at me until I cut them down again."

A slight smile came across the young boy's face as he said, "Perhaps I can help you."

"Do you have a hoe?" asked Mugabe.

The boy jumped back, looking frightened. "Oh, no sir, I don't have a hoe. I have never used one. But I am very good at pulling the weeds out by the roots, so they will not come back at night." The boy knelt and attacked the weeds like an enemy to be defeated without mercy.

Mugabe resumed his hoeing. Before they reached the end of the row, he found out the young man's name was Isaka, not an uncommon name in his country. Isaka told Mugabe that he thought himself to be 12 or 13 years of age. He did not know his last name, or where he was born. He was ambiguous about whose pot he put his hand into.

Mugabe respected his privacy, so the two worked on in silence.

Watching him out of the corner of his eye, Mugabe had to turn his head away, tearing up, realizing anew he would never have a son like this boy, to work the fields and share the harvest with him, or to grow together as disciples of the Lord.

Mugabe was hungry and knew Diolinda would have some food prepared for him. He told Isaka he had no money, not even any beans yet, but he would like to repay him by allowing him to put his hand in his pot.

At first Isaka was reluctant, but soon hunger replaced whatever reason he had for refusing, and he followed Mugabe to his hut.

Mugabe went behind the hut and poured water he had hauled from the river and washed his hands, then splashed it on his face. As he dried himself with a rag hanging from a tree, he motioned to Isaka that he was welcome to do likewise. Isaka was reluctant and backed off until Mugabe smiled and jokingly reminded him that pulling weeds was a dirtier job than hoeing them.

Isaka washed his hands and splashed a little water on his face. When Mugabe offered him the rag to dry himself, he declined, shaking his hands to dry them. He followed Mugabe around to the front of the hut, where he stepped aside and offered Isaka the privilege of entering his home first, but the boy stepped back, appearing to have changed his mind again.

"No, I can't put my hands in your pot," he whispered. "I am not worthy." He turned and ran, not looking back.

Mugabe, stunned, wondered what had happened. He entered the hut and sat on the floor as Diolinda brought him his meal. While eating together, as had become their habit, and which was frowned on by some of the men in the village, they talked about Isaka.

"What do you think his reason was for not putting his hand in our pot?" Diolinda asked. She had seen him out back with Mugabe She was certain she had never seen him before. "I mean, he couldn't know what a bad cook I am." She chuckled as she poured more maize into Mugabe's bowl.

Mugabe laughed with her, held up his bowl for more, then turned serious again. "It may be the rebel's supply of food, even more than their whiskey and guns, that draws boys to join up with them."

"It may seem better to them to die in war than to starve to death," Diolinda replied thoughtfully.

Mugabe, setting his bowl aside, heaved a sigh. "What future does a boy like Isaka have? He's probably escaped from the rebels, has nowhere to live, no family, and is moving like a nomad from village to village. Let's ask God how we can minister to him."

Dr. Nichols centered his chair at the front of the room so Mrs. Van Pelt could sit as she spoke to the class.

She's definitely from the old school, Murphy thought. *She looks like every man's grandmother.*

Her matronly dress sprinkled with pink flowers amply covered her knees. She kept her black pumps solidly on the floor. A trace of lipstick outlined a gentle smile, below compelling eyes. Wavy white hair framed her face and crowned her with dignity.

Murphy wondered what she would talk about. Dr. Nichols had spoken several times of being challenged by her stories, yet Murphy was surprised by the strength of her firm, but gentle voice that belied her eighty-two years of life.

Beverly Van Pelt and her husband, David, had gone to south China as missionaries when she was twenty-four. Together they ministered as teachers and ran an orphanage in a village a mile from the city of Kunming. They took only two furloughs in the United States during the years of raising two biological children, Sean and Shannon, and hundreds of discarded children considered "throw-aways" by their culture.

In 1949, the Communists literally threw the Van Pelts across the border into the New Territories, north of Hong Kong, where they worked for nineteen more years with Chinese refugee children.

Twelve years ago David had died and joined many he'd introduced to the Savior. Sean was a missionary in Africa with a family of his own. Shannon, her husband, and three children, were missionaries in Brazil.

Mrs. Van Pelt now lived in a home for retired missionaries, south of Los Angeles. Due to a debilitating heart condition, she had to give up her ministry on Hollywood Boulevard with young street girls.

"I'm told that I'm the second woman to have the privilege of addressing this class." She smiled and bowed her upper body towards them. "I am a liberated woman—liberated by my Lord Jesus Christ to be the wife of one, a mother of two, and grandmother of six. My life is full. I love every day, especially this one, surrounded by some of tomorrow's missionaries perhaps." Then she added with a twinkle in her eye, "Even if you aren't women."

Murphy looked around the room, wondering if she expected them to be chauvinists.

"You probably know that women are vital participants in China's House Church. I went back to China after it opened up again in 1981. I've been there six times since, visiting dear sisters we missed terribly during the years of Mao's tyranny and our exile."

"What impressed me most was their acceptance of the pain and suffering during Mao's regime, as the normal Christian life. One lady spent seven years in a prison labor camp because she refused to denounce Christ. When I expressed pity, she looked at me like I'd come from another planet and said, 'Oh my sister, it was wonderful. It was like seven years of Bible school, and Mao paid my tuition!'"

The class didn't know quite how to react, so they remained very quiet.

"Let me tell you about Dr. Hwang. She lived in Peking, as it was then called, now Beijing. After she was led to the Lord by missionaries, she went to medical school in the United States, becoming a surgeon. Unlike many who studied abroad, she returned to China to minister to her own people.

"During the terrible convulsive days of the Cultural Revolution, Mao started to lose control and turned the country over to the Red Guard, made up of young people, some as young as 12. They literally took over the country. They were a law unto themselves. They closed universities; they burned irreplaceable libraries. The Red Guard dragged people from their homes, accusing them of crimes against the state. They were judge and jury, sending people to labor camps, prison, or killing them in their homes.

"Dr. Hwang and another surgeon at the hospital in Peking were taken out of the operating room one day into the square in front of the hospital and were subject to a confession meeting. They were apolitical. They had nothing to confess. But they were still found guilty and sentenced to hard labor. These two surgeons were assigned to clean the hospital latrines from early morning to late at night. These were not your porcelain toilets with flushing capabilities. These were long troughs.

"Dr. Hwang excitedly told me how the two of them were given a rag and bucket of water. On their knees, they poured water into the troughs, and then used the rag to move the excrement to the end of the trough and push it down a hole. There were no rubber gloves. They did this twelve hours a day, seven days a week, for six years.

I was aghast, commiserating. "Oh, how terrible!" I said.

"But *she* comforted *me.* With a glowing face, she exclaimed, 'Oh no. It was wonderful. You see, each morning we would kneel at the latrine and confess to our lovely Jesus, 'Oh Lord, our hearts were like this filthy latrine before you came and washed them clean.' As we poured the water into the latrine, we thanked God for His cleansing Holy Spirit. As we pushed the filth with our rag, we thanked Him for His Word. We had the cleanest latrine in Peking, because we wanted to show our Lord our gratitude for cleansing our hearts.'"

Mrs. Van Pelt reached into her pocket for her handkerchief. Wiping tears, she continued. "Dr. Hwang gave me another 'what planet are you from?' look and asked me, 'Doesn't God say all things work together for good for those who love the Lord and are called according to His purpose?'"

Murphy thought Mrs. Van Pelt's spirit had momentarily returned to the land and people she loved so much. She seemed far away. Her body seemed to be shrinking.

"I'm not feeling up to the lecture I planned for today, but let me give you two more illustrations of a woman responding to God's love, with love, then I will leave you to your studies.

"Last time I was in China, I was introduced to Mama Lee. (Mama is a title of respect for matriarchal leaders in the church.) I had heard an awesome story about her and was privileged to meet her. She is a nurse and her husband was an engineer. One night Red Guards broke into their home, accusing her husband of crimes against the state. They tore the house apart looking for a Bible but found none. Then teenage soldiers beat her husband and oldest son to death, before her eyes, while her hands were bound. They then took her younger son away. He later was beaten to death, as well, for refusing to denounce his Lord.

"Now move ahead about eight years. The Cultural Revolution was over. One evening, a messenger came to her from a village a three-hour walk away. The son of the Cadre leader of the village was desperately ill, needing a particular medication.

"Now you have to understand that in China, you are only allowed to have one child, and a son is very precious. To have a girl is a failure on the part of the mother. The father, for a small amount of money or food, can bribe the doctor to drown a girl infant, so he can try for a boy. This is the norm, even today. I am told by my friends in China that there are villages today where there is one girl to twelve men.

"Well, Mama Lee walked the twenty miles to the Cadre leader's house. She spent several days medicating and nursing the boy to health. What everyone involved knew was that eight years before, this Cadre leader was the Red Guard who had ordered this nurse's husband and sons killed.

"I began to sympathize with Mama Lee over the difficulty of this ironic situation.

"'But sister," she said to me, "isn't that what our Lord Jesus taught us—to forgive others as He has forgiven us? After all, we too killed someone's son, and in a much crueler way. I am told that her willingness to nurse the Cadre leader's son back to health was as powerful a message as any of our Lord's servants could have preached to that village."

The silence in the room was almost tangible. Murphy thought of Mr. Maxwell and his son. *Forgive us our trespasses, as we forgive those who trespass against us*, ran through his head.

"Let me leave you with one more illustration. Mai was nineteen when she refused to denounce Jesus Christ to become a revolutionary for Mao. Her bleeding, swollen body was thrown into an underground prison cell. There was no bed; the floor was slippery with human excrement. Rats and vermin were everywhere. She told me how, as she sat on the floor, taking up as little room as possible, she began to thank her Lord that she was worthy to suffer for Him.

"Now remember, all she had to do was denounce the Lord as her Savior, but she steadfastly refused. She told how she sat, all alone, deserted by the world, but not by her Lord, bleeding and weeping tears of joy as the cell became a place of worship. Without rancor for those who imprisoned her, she asked the Lord for strength and wisdom. All she wanted to do was continue to preach His gospel to the lost.

"While singing a hymn and praising the Lord, He gave her this message: 'This is to be your ministry!'

"'But' she objected, 'I am all alone. Who can I preach to?' She continued to pray that her ministry would be fulfilled. One day, like a bright light, an idea filled her mind. She called to the guard. When he came, she said, 'Sir, can I do some hard labor for you?' She told how the guard looked at her with contempt, mingled with surprise. No one had ever made that request before.

"'Look,' she exclaimed, 'this prison is so dirty; there is human waste everywhere. Let me go into the cells and clean up this filthy place. All you need to give me is water and a brush.' She soon found herself on her hands and knees, with opportunities for scrubbing and preaching. She told about looking into the faces of people who were hardly recognizable as human beings. Through ongoing torture, they had lost hope of ever seeing a human being who wasn't going to beat them.

"When they heard they could have eternal life, they believed and repented of their sins, crying and kneeling. And do you know what? Very soon almost all the prisoners believed in Jesus.

"The Communist officials found out what was happening and they were furious. They had lost control over their prisoners. They yelled at them, threatened them, and beat them, but the prisoners would only say, 'I forgive you in the name of Jesus Christ.'

"One day the guard hauled her from her cell, beat her, gave her paper and pencil, and told her to write her confession how she had sinned against Mao and all the people of China. She cried out to her Lord, 'I have done nothing against the State or the people, except clean up this dirty place. What can I write?'

"'Gradually,' she said, 'the words came, then faster and faster. She told me, 'I finally finished, and with aching fingers, handed the confession to the guard to be delivered to the warden. Soon the warden called me to his office. He was trembling with rage. He shouted at me, 'How dare you write such anti-revolutionary things!' He then read her confession to the guards and others who worked in the prison. It was confessing the very words she spoke to the prisoners, telling of God's offer of forgiveness and eternal life.'

"As he read it aloud, he started slowing down as though trying to grasp the meaning of every word. The guards, silently, took her back to her cell and left her without so much as a shove.

"She said, 'The next morning several guards came and got me. I thought they were going to kill me, but instead they pushed me through the prison gate and shouted, "Never to come back. You are a troublemaker!' Young men, she was free! Inside and out!

"I'm an old woman, but the message God gave me for you future preachers is that He can use old *and* young, women *and* men, weak *and* strong to preach and teach. And remember, your greatest messages will not be given from behind a pulpit, but in the midst of personal suffering. That's when people will know if you really believe in God's redeeming love."

Murphy saw that though Mrs. Van Pelt's heart and body were weakening, no one could ever say that about her spirit.

Eighteen

Days passed as Mugabe continued to hoe the fields and Isaka pulled the weeds. Diolinda continued her work of molding and firing pots to sell in the marketplace.

Isaka eventually accepted Mugabe's offer of meals and a place to sleep, but he would not go into their hut. He chose to eat and sleep outside their door.

Mugabe's and Diolinda's conversation and prayers centered around asking where the Lord wanted them to minister. They were loved by their village, but Brother Jonathan knew God had plans for them to build another church.

The answer to their prayers came late one evening when Pastor Jonathan came to their hut with Brother Nehemiah. Mugabe enthusiastically greeted the man whom Via Mahondra had also discipled and given the biblical name Nehemiah because of his passion for working in villages where churches had been destroyed by witch doctors. Brother Nehemiah believed Christians were not taken seriously until they had their own church building that the people could see. A building demonstrated their commitment to remain in the village.

Brother Nehemiah had heard from the gossip circuit that Mugabe had returned to Mozambique. He was elated that they were now standing together in his hut. As he spoke excitedly, as was his norm, he told Mugabe, "There's a village with a powerful witch doctor who has wrapped a white cloth around a tree at the entrance."

Mugabe, as well as Isaka who was listening from outside, knew this meant that the village was controlled by the demons, and that all demons were welcomed.

"They had a church there," Brother Nehemiah said, "but this witch doctor and his followers burned it down. Not once, but twice, and threatened to kill anyone heard singing the Christian's songs or praying. He promised to burn any hut that contained a Bible and chase the owners from the village before the evil spirits got angry and punished the entire village. I heard him as he stood in the ashes of the church he burned down, shouting how he would personally kill any Christians he finds in his village so everyone would know his god is greater than the 'Christian god.'"

Mugabe, Diolinda and Pastor Jonathan each sensed, individually, that the Lord had sent Brother Nehemiah to show them where to go. As Brother Nehemiah bid them good-bye, Mugabe and Diolinda had a new mission. It was not a matter of whether they would leave their village, but how soon.

Isaka, lying on the ground outside the front door, strained to hear every word, fearing being left behind.

Three days later, Mugabe lifted Diolinda onto the back of an old truck already loaded with people and their bundles. They had wrapped their few earthly possessions, which included a change of clothes and cooking utensils, inside their sleeping blankets.

Isaka stood back and watched as Mugabe lifted the bundle onto the truck. Diolinda held onto their Bibles and the broken wedding hoe. Then another passenger grabbed Mugabe's hand and helped him up.

Isaka raised his hand in a sad farewell, but Mugabe grasped his hand and, with a hearty pull, lifted the boy onto the back of the truck. No words were spoken as Isaka squatted by Mugabe's belongings. None were needed.

The driver came to the back of the truck, muttering, "No more, no more room."

People begged to be let on. The driver was adamant as he got in the truck, "No more. There'll be another truck. One or two days. You must wait."

Some cursed, come cried, but most accepted it as part of life, one that never got much better.

After some coaxing, the motor's roar turned into an encouraging, steady rumble. There was a grinding of gears as the truck leaped forward, creating a cloud of gas fumes and dust. One man fell off; several hands grabbed him and lifted him back on board.

Those left behind picked up their luggage, took their children by the hand, and left to wait for the next truck.

Seven hours later, three choking, dust-covered, weary travelers slid off the truck to the ground. They were the only ones to get off. The truck belched and continued its journey.

They stood in a crowded marketplace. Mugabe immediately saw the white rag wrapped around the tree truck at the village entrance.

The palpable hostility that met them was uncommon for the usually friendly villagers. The three bedraggled strangers looked for Brother Nehemiah, but he wasn't there.

Mugabe noticed a young man break from the crowd and take off in a run.

Another young man walked past Mugabe and quickly whispered, "Nehemiah couldn't come. I'm Aaron. Follow me."

Aaron moved ahead of the three to hide the fact he was their guide. Villagers stared at Diolinda, carrying the broken hoe and their Bibles. Only the children followed them as they went down a dusty road. After the children lost interest and returned to the marketplace, Aaron slowed down until the three caught up with him. "Come, we have three huts to choose from. You pick which one you want."

Mugabe set his luggage down and asked Aaron if they would be less conspicuous if Isaka stayed behind with the luggage while he and Diolinda went to see the three huts. Aaron agreed. Mugabe and Isaka set their luggage down for Isaka to guard, but Diolinda tightly held onto the Bibles and the broken hoe.

An hour later the three returned for their luggage. Mugabe asked Aaron to go tell Brother Nehemiah they had arrived safely. Aaron smiled and took off running.

A short time later, Mugabe had the hoe on their wall, Isaka had gathered fire wood and water from a nearby stream, and Diolinda was preparing maize she had carefully stored. Soon they would eat their first meal in their new home.

Isaka still insisted on taking his meal outside. They knew that arguing with him was useless.

The long day came to an end. Mugabe and Diolinda lay down on their blankets. Turning their heads toward the opening, which lacked a door, they saw Isaka's sleeping body stretched out, machete in hand, guarding the doorway.

Diolinda rolled onto her side, facing Mugabe. "What do you think will become of him? He'll probably leave tomorrow. Where do you think he'll go? Where will he end up?"

Mugabe, lying in his thinking position, hands under his head, replied, "Well, we can be sure of one thing, it won't be political forces that decide his future. It's spiritual forces that will wrestle for his soul, the same for everyone in this village. I suspect everyone watching us arrive today is anticipating watching us be destroyed, just like the church was destroyed."

Diolinda rolled over with her back to Mugabe, saying, "I'm sure you're right, but the force of a seven-hour bus ride just about destroyed me."

Mugabe rubbed her back and asked their God to heal her bruised body.

Arm back under his head, he saw the moon through the hole in the roof and began to think of the witchcraft that he was sure to encounter. He knew the power tribal religions held over the lives of his people from birth until after death. Even though the Portuguese brought Christianity with them, they incorporated so many of the superstitions of the tribal religions that the curse of syncretism made it hard to discern where one religion ended and the other began.

The people believed their children died of malaria because the demons were let loose by a dead ancestor who was displeased with the offerings of the living. They believed every material object was associated with a spirit who, if not appeased, would seal the heavens or release the grasshoppers. They fearfully listened to their dead ancestors dictate and obeyed.

To build a Christian church in this village, Mugabe realized, he would have to face the witch doctor who led all the forces that hated the church's Jesus.

Witchcraft, that supposed power of a person to harm others by occult or supernatural means, is an invisible force, terrible, mysterious and deadly. It creates and perpetuates a culture of violence. Irrespective of what famous anthropologists may say, there are some things in every culture that need to be destroyed.

Mugabe knew that the moment he and Diolinda and Isaka passed that white cloth on the tree, the battle began. He also knew that in a war, it is always wise to keep track of your enemy. Of the three huts available, this one was in the poorest condition, but it was right next door to the witch doctor.

"My life's a disaster. I'm still living with the guilt of what happened to Roger. I just can't shake it." Murphy's words were more a plea than a statement as he sat draped across the armchair in Mr. Maxwell's office.

Maxwell turned his swivel chair to look intensely at his young friend as he listened carefully to his heart as well as his words. He silently prayed, *"Now also when I am old and gray headed, O God, do not forsake me, until I declare Your strength to this generation…"*

"This generation" threw up his hands, rose from his chair, and declared to God and man: "Life sucks."

Mr. Maxwell smiled as he motioned for Murphy to sit down. "So do little lambs. But they seem to survive. Maybe they see it as a nurturing, growing experience, to make them stronger."

Murphy sat back down, blushing, embarrassed for the language he had used. "Sorry, guess I confused your office with the dorm."

"I've heard worse." Mr. Maxwell stared at the picture on his desk. "And you know, you're right. Life does, as you say, 'suck.' I guess that means life isn't going as planned, is that right?"

Murphy sighed deeply. "Yeah, I wish I could go back a few months and try again."

"So that, like me, you could make the same mistakes over again, only with more, using another of your words, *pizzazz*?

"You know, Pastor Murphy, your generation has had it so easy that you find it difficult to handle those events in life over which you have no control or that can't be solved with some quick fix. You want to go out and get drunk on the latest religious fad, and move on. I even saw a book on the Beatitudes entitled something like the Be-Happytudes. The

Lord never promised to make us happy, only blessed."

Murphy smiled, shaking his head.

Maxwell leaned back in his chair and put his feet on his desk because his legs ached and this often brought relief. "A great help to me during a very difficult time, different than yours but no less painful, were the words of an old English preacher. Maybe you've heard of him—G. Campbell Morgan?"

Murphy nodded that he had.

"In his book, *The Crisis of the Christ,* he wisely pointed out an important principle when going through a crisis like you are right now. He said, 'In all the works of God there is to be discovered an unvarying method of process and crisis.' He says the process is slow, and difficult to watch, but on the other hand the crisis comes very suddenly. Like a bolt of lightning on a dark, stormy night. In the pitch dark, you stand frightened, lost, wondering which way to go, and suddenly a strike of lightning shows you where you are, where you've been, and the direction to take for safety. That bolt of lightning, that is to say the 'crisis,' is not an accident of nature, but a gift from the Lord."

Mr. Maxwell got up, walked to his bookshelf, and pulled out a well-used old book. He thumbed through it, turned, and began reading: "'The crisis is not a catastrophe...but a state in an orderly method.' But then all of our Lord's ways are orderly, aren't they? I'm sure we both understand that the process sucks, but it is during the process we learn, sometimes by trial and error, the purpose behind what we saw during the lightning flash."

He read on: 'This lesson once learned, we see that crisis, actually a gift from the Lord, has initiated a new movement, and commenced a new process.' Mr. Maxwell closed the book. Murphy took note where he put it on the shelf.

"So," Mr. Maxwell continued, "a crisis is not an accident, nor a catastrophe. But none of us *likes* to face a crisis. I'm sure you're not enjoying what you're going through right now."

Murphy shook his head.

"We often try to solve the crisis on our own, using our own wisdom. Or we ignore the crisis, hoping it will eventually work itself out. Or we look for a way of escape, some way to avoid thinking of why

God might have allowed the crisis. So what was meant as a gift from God to form me spiritually and prepare me for greater ministry becomes a disaster. You know I speak from experience."

Mr. Maxwell put his hand up to his chin. It replaced a reflexive action born out of years of putting his pipe in his mouth, lighting it, and blowing smoke. It had given him time to think what he wanted to say. The pipe was a habit he had given up, but not the time to think.

He opened his Bible. "It should come as no surprise that our Lord's life was one crisis after another. Morgan points out our Lord went through seven crises, seven crucial, significant events. I won't take time to go into them, but come in and get my book sometime and study them. To whet your appetite, just let me list them. His birth, baptism, temptations, transfiguration, crucifixion, resurrection, and ascension. As you are aware, none of these events came close to being a disaster for our Lord."

"These events follow an orderly sequence, and in their entirety contain the entire story of His work of redemption for us. Each significant event prepared him for the next. Just think for a moment. If our Lord had attempted to escape the crises that he faced, or skipped the process, or had only applied Himself to finding a fix, where would we be today? We would be people without hope."

"Wow!" Murphy exhaled. "I never thought of it that way."

"Roger's life turned into a disaster, but yours doesn't have to, my friend. Roger's disaster is your crisis. Learn from it. Be humbled by it, but don't give in to temptation to despair. Remember, Jesus said, 'My strength is made perfect in weakness.' Did you hear the 'is made'? You are in the middle of the process of being strengthened. Be patient, my friend."

Murphy fell to his knees. Mr. Maxwell joined him.

Nineteen

When Mugabe and Diolinda went to the marketplace, the social center of every village, they were treated with measured acceptance. However, on the way home from market, people crossed to the other side of the road, upholding the tradition their culture dictated of not being friendly to outsiders.

Yet, when Mugabe and Diolinda were praying, they saw something more behind such discourtesy. They saw a people crying out to be rescued from fear that permeated their lives and literally kept them prisoners in their own bodies.

Surprisingly, the ray of light that kept total darkness at bay was Isaka. He strolled around the village like he had lived there all his life. His infectious smile drew outbursts of affection from the children even if the adults only gave carefully controlled smiles in return. Mugabe was sure the Lord had given them Isaka to be the key that would open hearts, and then doors, for their ministry.

Mugabe and Diolinda had awakened the first morning in the village and found him missing. They feared he could have been kidnapped but felt he probably had left on his own volition.

They sheepishly looked at each other when they did see Isaka, smiling as though he had just conquered the world. At his feet lay his gift for them, a pile of branches cut with his trusted machete. Wiping his brow, he proudly pointed to the branches. "No more lying in bed at night and looking at the moon. If that is not enough for the new roof, I know where there is plenty more."

He also took seriously his self-appointed responsibilities at the front door of the hut, with the machete on his lap, like one of David's soldiers manning his post. It gave joy and comfort to both Mugabe and Diolinda.

Not so joyful was the fact he still held his head down when talking to Diolinda and refused to enter the hut to put his hand in their pot.

He and Mugabe spent their days clearing land next to the burned-out skeleton of the church. Brother Nehemiah had told them the land still belonged to the church. They were preparing to grow beans, turnips, and corn. Isaka pulled weeds while Mugabe hoed.

Brother Nehemiah was still apparently off building a wall somewhere else, but certainly not in this village where his previous "tabernacle" remained a pile of ashes.

The one constant in all three of their lives was waiting for the inevitable encounter between Mugabe and his neighbor, the witch doctor. Mugabe was sure they were not the only ones who anticipated that fateful moment. They did not have long to wait.

A wailing sound, like that of a wild animal, penetrated the darkness of the early morning. Mugabe and Diolinda sat upright in bed, staring into the darkness. Isaka stood at the door, holding his machete.

Mugabe had heard the sound before, and as it had then, it caused his blood to run cold. It was a shrill wail announcing the visitation of the spirit of death. Mugabe knew that a very old man, whom the witch doctor visited daily with all his paraphernalia, lived a short distance away. The cry became more virulent as others in the village picked it up and ran through the village, crying out the old man's name. The old man had died.

The paradox of death bringing a village to life did not escape Mugabe. Through past experiences, he knew that a witch doctor and his demons used a death to increase their power, elevating the people's fear. Death was also an opportunity for people to give the dead person's life worth through their weeping and wailing, giving the dead strength needed to propel himself through the deep, dark waters that flow beneath the earth to the voodoo spirits.

Mugabe heard the sounds of feet running toward the house where the old man had lived. He stood in his doorway, sure of one thing: the witch doctor had already planted the seed in the minds of his followers that the old man died because a Jesus follower lived in their village.

From past experience, Mugabe also knew the routine. The witch doctor was already taking control, setting down rules to be obeyed to please the evil spirits, or there would be all hell to pay by the survivors.

Mugabe and Diolinda lay down again. This was a time to stay indoors, praying. Mugabe told Diolinda, and Isaka who was listening from outside, fearful of what would happen in the village during the next couple of days. He remembered it from his childhood, before he became a follower of Christ. He found it frightening then, but terribly sad now.

Mugabe knew the beliefs behind the ritual. As life leaves the body, the soul lingers near. It moves about the hut and among the people who gather, all of whom want to be sure that when the dead man departs, it will be with good memories of those who came so quickly. The men then go outside and stand quietly as the women wash the body. The men listen as the women sing and talk to the deceased, telling him what a wonderful man he was. They don't want him taking revenge for being ignored.

After the light of morning came, it all seemed less threatening, but no less sorrowful. Because the house of the dead man was only a short distance away, Mugabe and Diolinda sat just inside the hut to watch, but where they could not be seen. They saw men coming out of the house, carrying the dead man's belongings, taking them to be burned. This act was the line of separation between the dead and the living.

Suddenly, Isaka, watching from behind the hut, pointed with youthful excitement. "Look, they're putting a purple curtain across the doorway!"

"Yes," replied Mugabe, "that's what they did for my grandmother. Purple is the symbolic color of mourning."

As they continued to watch through the door of their house, they saw several men coming down the street carrying a plain wooden coffin. Mugabe explained to Isaka that one of the men would tell the mourners at the house he had a vision that the spirits were about to carry the old man away and they needed a coffin.

The family does not bicker over the cost of the coffin that just happens to be available. The witch doctor looks on as the family is given the price. His face remains immobile, but his mind is doing some calculating as he looks at the coffin supplier with a rather pleased expression of a job well done. The family will do whatever they must to pay whatever it costs. They will go hungry in the days ahead to be certain that the deceased has a proper departure.

Several men, followed by the witch doctor, carried the coffin into the house. Though Mugabe could not see inside, he knew what was going on as he explained to Isaka: "They lay the dead man in the coffin. For the rest of today, and much of tomorrow, the women will serve tea and coffee. The men will gather outside to gamble. This will go on all day and night, punctuated by random sobs and wails. Then the men will stop playing cards to exchange stories of what a great man the dead was."

Isaka suggested they do some land clearing, but Mugabe advised against it. "I think it's best to stay out of sight. Don't forget: we are the enemy."

Early in the afternoon, Mugabe, Diolinda, and Isaka sat behind their hut and discussed whether they should pay a visit to the deceased. It would be their first close encounter with the witch doctor.

After a time of prayer, they decided it would be the appropriate thing to do. They went into the house and put on their nicer set of clothes while Isaka waited outside. He was wearing all he owned.

The three of them walked solemnly down the street and turned into the yard of the home of the dead. It was a solemn procession, led by Mugabe. At an appropriate distance behind him and a little to his left was Isaka. As custom dictated, he was followed by Diolinda. This was a time when culture, and not personal preferences, prevailed.

They walked past the men and children sprawled on the ground. Some were sleeping, others passed out from too much "men's tea," some still gambling, and a few weeping quietly. Mugabe slowed down as he felt the oppression. Demons pervaded the air. Someone slid the purple curtain aside.

The witch doctor squatted at the head of the coffin but made no attempt at eye contact. He pointed to the deceased, as if Mugabe couldn't tell the difference.

Tears came to Mugabe's eyes. Hardly able to breathe because of the heaviness of the air permeated with incense, burning candles, and human sweat, he felt nauseated. He had never seen the deceased, but his heart went out to the old man as he thought, *Oh my brother, Jesus died for you for something better than this.*

He glanced at the witch doctor. To Mugabe's surprise, the witch doctor looked directly at him, their eyes meeting for the first time—for just a moment. He quickly looked down again and quietly chanted.

Mugabe's heart cried out to the Lord and his lungs cried out for fresh air. He and his family turned, exited the dead man's house, and silently walked back to the hut side by side. Even Isaka said he felt the darkness of unredeemed death. Never again would they wonder what they were doing here and what their ministry would be.

Early the next morning, people from the village gathered at the dead man's house. Mugabe explained to a fascinated Isaka what was probably taking place inside the house as they prepared the body for the trek to the graveyard for its final burial.

Isaka excitedly asked, "Where is the 'big man'?"

"The witch doctor is inside the dead man's house. If you listen carefully, you might hear him vigorously shaking a rattle. To be effective, the rattle must be heard outside the house. They believe that the personal spirit, the *lawa*, remains in the dead man's head and must be set loose before they bury him.

"Listen carefully; you'll hear the witch doctor call out when he sees the head of the deceased move. This will tell everyone that the spirit has left the body."

When they heard the call of the witch doctor, indicating the spirit had left, the people outside shouted in victory, then became very quiet.

Mugabe explained what was happening next: "The spirit of the dead is now thought to be looking for a new place to live, usually in a family member. They will wait in quiet and some dread while the spirit makes its choice. Inside the house, the witch doctor will use his ceremonial scissors to cut a few locks of the dead man's hair and clip several fingernails, and then place them in a pot, to assure the people the deceased will not be used for any evil purpose."

Isaka asked skeptically, "But only the big man sees the dead man's head move?"

"Yes," replied Mugabe, "only the witch doctor sees the dead man's head move. It is another of his secrets of control."

Both watched as several mourners went into the house and came out carrying the coffin on their shoulders. They were followed by the witch doctor, who never stopped the quiet chanting in a language known only to him.

Isaka laughed and said, "I wonder what the big man is saying. Probably something like, 'Let's get this thing over with so I can get back to my hut and count my profit and have a whiskey.'"

Mugabe, while stepping outside their hut to join the procession as it came by, replied, "Yes, you're probably right, but I wouldn't say it too loud. OK, let's put on our mourning face. On the way to the graveyard, those carrying the coffin must pretend to get lost. This confuses the dead person so he'll not be able to find his way back to his hut from the grave. That's why the graveyard is outside the village and behind thick trees."

Most painful for Mugabe and Diolinda to look at was the cross on the top of a pole that led the procession. They knew there was a time when that cross represented Christ, but most villages had completely rid themselves of Christian symbolism. For most, the cross only symbolized the crossing of life to death.

"The ceremonies at the graveside are simple and led by the witch doctor," Mugabe whispered. "The sun is hot and the men are thirsty, and they need something to mask their dread of one day being the lost one unable to find his way home."

As the public service ended, Mugabe, Diolinda, and Isaka walked back to the village. The other mourners made no effort to join them, walking ahead, behind, or across the street. But before they walked very far, they heard a new outburst of wailing from the graveyard.

Mugabe explained to Isaka, "The family, no matter their age, is required to stay at the graveyard until they have done everything to satisfy the dead."

As the sun set and the candles were extinguished in each of the homes of the dead man's relatives, the ritual continued that would last another six months. Every day family members would take food to the gravesite. The size of the deceased man's appetite would be measured by how hungry the rodents were that lived nearby.

"The mourners will continue to live in fear as they talk to their dead, and assure him that he is greatly missed, adding that in spite of that, he would not want to come back to this difficult world. The family will set up an altar in front of and inside the home supplying the dead each day with food and drink, so that he will not travel with an empty belly while in the process of the final journey into invisible waters. From time to time, the family members will take the pot holding the deceased man's hair and nail clippings, light a fire, and pass the pot over the flames so the dead will not feel cold."

Isaka interjected, "They must do a good job. I've never heard a dead man sneeze."

"That is another thing I wouldn't say out loud if I were you. Whether the dead man catches a cold or not, his control over the family continues. They'll ask him for the secrets of life and for wisdom, as the spirit of the dead slowly flows back into the mainstream of the survivors' lives. The dead will instruct his self-appointed representatives, the witch doctor and his assistants, which medicines they must purchase to heal any illness. I'll let you guess who they'll buy them from."

"I wish those who tell us to leave these people alone could witness what we have these last two days. Would they still try to convince us that the people of this village, and hundreds of others, are completely satisfied with their way of life, that it is their culture and Christians have no right to recklessly destroy the culture? If only they could witness the fear that permeated every second of this day. If only they could see the hopelessness in the people's eyes, both young and old."

"Oh, how I love Jesus," Diolinda quietly sang, with a renewed determination in her voice. "Oh, how...." Mugabe put his arm around her and joined in. Isaka hesitantly picked up on the unfamiliar words.

Murphy opened the door to Maxwell's office, not bothering to knock. He flipped on the light and saw Mr. Maxwell, sleeping. He turned quickly to leave, but Maxwell called out for him to come in.

Maxwell sat up in his chair, rubbing his eyes. "Sorry, but I had a bad night."

"You don't look very good. Are you sick?"

Mr. Maxwell leaned back and sighed. "My young friend, I wish it were that simple. I wish a pill could fix things."

"I'll get some aspirin. I've got some in my desk."

Mr. Maxwell motioned him to sit down. "I'll be okay. It's just that yesterday I attended the funeral of a friend and heard some disturbing things. Got a minute?"

Murphy settled into his chair. "That's why I'm here. I love to listen, and learn."

"Good. Maybe talking about it will lead to some insight about Christ's Church, for both of us."

Murphy opened his notebook, ready to take notes.

"James MacGregor was an acquaintance of mine. He was born and raised here. I met him fairly recently. He didn't go to church here, but down on Fifth Street. He was a stalwart, frugal old Scotsman, a little older than me. A carpenter all his life, and I understand a good one. He pounded so many nails his body rebelled, and he retired four or five years ago. He hadn't saved much money, never made much. I understand he spent too much of his time doing what lawyers call pro bono work, offering his skills free to those who couldn't afford them. Only he didn't do it for publicity, or to gain customers, or even to salve his conscience. He did it out of genuine concern for the poor.

"His wife, Edna, died young, leaving him alone to raise their young son, Matthew. I'm told that as a high school student, Matthew led anti-war demonstrations and was practically run out of town. But yesterday, he showed up for his father's service, and asked to deliver the eulogy. They could hardly turn him down. He was Mac's only kin.

"There was a noticeable stirring in the congregation over a 'sinner' in their midst. Matthew looked straight ahead as he walked to the pulpit. He's a handsome man, looks like I imagine his father looked at that age. Neatly dressed in a dark suit and tie, face composed, he looked and sounded more like a Sunday school teacher than the 'terrible McGregor boy' I'd heard about.

"He introduced himself, although many remembered him. He said their prayers had been partly answered: He'd shaved his beard, and his wife had cut his hair. He didn't carry picket signs anymore, nor yell at the police.

“Now he lived in Chicago, he said, with his wife and two sons. They didn’t come to the funeral, wanting to remember their grandfather as they last saw him, praising and cheering them on. Their summers will never be the same.

“Although he and his dad were at opposite poles on some issues, he never doubted his father’s respect and love for him as a person and a son. They didn’t always agree, but respected each other’s convictions as being as Scripture based as their own, just different interpretations.”

“He spoke of a memorial service held for the Darby boy, killed in Viet Nam. A matriarch of the church had indignantly confronted his father, saying his son was a traitor and partly to blame for what happened. Matthew said he’d never seen his dad so angry. ‘That young Darby boy died to protect other’s freedoms!’ he said between gritted teeth.

“The woman tried to back off, but Mac didn’t give her one inch. ‘Don’t you forget my son has the freedom to *object* to the war that killed that boy!’

“He said he had such love for his dad at that moment, but he told him he didn’t want anything to do with church when people judged him so harshly. His dad told him he was sorry he’d been hurt, but that he was sure the people loved Jesus and Jesus loved them.

“That was fifteen years ago, and this funeral was the first time he’d been in a church since. He hadn’t rejected his dad’s Jesus, but he had rejected church for attacking and condemning him and his dad.

“But that incident was one of the reasons he considered his dad his best friend, his advocate, and his conscience. His dad had an indomitable and unquenchable spirit of love that considered what happened to others as being more important than what happened to himself. Matthew said he didn’t inherit that trait, but loved it in his dad.

“Then Matthew made a startling statement. He said his dad didn’t have to die. That caused a considerable stir in the room.

“It seems Matthew talked to his dad’s doctor. He knew they’d been friends for years. The doctor showed him his dad’s chart and told him his death confounded him because his diseases were very treatable. The medications he prescribed should have controlled them. About a year ago, the doctor gave him a new prescription, but he quit coming in. The doctor was concerned but assumed he'd moved to Chicago to live with Matthew. He was shocked when he saw his obituary. He didn't realize his friend had still been in town, nor did he understand why the medications had not worked. He shouldn't have died!

"This week, while emptying out his father's apartment, he found a folder of his dad's financial stuff, Mac's checkbook. Social Security was his only income. After tithing and supporting a missionary couple in Irian Jaya and another in Japan, he paid for food and utilities—only the very basics. Medicine, only $35.00 a month? His father was diabetic and had arthritis. Where was his insulin? His testing strips? He had heart disease, but where were the medications? There was only one drug sent to him automatically each month by AARP: painkillers.

"He'd not had any of his prescriptions filled because after paying his tithe, supporting missionaries, paying utilities, and buying food, there was no money left. He died for lack of $331 a month!

"Matthew hung his head and sobbed. He felt guilty over not having known, and not having seen him since last summer. He was struggling with bitterness over his rejection by the church for his nonconformity, yet his dad gave his all to his church family while he deteriorated before their eyes. Matthew thought someone should have noticed how he was failing and visited his home to find out what he needed. He was pretty upset, suggesting the church didn't help the poor, the sick or the dying, but waited for the government to do it. He said there was always money for padded pews or trips to visit missionaries, but nothing for the widows and orphans. Finally he calmed down and cried, 'Why didn't I see? Why didn't I help? My dad seems to be the only one who had a heart the think about others more than himself.'"

Mr. Maxwell handed Murphy a paper. "Here's the program of the funeral. On the back are some figures. Eight people from our church just visited Asia to 'encourage our missionaries and see firsthand how they are blessing the people over there.' You can see the figures: eight times eight hundred would be the approximate cost of their airfare."

Mr. Maxwell continued: "Then there were the hotels. And of course there were other places they had always wanted to visit and it would be good stewardship to do it as part of this trip. Add another sixteen hundred dollars. A rented car, restaurants...And of course, how could you visit Hong Kong and not buy watches and have suits made? You see the total. Divide it by the price of Mr. MacGregor's prescriptions, and if the doctor is right, he could have lived many more years. Longer than the fake watches will run or the tailor-made clothes will stay in style before they go to Goodwill."

Murphy stared at the numbers. As he placed the program back on Mr. Maxwell's desk, he replied, "No wonder you couldn't sleep. That's a lot to think about. Kind of hard to forget."

Mr. Maxwell dropped the paper in the wastebasket. "I never will."

Twenty

Some merchants still refused to sell Diolinda anything, but she took it stoically and found another merchant who would, though at a higher price. Secret messages were whispered to her, hinting that when Mugabe and Isaka were ready to harvest their garden, the chief would confiscate it. People still walked to the other side of the road rather than greet her on her walk home.

The only time Mugabe saw the witch doctor was while taking their morning bath in the stream they shared behind their huts. There was still no eye contact on the part of the witch doctor, though Isaka would shout a greeting when he was with Mugabe. Isaka remained the bright spot in their existence.

One day Isaka was walking by himself and heard his name called. He looked back and saw a very old man sitting in the doorway of a dilapidated hut that looked as weathered as the man. He asked the man how he knew his name.

A smile spread across the man's toothless, wrinkled face. "The whole village knows your name. You're Isaka, your father's Mugabe, and your mother's Diolinda."

Isaka corrected him, explaining they were his friends, not his mother and father. Isaka's eyes were glued to the man's huge, misshapen hands.

"I dedicated these hands to the service of our Lord Jesus to rebuild our church the first time they burned it down, and to play my guitar to His glory," the old man said in a broken voice. "Before we could get it built, your neighbor sent hoodlums to visit me."

Tears rolled out of his milky eyes as he held his hands in front of Isaka. "They crushed my fingers with rocks, beat me, and destroyed my guitar. But I couldn't play now, not with these hands."

Isaka felt sick. He took the disfigured hands in his callused hands.

"We are building a new church, and when we get it built, I'll get you a guitar and you can come and lead us as we sing together."

The old man squeezed Isaka's hands and forced out the words, "The Lord willing, the Lord willing."

Their visit ended as a woman called the old man inside.

At the end of a very tiring day, Brother Nehemiah appeared without explanation or apology. Mugabe asked for neither. Both were eager to hear what the other had to say. They talked as they ate Diolinda's simple supper.

Brother Nehemiah felt called by the Lord to move into villages and help people realize they did not have to live under spiritual tyranny. He had a greater understanding of witchcraft than Mugabe did. However, he could only be in one village at a time, and that is where Mugabe came in. Nehemiah cried out in exultation, "Look, my brother! Our Lord has given the three of you the privilege of answering the Lord's call to set this village free, just as our Brother Paul did in his day."

Brother Nehemiah's enthusiasm was contagious. Diolinda sat up straighter with hope on her face. Isaka, who had been secretly listening outside, leaned his head around the doorframe. No one could miss the excitement in the missionary's eyes.

As the evening progressed, Brother Nehemiah and Mugabe moved outside to the back of the house to take advantage of a slight breeze. Isaka, already there, got up to leave as they sat down. Mugabe motioned for him to stay.

Brother Nehemiah pressed Mugabe. "You must start rebuilding."

"First, I have to get them to talk to me."

"No, when you rebuild the church, the secret believers will see you are serious. Then they will talk to you, and to each other."

He leaned in closer and pleaded, "Believe me, Mugabe, having a real church building tells the villagers you are not leaving, and it encourages the secret believers." Nehemiah looked at Isaka with a smile and patted him on the leg. "And your wife and son here can help you. As your home tells people, your neighbor included, that you've taken up residence here, so a church building tells people that our Lord Jesus resides here. A building sends a powerful message that you and your Lord are committed to this village."

Brother Nehemiah pulled an envelope out of his pocket. "It's not much, but three villages have sent it as a love offering to the Lord.' He handed it to Mugabe. "It will help put maize in your pot and a few simple tools in your hands."

"I'm embarrassed at my lack of faith. When you visit these brothers and sisters again, please tell them our pot would have been empty tomorrow. This village sees a white rag around the tree, but this offering helps me see the one true God is here. With the help of this offering we will help build the church."

Brother Nehemiah slapped Mugabe on the leg, as he had done to Isaka. "I know you will—all three of you!"

Isaka stood with the others and cleared his throat, as though he wanted to say something.

Brother Nehemiah smiled. "Isaka, you've been very quiet all evening."

Isaka looked at the ground, as if getting up nerve to address this missionary. "Sir, there's an old man with broken fingers..." He gave the details of his meeting with the old man a few days before.

While listening, Brother Nehemiah's interest grew. Leaning closer, he nodded but was careful not to interrupt Isaka. When he finished, Brother Nehemiah said, "The man you encountered is named David. He's the one man the witch doctor and his followers fear most. He's a godly man and is called David because of being a man after God's own heart, and because of his ability to play the guitar and sing psalms and hymns in times of joy and distress. Many came to church just to hear him. As the ungodly feared David of old, so the witch doctor and all his followers feared this David. You saw his hands?"

"Yes, they look like they've been broken many times."

"No one could prove who did it, but the gossip circuit was not deceived." Brother Nehemiah took hold of Isaka's hands and prayed for his protection, that neither his fingers, nor his youth, nor his zeal would ever be broken. "Lord, use these young hands to build your church." He then prayed for Mugabe and Diolinda, and as quickly and unceremoniously as he had arrived, he disappeared into the night.

The darkness of night always weighed heavily on Mugabe. He envied Diolinda, who could roll over at night and in moments be deep in a sleep of faith, sound effects and all. He tossed and turned, never satisfied with his day, wondering if there was something he should have said, but more often wishing he could take back something he had said. His last thoughts were often of Diolinda. Then he smiled and thanked the Lord for her faith and love. He gently put his hand on her shoulder, careful not to awaken her from her well-deserved rest. She might stir, but never awakened, as though assuring him all was well.

Tonight Mugabe thanked the Lord for the joy of his growing relationship with Isaka. He still wondered why he would not enter the house and why he held his head down when talking to Diolinda, but she believed he was just bashful, and they were both encouraged to see him loving Jesus more and more each day. With that comforting thought, Mugabe joined his family and all of God's creatures in adding to the symphony of sounds that spoke of sleep and peace.

The next morning Mugabe said good-bye to Diolinda in the hut and joined Isaka outside. Together they walked through the quiet village, which was just beginning to stir. They were alone on the street but knew they were being watched.

They arrived at the burned-out church. Isaka appeared to be deep in thought. Mugabe leaned on his hoe and waited for him to speak. "I noticed that when someone believes what you believe…"

Mugabe smiled and added, "You mean as a disciple of Jesus Christ?"

Isaka nodded. "Yes. Why do they change their name? Like Brother Nehemiah. That wasn't always his name, was it?"

"No, I don't know what his tribal name was, or what his family calls him, but I do know that his new name was given to him by Via Mahondra."

Mugabe moved closer to Isaka, who was giving him his full attention. "When our Lord called Peter to be one of his disciples, his name was Simon, but Jesus said, 'Your name shall be Peter, a rock.' It described what Peter's ministry would be. He would be as solid as a rock."

Isaka nodded in understanding. "What does Nehemiah mean?"

Mugabe squatted down, still holding onto his hoe. "Nehemiah means 'Jehovah's Comfort,' or one who comforts as he's been comforted by the Lord."

"That's Nehemiah," Isaka said. "He's very kind and it is comforting to have him around."

"The Nehemiah in the Bible was a man God raised up to rebuild the walls around Jerusalem, the Holy City, which had been destroyed 70 years earlier when the Jews were carried away into captivity by the Babylonians as punishment for disobeying God. God used the Babylonians, a pagan people, to punish the disobedient Jewish nation. Next God used the Persians to punish the arrogant, ungodly Babylonians. Then God wanted to comfort the Jews and enable them to return to Judah and rebuild Jerusalem."

"Like our own people leaving the gold mines in South Africa," Isaka interjected, "then coming back to their families and loved ones?"

Mugabe's face lit up with delight at Isaka's comprehension. "Yes, exactly. You see, the walls around Jerusalem were seen as a threat to the Persian authority over the Jews, so of course there was opposition to rebuilding the walls. To the Jews, the walls represented protection. Without walls around their city, no one was safe, like a village with no protection. Rebels can rape and loot and easily get away."

Isaka looked at the ground.

Mugabe continued, "They needed to rebuild the walls around the city considered God's home."

He paused as they both moved into more comfortable positions. "Whenever God's people really wanted to return to their God, the Bible says He raised up a man to lead them. Nehemiah was a cupbearer to the Persian king. The king saw Nehemiah grieving over the state of what had once been God's dwelling place. God moved the king's heart to not only allow Nehemiah to rebuild the walls, but to assist him so the Jews could once again have a place to worship God. However, when Nehemiah started to rebuild the sacred walls, even though he had the King's blessing, he faced severe opposition led by a man called Sanballat. Nehemiah simply told those who opposed him, 'Leave me alone, get out of here, I have a wall to build.' And build it he did—in fifty-two days!"

Mugabe looked at the ashes of their church and said to Isaka, "With God's help, Nehemiah and his followers did the impossible. The Jews could now come home. The walls of their city had been rebuilt.

The Jews now had a place to worship their God."

Isaka quietly repeated, "Fifty-two days...fifty-two days..."

Dr. Nichols often told his class that one of his jobs as a teacher was, whenever possible, to make opportunities for experts in their field to speak for themselves. Just as he finished this latest reminder, the door to the classroom opened. A man in his mid-sixties entered, attired in mismatched corduroy jacket, tie, and shirt that cried out for distance from trousers that appeared to have never been pressed in their obviously lengthy life. Below and partly hidden by the baggy trousers was a pair of scuffed shoes that looked as if they had never felt the buffing of a shine cloth.

Dr. Nichols motioned to the guest, inviting him to join him at the lectern. He looked at the students with a mischievous smile and put his arm on the shoulder of the guest, giving the students permission to relax. "Dr. McHenry is a historian, not a fashion plate."

The guest joined in as the students laughed, and Dr. Nichols added, "But I assure you that his color blindness does not hamper him as an historian, and a very good one."

Dr. Nichols used humor to defuse any matter that might distract from the business at hand. With everyone relaxed and the issue of haberdashery settled, they could get to the business of learning. "As I promised you yesterday, this is Dr. James McHenry, whom many of you know as Professor Emeritus of History at another of our fine universities."

"Thank you, Philip, for this invitation. I've been retired for two years now, and one of the things I miss most are students. There are few things in this world that give a man who was born to teach more joy than seeing the eyes of students light up when they grasp what it is you are teaching. I remember when my history professor at Stanford said something that changed my life. 'Man only records history, but God in heaven makes history.' I committed myself that day to expound that truth as a history teacher. And now here I am, forty-three years later, not only expounding it, but believing it more than ever. Allow me to give you an illustration.

"We, who believe God created man, also believe God uses all kinds of men to fulfill His plans. I'm sure you're all aware of the story of Cyrus, the pagan king of Persia."

The students nodded as he continued: "As we see in Isaiah, Chapter 44, God raised up this pagan king, who had never heard of the four spiritual laws, let alone that God had a wonderful plan for his life, but He used him as an instrument to put down nations and to overthrow existing powers. Cyrus obeyed God without ever really knowing or believing in Him personally."

"Now the question I would like to pose to you this morning is a simple one: Does God still use the ungodly to build His Church?

"Allow me to give you a modern-day example. In 1949, not that long ago, Christians in China numbered about 900,000, out of a population of 800 million. This included every stripe of Christianity. The Church was in serious decline and had become more political than spiritual. Their numbers were decreasing rather than growing. There were American missionaries who were vocal in their belief that Marxism was the answer to China's future. In the middle of this historical tragedy, God raised up a Cyrus, an unbeliever. Do you know his name?"

Several students replied, "Mao."

"That's right, Mao Tse-Tung. God's modern-day Cyrus was given absolute control over the largest nation in the world. So how did God use Mao to build His church? Understand there were some real problems that had stymied the growth of Christianity that the home missions committee could not solve, no matter how well orchestrated a fund drive it might have been. Instead, this problem would take a godless dictator, whose ego convinced him he was in control of his own, private universe. Mao did for the Church in China not only what Cyrus did in his day, but also what the Roman Empire did for the New Testament Church.

"Just a little background: Mao decreed that he was the supreme leader, meaning the 'new god of China.' He had people saying grace before their meals, assuming they had any food. They bowed their heads and thanked Mao for the bounty before them, real or imagined, present or future. To solidify this control, he needed to have a Bible people could use during their prayer and study times. He put some of his men to work to collect the thoughts of Mao, often called the plagiarized Proverbs by others than his minions, into what they called, *Mao's Little Red Book.* His orders were to place one of these books in the hands of every man, woman, and child in China. It was designed to do something never before been done in China: unify the minds of the people.

"To fulfill Mao's wishes, some momentous problems had to be addressed. What were they? First, being such a vast country, there was the matter of transportation. Before 1949, it would take missionaries weeks to reach missionary stations. The outreach was extremely limited by having few roads. When Mao took over, there were only 75,000 kilometers of serviceable roads. He realized that not everyone could have the benefit of a copy of his *Little Red Book* to make them into one great family, with him as god, if there was no means of distribution."

Dr. McHenry stopped, smiled, and continued: "Now, we all know that there is no unemployment in a socialist society. You know how it is, 'each according to his/her abilities, each according to his/her needs.' But Mao, in his great wisdom, did not overlook the fact that about 200 million people were unemployed. Or at least standing in lines getting ration cards so the government could feed them. So why not give them picks, shovels, a map, and a command to get the roads done, or else! When Mao died in 1976, there were 189,000 kilometers of new roads. That's an increase of 114,000 kilometers, and not one labor strike in the process. He got those *Little Red Books* moving."

"Missionaries in China had also faced the problem of languages and race. In 1949, when Mao wanted to communicate with his people, he had to address 4 races and 57 tribes, who spoke in 300 major languages and 1000 dialects. The question arose in Peking of how the roads would help Mao's lordship if the *Little Red Book* was put into the hands of waiting disciples who could not read them."

"A dictatorship does have its advantage. Comrade Mao then declared Mandarin the official language of China. To encourage the benevolent masses, he set a deadline when employment would be reserved for those who spoke the new official language. The unemployed could not get a ration card for food or housing unless they could apply in Mandarin.

"Solving that problem brought to light another one. The printed word, designed by Confucius to keep everyone but the elite ignorant, had an alphabet of 47,121 characters. To print Mao's inspired thought would take more than a *Little Red Book,* but a very large book, whatever the color."

"Again, problem solved. He commanded scholars to do to the majority of characters in the language what he had done to those who opposed his revolution: get rid of them. Soon, instead of 47 thousand characters, there were only 1,556. It would now be possible to make Mao's *Little Red Book* truly little.

"But what good was a nice road on which to deliver an easily digestible *Little Red Book* if people could not read, even if they could speak Mandarin? In 1949, when Mao took over China, illiteracy was at 91 percent. The slogan of the day became 'read or perish.' Mao began a program that continues today, taking the country from being 91 percent illiterate to being 89 percent literate today."

"There was another problem to be faced: religion. The Chinese are a religious people. China was a land of 1000 religions. Mao told them, as dictators can do, that from then on there was only one religion in China, Marxism, and one god, Mao Tse-Tung. To make sure there was no competition, churches and mosques were closed. They were turned into granaries, which remained empty because of a disastrous program called the 'Great Leap Forward,' which is another long story. But Mao's original intent was carried out and there was nowhere for worshipers to meet, except in their homes. In addition, Bibles, Korans, and other religious books were burned. To be caught with a Bible was a capital offense, with a minimum prison sentence of seven years in solitary confinement.

"So Mao had a message, a transportation system, a simplified language, literacy, and supposedly no competition. He issued orders that all people, in all villages and cities, no matter how large or small, were to gather in small groups for 'Mao book study.' It involved studying Mao's writings, and then holding self-criticism sessions where everyone in China had to write a confession of their sins against the state and promise to do better. That was a tremendous change for people careful to never show outward emotion, and to always save face, especially in public.

"There was not even a word in their lexicon for *sin* or *repentance*, so they added one to Mao's dictionary. Now people knew a way to confess their sins of failing Comrade Mao.

"Finally, Mao did what the missionaries had not accomplished while still welcome in China. The constant chaos that wracked China for 30 years created the best possible climate for conversion. How? Simple, it's universal. It applies to each of us in this room. Man is most ready for 'conversion' of any kind when there exists these five things: 1. a painful uneasiness or anxiety; 2. a loneliness amongst togetherness; 3. a feeling of mental fatigue, tired of one more campaign; 4. a feeling of separation from the rest of the world; 5. a feeling of pointlessness, that there is no real future.

"So what did Mao do for China? He taught them obedience to authority, brought them together as one people, gave them a transportation system, a common language, literacy, made them a nation of 'one sacred book,' taught them the concepts of sin, repentance, and confession, and of course, got rid of the competition."

"Before Mao died, he led his nation through one of the greatest church growth movements in the history of mankind, producing the largest body of believers in Jesus Christ in all of history: those 900,000 in 1949, multiplied into a body of believers today numbering from 20 to 100 million."

"How many believers does China have today? A member of the Party summoned the head of the House churches to Peking, just three years ago, to warn him that there were too many people in the House and Official churches. They numbered as many as the Communist party. He then caught himself, but it was too late. The Communist Party membership at that time was 100 million."

"But there is no bowing down to the altar of statistics in China. The numbers are not the important thing. The spiritual life of the church is what really matters. You will note that the followers of Christ are known as believers, even by government officials. Christianity means a big nose, big ears, and round eyes. In other words, a Westerner, in the same way we think of everyone from the Middle East as Muslim. However, believers are those who have confessed their faith in the Lord Jesus Christ as the Lord and Savior of their lives, and live daily under his Lordship, and who have and still are willing to pay any price to follow Him.

"I'm sorry, I've run over time. But here's my point: Man may write history, but God in His sovereignty makes that history and is not limited to our methods. No one could have imagined, prior to 1949, that God would use a modern-day Cyrus to prepare a nation for the largest revival in the history of man—a fact, by the way, ignored by most of today's historians."

"So let me conclude today with some final words from the Creator of all history, from Genesis 50, verse 18. Joseph's brothers are about to meet him for the first time since they attempted to kill him, and they are frightened. When they meet Joseph, another man God raised up to build his Church, he says to his brothers, *'Do not be afraid, for am I in the place of God? But as for you, you meant evil against me but God meant it for good in order to bring it about as it is this day to save many people.'*

"But get this: had missionaries like Hudson Taylor and thousands of others not given their lives to China, none of this would have ever happened. Tertullian said that persecution is the seed of revival, or words to that effect. Far be it from me to argue with Tertullian, even if he was not dead, but I think he is wrong in this case. The seed of revival is God's Holy Word. It lies in the ground until the blood of the martyrs, millions of them in China's case, waters and nurtures the seed until it breaks forth into a vital body of believers. Lord, may it be the same for us one day."

The students stood and applauded as Dr. Nichols met Dr. McHenry and embraced. The students talked about the message for days afterward. The professor's attire was forgotten.

Twenty-one

"Don't worry, Isaka's a big boy. He's often out early in the morning. He'll be back for breakfast." Mugabe took Diolinda's hand and kissed it gently. "Come, let's eat."

They barely got their bowls to their mouths when they heard noise from behind the hut. Diolinda smiled and filled another bowl with maize. They both recognized the sound of Isaka washing up.

When he took his place on the ground at the front of the hut, Diolinda handed him his bowl. He smiled, thanked her, took a big swallow and licked his lips. Speaking loud enough to be heard inside the hut, he said, "I couldn't sleep. What you told me yesterday about Nehemiah kept floating around in my head like smoke from a cooking fire. I kept hearing, 'Rebuild the church, like Nehemiah rebuilt the wall.' Then I thought, *Would I get a new name?*"

He lifted the bowl to his mouth and with one large gulp, devoured the maize. Watching from inside the hut, Diolinda took his bowl. "I'll get you some more. You're a growing boy."

Isaka gave the bowl back with one hand, wiping off his mouth with the other. "No, I've had plenty. Full as usual." He patted his lean stomach. He knew that food was scarce.

Diolinda pretended to scold him, took the bowl, and turned back to the cooking pot. "You've had a long night, and a long day is ahead of you. You need food. This pot is like our prayers. Our Lord keeps filling it." She handed him another bowl of maize.

Isaka didn't argue.

Mugabe and Diolinda sensed he had more to say. They silently, prayerfully waited.

Isaka set the empty bowl down. "Since I couldn't sleep I decided I might as well work in the garden. When I got there, it was still dark, but I saw someone sitting in the rubble. I started shaking, sure it was the witch doctor. I turned to run and heard, 'Don't be afraid, it's only me. You're not afraid of an old man, are you?' It was the voice of David, the old man with the broken hands.

"Even though it was dark, I could see he was motioning me to sit by him. I did. He said he used to sit there with his guitar, and people came to listen to him sing Jesus songs he learned from the missionaries, before they had to leave the country. He said Jesus put new songs in his heart and hands when he worshiped Him; even the pagans listened.

"As it got light, I saw tears in his eyes. He told me there are two ways you can tell a village is run by the devil and his demons. When a white cloth is wrapped around the tree. And when the devil owns a village, he doesn't allow music. He asked me if I'd heard any music since I'd been here. I told him I hadn't, except when passing his hut, or when we sing. But that I had heard chanting during the nights."

"He told me pagans chant, but believers in Jesus sing. I think he said 'one speaks of death, the other of life; one of despair, the other of joy; one of being lost, the other of being blessed.' He said it was time to bring music back to the village. Then he pointed towards the forest and said, 'God will provide what you need.' I walked with him to his home. He was singing some song about 'amazing.'"

Mugabe went out to Isaka and put his hand on his shoulder. "Come on, get your machete. We have walls to build."

The villagers did not notice that Mugabe carried a machete, as well as a hoe. No one noticed Isaka carried a pot with their lunch, as well as his machete.

Surrounded by blackened stumps of what was once the church walls, Mugabe walked deliberately from corner to corner, calling out the number of steps making up the circumference of the building. Reaching the spot where he started, he said, "We need fifty trees for poles to hold up the walls, and twenty more for the roof."

"No," said Isaka, "we must cut down a hundred trees."

Mugabe looked at him, puzzled. "A hundred? Why a hundred?"

Excitement shone in Isaka's eyes. "Last night, I thought we must make this new church twice as big as the one they burned down. Then they'll know if it's burned again, we'll just build again, but twice as big."

Mugabe could see he was serious but did not share his excitement. "I can see you haven't cut many trees; let's see how you feel by the time we have fifty."

"We'd better hurry; we only have fifty days left," Isaka said. "That's two trees a day."

They headed for the forest with their machetes. Mugabe had already scouted out trees to be sacrificed for the sanctuary.

"I've been exploring and found a stand of trees that might be better than these. They wouldn't burn as easily as the others," Isaka said, humbly. "They're harder to reach, but the villagers won't see us."

Recognizing Isaka's wisdom, Mugabe motioned for him to lead the way.

Day after day, they walked to the burned-out church with their hoes, machetes, and food pot, prayed, and disappeared into the forest, reappearing at the end of the day. Eyes peering out at them through the gathering dusk could see they had spent a day in hard labor, and that their gait had slackened to a controlled stumble.

The routine continued, but now included stripping the cut trees of all branches, turning them into poles.

After weeks of back-breaking work, Mugabe told Diolinda, "With God's help, we have the poles. Tomorrow we'll carry the rest of them to the church site."

"A hundred of them," Isaka chimed in from outside the front door.

Mugabe rested as Diolinda served her men their bowl of maize. Brother Nehemiah had dropped by with another small offering. It was just enough for turnips and maize.

As Isaka sat at the front door eating and listening, Mugabe told Diolinda, "The last three mornings, our pile of trees has multiplied during the night. It's like a miracle. That's why we have enough trees cut already, along with the branches for the walls. Tomorrow we'll bring them in to the church site and start digging."

"Sanballat is going to be furious," Isaka interjected, then continued eating his maize.

"You're right, Sanballat and his followers are going to be angry." Mugabe was silent for a few moments. "But we must trust the Lord as Brother Nehemiah did."

Isaka passed his empty bowl back through the door. Mugabe heard him saying, "We need to get up early tomorrow. We only have thirty-seven days left."

Isaka was up and ready to go before the sun came up. Mugabe suggested that because it was Sunday, maybe they had earned a day off to celebrate how much the Lord and their "angels" had accomplished.

"But God would want us building a house of worship on Sunday, wouldn't he?" Isaka asked.

Mugabe got ready to follow Isaka to the forest, muttering, "I guess if Jesus healed on the Sabbath, we can build a house of worship. It's sort of a hospital where the sick can come for healing."

As they approached the church site, they were astonished at what they saw. The night before they had carried ten poles from the forest, but in front of them were all the poles they had cut, enough to build a church twice the size of the one that had burned down.

Mugabe looked up. "Thank you, Lord. You not only multiplied the fish and bread, but the poles as well."

God's "angels," whoever they were, had worked throughout the night. Sitting on the pile, with a great smile on his weathered, ancient face, was David.

As they approached him, he looked up. "I think the Lord surrounded these poles with His angels last night. There are people who know the poles are here, but they are not the ones who carried them up from the forest."

As the sun rose, the light of a new day shone on poles that would soon come alive again to give glory to God.

Each day villagers squatted on the ground, never saying a word, except to hush their children, watching as Mugabe and Isaka continued, uncomplainingly, to sweat and work. The villagers knew "Jesus people" had come back and were not going to leave. They were building themselves a worship house. Isaka let it be known that if it burned down, they would build another one, with two hundred trees.

The tension in the village rose as they dug holes for the poles. It made the labor of cutting and stripping the poles seem easy by comparison. A machete was not made for digging postholes, but it was all they had. Mugabe cut through the dirt, and Isaka used his hands to remove it.

Having an audience made it easier.

One day the chief of the village appeared at the back of the crowd, arms folded in disapproval. He made no attempt to interfere as Mugabe and Isaka spent several days digging and scooping out dirt. It was a slow process. It didn't look like they could get the walls up in fifty-two days.

The next morning they discovered the rest of the holes had been dug. Not with machetes, but with proper tools. The "angels" had paid them another visit.

The audience grew the day they dropped the first pole into its hole. Mugabe held it straight as Isaka scraped dirt back into the hole, and stomped it firm. When Mugabe let go of the pole, it stood erect, pointing to heaven. They stood back, grinning in undisguised triumph. Their audience, including the chief, showed no visible signs of sharing in their exultation, though Mugabe was sure that some of their "angels" were there.

A buzzing from the audience caused Mugabe and Isaka to look at the crowd. Standing behind the village chief was the witch doctor and one of his assistants. The crowd opened up as the witch doctor, wearing only a grass toga and multiple talisman, strutted forward, followed by his disciple. He stopped a few feet in front of Mugabe and Isaka and purposely turned his back on them, making no eye contact. The atmosphere was electric with anxious anticipation.

He pointed at the one erect pole. Spit flying from his mouth, he raged, "What are these weaklings doing to our village? They are insulting us, they are mocking us, they will bring sickness and evil to our village that we will not be able to cure. Our women will not have babies in their bellies, and the children will get sick and die. The ground will not give back its seed. We will all starve!"

The crowd shouted agreement as he continued. "We must not anger our ancestors. These Jesus people must stop! Not one more pole in the ground! They must leave our village forever!"

Those in the front raised their hands and shouted, "Burn it down, burn it down!"

Before it could become a chant, his disciple handed him a beer bottle. The witch doctor ceremoniously held it high above his head, then poured blood out of the bottle in a line extending across the entire front of what was to be the church. "Anyone who steps across this line of blood, which has been sacrificed to our gods, will die!"

He paused for effect, slowly turned to look at Mugabe and Isaka, and shouted so all could hear, "And if necessary, with my own hands!"

There was complete silence. The crowd separated as the witch doctor left. One by one, the crowd dispersed, leaving only the chief. He stared for a moment at them, then turned around and walked away.

Mugabe remembered the prayer of God's people when Sanballat threatened them. *"Hear us, Oh Lord, for we are being mocked. May their scoffing fall back upon their own heads. Do not ignore their sins. Do not blot it out, for they have despised you in despising us who are building the wall."*

Isaka nodded, picking up a pole. As he dropped it in a hole, he said, "Let us not be frightened by a beer bottle full of some poor rooster's blood. We have a church to build."

As Dr. Nichols took Jason's seat, Murphy stirred nervously. Jason and he had discussed at length what he was about to say. Neither of them expected it to happen so soon. They had even prayed that Jason would be one of the last to be called forward to "preach, pray, or die." They agreed that when it did happen, Jason would preach and Murphy would pray, hoping no one would die.

Jason, well-liked by his fellow students, was known for the hard questions. He was never arrogant but genuinely searching his own heart and mind to answer Jesus' question, *"But who do you say that I am?"*

Jason put his notes and Bible on the lectern and looked with pleading eyes at Dr. Nichols, hoping for a reprieve, or possibly a sign to change his message. He respected Dr. Nichols and had already discussed with him what he was considering talking about. Dr. Nichols not only gave his permission but encouraged him to speak out. He had assured Jason that though he didn't totally agree with his theology, he felt his views should be heard and respectfully considered by the class.

Murphy turned slightly sideways to look in Dr. Nichols' direction. As Dr. Nichols smiled and nodded for Jason to proceed, Murphy turned his gaze toward Jason and gave him a "Let's do it" sign.

The students watched the silent exchange, picking up on the tension.

"I've spent a lot time lately wishing I could have been in the upper room at Pentecost. I read somewhere that the significance of Pentecost wasn't in the realm of devotion or zeal for the salvation of souls, but rather, that day marked the beginning of something supremely historical. I'd like to have been a front-row witness on opening night.

"It was that day when those chosen by the Lord to be His disciples (as we have been) realized for the first time what God the Father had done for His children by sending His Son, Jesus Christ, to die, and be resurrected, for them. Those first disciples weren't thinking of evangelism or discipleship, but were simply telling everyone they met about the gift of forgiveness and salvation God gave through His Son, Jesus. It was all about Jesus.

"What happened?" Jason appeared grief-stricken as he looked at Dr. Nichols, then his fellow students. "Who has that kind of excitement about Jesus today? I suspect the Church's loss of compulsion to share the good news about Jesus was a gradual process, unnoticed until it was too late. Slowly the fire began to go out. The hot coals dropped from heaven weren't stoked well enough to produce even a spark.

"But the Church got organized. Instead of committing to the initial charge of Pentecost, to pass on the good news that set fire to the hearts of people of every nation and tongue, the Church became managers, organizers. Seminars replaced waiting in an upper room. Churches started schools of evangelism and discipleship, while the Holy Spirit wasn't even invited to participate."

He paused, embarrassed. "I'm sorry. I guess I get carried away. It's just that I've been wrestling for several months with what I read about first-century Christianity and my own empty experiences in the Church. I've discussed this with Dr. Nichols and Murphy. I'm not suggesting they agree with me totally, but they were good sounding boards."

"Before coming to seminary I cried out for a personal Pentecost. I see now what I really wanted was an experience. I'm not sure that I wanted the Holy Spirit in my life as much as I wanted Him to add something to it. I guess I wanted Him to give me some supernatural gift that people could see.

"However, there have been times when I realized that I was not the one in control. There were times when all I could do was weep—sometimes in repentance, sometimes in joy. There were times when people who hadn't been willing to listen to me before came and asked me to tell them again about Christ's forgiveness. I found myself wanting more than anything to have the mind of Jesus, to think like Him. I'd be reading things that had been meaningless, and suddenly they burned my eyes and my heart.

"You've probably had these experiences as well. But I think there is more to Pentecost, more to having the Holy Spirit come upon us. I'm not going to give up waiting for the Holy Spirit to fill me, again and again. I want to be compelled by what God has done for me to wholeheartedly give myself to Him.

"Do I speak in tongues? That's not the issue. What is the issue? I know some of you will strongly disagree with me, but this is what I believe.

"First, I believe that the Baptism of the Holy Spirit does not happen as a result of something I do, nor is it the result of what someone else does. The Lord is the initiator and baptizer. There are those who have told me that I could have this experience anytime I want it. But John the Baptist said of Jesus, 'He shall baptize you with the Holy Ghost and with water.' Jesus Christ is the giver. I remember going to a church once where they announced their yearly revival meeting the last week in March. 'Come and meet with the Holy Spirit.' It was like they were telling Jesus to put that in his date book.

"I believe that miracles are for this century as much as for the first-century Church. I've heard about many miracles in other countries where people don't have as many resources as we do—resources that tempt us to put our trust in them, instead of in God.

"I believe all the gifts of the Spirit can be found today within the Body of Christ, but they must be distinguished from natural talents.

Gifts given by the Holy Spirit equip believers for their place in the Body. Tozer wrote, 'Religious work can be done by natural man without the gifts of the Spirit, and can be done well and skillfully. But work designed for eternity can only be done by the eternal Spirit.'

"I don't think a multiple-choice quiz is an appropriate way to discover our spiritual gift. The Holy Spirit gives the gifts as He wills, not as we want. We do not choose a gift and then attempt to use it. We just do what the Spirit leads us to do, often unaware that the gift is operating in our lives. We often recognize each other's gifts more easily than recognizing our own. I've found it helps to give and receive encouragement when a gift is recognized.

"I believe the Holy Spirit is the invisible third party living within us, opening our eyes to see Jesus. He is the giver of that vision without which people perish. He opens my eyes when I'm unaware of people and their point of need. He opens my mind when I shrink from too much reality. He's teaching me that if I am open towards God, I am open also to the beauty and brutality of the world. He's showing me that if I am closed against being hurt, I inevitably close myself off from God as well.

"As my theology is being refined, I've come to believe the Director in the historic mission of the Body of Christ, since Pentecost, is the Third Person of the Trinity. The mission hasn't changed since Pentecost: Focus on the Person of Jesus Christ. I feel we may be frightened of what might happen if we had a personal Pentecost, but sharing this with you today and seeing your response has removed much of that fear."

Jason took a deep breath. "So I'm going to mention two other issues that I'm hoping some of you will want to work through along with me.

"One is an issue raised by Martyn Lloyd Jones, and that is the possibility of being born-again, but not yet filled with the Holy Spirit. He wrote strongly in defense of that possibility, but that particular book is very hard to find. I'm wondering why we aren't discussing this. It seems important.

"The second is the history of Puritanism and Pentecostalism. Both have been accused of excesses, and rightly so, but it seems they have been convicted and sentenced to a life sentence of ostracism, without possibility of rehabilitation. Don't you think Christianity would have gaping holes in its world influence if we didn't have the words of Puritan preachers to guide us back to the fundamentals, or if the Pentecostals hadn't spread out from the Azusa Awakening, playing a significant role in post World War II missions, especially in Asia?

"I'm not sure what I believe about these issues, yet, but that's why I'm here, to wrestle with the hard questions."

As Jason passed Murphy, he let out a stream of breath and whispered, "I didn't die!"

Murphy gave a gentle punch and a grin. "Awesome, man!"

Twenty-two

Mugabe and Isaka stood together in awe, looking overhead. Neither of them spoke. The last pole was set in place. Branches filled in the walls and framed the roof. Light from the setting sun glowed through the doorframe and windows. It was the end of the fifty-first day. Tomorrow they would return and hang the doors and put up window shutters.

Still not finding words to express their feelings, they silently walked out the door, ready to go home, eat, and rest.

The village chief approached, carrying a letter and calling Mugabe's name. He was very careful to not cross the witch doctor's bloodline, although it no longer existed. Mugabe and his hoe had made sure of that.

"I have a letter from the chief-of-many-villages in the capital."

Isaka stiffened.

"That building you've just completed is causing much grief in our village. The witch doctor has warned the chief-of-many-villages at the government central office. He demands the church building be torn down or it will be burned down."

Mugabe said nothing.

The village chief raised his voice in anger, shaking the letter at Mugabe. "I have four letters like this. You must go to the chief-of-many-villages and talk to him."

Mugabe spoke respectfully. "Chief, please understand that I'm not here to fight the witch doctor, but to give the people of this village a chance to know the peace our Lord Jesus Christ can give. I will not be preaching against the witch doctor's religion, but will be proclaiming the words of our Lord Jesus Christ so that our people may choose whom they want to follow. I do not want to make trouble for you."

"You are in serious danger, as well as your son here and your wife," the chief said, "if you ignore the order from the chief-of-many-villages. You must obey his command; he is my superior and I am yours. It will be very bad for both of us if you do not obey."

Mugabe opened the Bible he always carried to work with him and said, "What is happening in your village is not new. It happened many, many years ago when a man by the name of Nehemiah followed God's call to rebuild the Holy City. Let me read for you. *Now it happened when Sanballat...and the rest of our enemies heard that I had rebuilt the wall, and that there were no breaks left in it, that Sanballat...and our enemies who did not want the wall rebuilt sent me a letter saying, 'Come, let us meet together among the villages in the plain of Ono.' But they thought to do me harm.*"

Mugabe looked up from the Bible. "Nehemiah realized it was a plot to kill him. Nehemiah continues: *Then they sent me a letter four times.*"

Mugabe looked up again at the village chief. "Nehemiah refused to honor any of them, and so must I. And like Nehemiah, I must say, *'Now therefore, Oh God, strengthen my hands.*" Mugabe held out his hands, callused by the cutting of trees and branches. "The wall was finished—in fifty-two days. Tomorrow we will finish the work the Lord has given us to do—in fifty-two days."

The chief shook the letter angrily. "But you cannot ignore the chief-of-many-villages. He's a very powerful man!"

"We must obey God rather than man." Mugabe put his arm around Isaka. "*As for me and my house, we will serve the Lord.*"

The chief cursed and stalked away, still careful not to cross where the bloodline had been. Though it had been erased from the ground, it still had to be erased from the hearts of the villagers.

That night there was little sleep, but much anxiety and prayer from the residents at the hut near the witch doctor.

Neither Mugabe nor Isaka spoke of it as they walked to the church in the morning, but both feared that it might be just a hacked-up pile, waiting to be burned at a time when all the villagers could watch.

The first encouraging sign was seeing David slowly walking to his hut after his now-familiar, all-night vigil to ensure the "angels stayed awake."

The people of the village were unaware of yesterday's encounter with the village chief, and most knew nothing of the parallel of finishing the building in the same number of days that Nehemiah rebuilt the walls of Jerusalem. However, not wanting to miss any action, villagers came and watched as Mugabe and Isaka hung the front door. They tested it a few times by opening and closing it. They hung shutters for the windows, which would remain open during services, except during bad weather.

The audience grew as women stopped on their way home from the market. Mugabe went to the people, ignoring the witch doctor's imaginary bloodline. "Tonight at seven we will hold the first service in our new church. You are all invited to come inside and join us."

Mugabe was ready to go home. Isaka scuffed dirt with his toe, as he did when he had something to say. "I have something important to do. May I come later?"

Mugabe was puzzled, but the bond established during the last fifty-two days gave him peace. Smiling, he laid his hand on Isaka's shoulder and told him he deserved some time off after all his work.

Isaka took off running. Mugabe watched him go, wondering what was up with this young man who had become such a vital part of his and Diolinda's life.

Supper came and went with no sign of Isaka. It was time to go to the church and prepare for the service. Mugabe hugged Diolinda and attempted to comfort her by saying that Isaka was probably waiting for them there.

They walked to the church, both thinking, *But what if Isaka was not at the church?*

Their spirits lifted as the church came into sight. A large crowd of people stood outside. As they walked toward the crowd, the people stared at them. The couple smiled. No one smiled back.

Mugabe called out, "Welcome. We will start in fifteen minutes."

The crowd continued to stare.

Mugabe and Diolinda walked inside. They looked at the empty room. There were no seats, so everyone would sit on the floor, if anyone dared cross the bloodline. Isaka had cut a pole in two and made a cross, which was nailed to one of the poles in the front of the church. Mugabe had not yet been able to build a pulpit.

They looked around. There was no sign of Isaka.

Mugabe looked out the front door, then turned to Diolinda. "The whole village is out there, except for two people: the witch doctor and the village chief."

He was certain Diolinda heard him. But her mind was elsewhere.

Suddenly, there was a murmur from the crowd. The couple was sure that the witch doctor had arrived. They stood frozen in place.

Directly in front of them, framed in the doorway, was a familiar figure. David walked through the door, announcing, "I've come to worship in our new church." He placed a small grass carpet on the floor and sat down. "I suspect you have many friends out there who, like new lion cubs, are afraid to be the first to come forward. Each of them is waiting for the other. I've seen it before. I promise you, when the service begins, they'll come in."

Mugabe went to the front of the church and sat down on the floor, leaning against one of the poles just below the cross. Diolinda sat in the middle of the church a few feet from David.

Mugabe was the preacher and this was his congregation. It was not a very auspicious beginning. Diolinda kept turning her head as though checking if any villagers were coming.

David asked, "Where's Isaka? I thought he'd be the first one here."

"He's off on a personal errand. Don't worry," Mugabe replied. "Let's begin by each one of us praying."

As they finished praying, a woman with three children entered. One of the children crawled onto her lap. They sat very quietly.

A young man followed them, sitting even closer to the front. A few minutes later, several older women came in. Mugabe noticed they had all walked around the invisible bloodline.

Diolinda anxiously and fervently prayed for Isaka. Mugabe joined her. Suddenly, a sob from David ripped through her private grief. Startled, she looked at him as he pointed to the back door.

Isaka stood in the doorway triumphantly holding up a guitar.

David stretched out his arms, and Isaka handed it to him.

Without saying a word, Isaka sat on the floor as if nothing had happened. He was just waiting with the others for the service to begin.

David fondled the guitar, rubbing his fingers over it. With one gnarled hand he gripped the neck and placed his other hand over the strings, ready to play.

Everyone inside and outside waited for what was to come.

David looked upward, tears rolling down his cheeks as he painfully and awkwardly strummed and sang, one word at a time, "A...maz…ing...grace...how...sweet...the...sound…" His voice became stronger as he continued, "That saved a wretch like me."

Now he looked outward and sang loud enough for the people outside to hear his testimony, "I once was lost, but now am found, was blind but now I see."

He nodded to the people to join him. The rebels may have broken his fingers, but not his spirit. Those fingers now led the people in singing a sweet offering to the Lord.

The people outside now crossed the invisible line to enter the church. Before long, the place was full. The village chief walked through the door. As he stepped inside, several people pushed against each other to make room for him. He sat down.

David's singing and playing, the blending of heart words and soul music, so like David of old, drew the people into the symphony of praise, singing, clapping, and raising their hands in worship.

Mugabe smiled at Isaka's new understanding of what was meant when Brother Nehemiah said David "sang in the spirit." David's gift of leading people in heavenly worship had not been destroyed by his suffering, but enlarged by his openness to forgive. Hearts, now prepared to listen to God's Word, became lighter and lighter until the guitar could hardly be heard.

David looked in Mugabe's direction.

Taking his cue, Mugabe stood up, opened his Bible, and preached his first sermon in their new church. The transition went unnoticed, but Mugabe knew the Holy Spirit was in control as he looked at the people, and they looked back with anticipation.

An hour later, Mugabe and David ended the first service in their new church, singing a wondrous truth Mugabe read from Nehemiah before closing his Bible. "*The joy of the Lord is your strength.*"

Dr. Nichols closed his folder, tossed it on the desk behind him, and rolled an electronic keyboard to the front of the classroom. "Afraid I'm going to play?"

He ran his fingers across the keyboard. Nothing happened.

Someone from the back of the room sighed. "Thank the Lord."

The comments were greeted by laughter as Dr. Nichols walked back to the lectern, saying, "We're doing something a little different this morning. Our 'preacher boy' (your words, not mine) has asked to give his message today because he cannot preach without his electronic piano, and he doesn't want to disconnect it and haul it over here every day. So, Howard, why don't you and I change places?"

As Dr. Nichols walked back to swap places, a hefty student made his way up to the lectern.

Murphy did not know Howard well, but he liked his easy way with people. They had sat together in the cafeteria several times, but Howard never volunteered personal information. They talked mostly about sports. He did not know Howard was a worship leader, let alone a musician.

In a quiet, yet rich baritone voice, Howard began: "As you know, my name is Howard. I'm a worship leader in a local church. There is no reason you should know that. I don't recall ever seeing any of you there. It's located where the freeways all come together. That's why I have this," he said, reaching over and to put his hand on the instrument. "It can be turned up loud enough to drown out the freeway noise. Now the fumes, that's something else. But we don't let that stop us from opening our mouths wide and singing praises to the Lord. We may cough the rest of the week, but it's worth it."

The students squirmed a little in their seats.

"I am sure everyone here loves music. It's the one subject where we are all experts. I may not be a great musician, but I do know what I like, like you, and that's what I tend to listen to. My favorite musician, songwriter, and singer is Neil Diamond. Surprised? Well, I like him for several reasons. First, all of his really important songs sound to me like a nice Jewish boy crying out for Messiah. Just listen carefully sometime to 'I Am I Said,' or 'Brother Love's Traveling Salvation Show.' I think you'll hear an honest, 'Where are you? I'm still looking!' And the pathos in his voice! Especially to hear him in person, which I do every time he comes to town. Don't get me wrong, I don't have a room full of his posters. I just appreciate the gift God has given him, and us, of music.

"Unashamedly, I'll admit that the only savings account I possess is to fund Neil Diamond concerts at the Greek Theatre, or at the Arena in San Diego. I mark it on my calendar, I count the days, and yes, in the end, the hours. I don't want anyone to come with me. I go alone. I arrive early. I even get expensive tickets so some middle-aged idol worshiper doesn't stand up in front of me and all I see for two hours are his buttocks. I sit and think about the songs he's going to sing, and even sing some to myself. Finally the moment arrives. The lights go down, and the orchestra starts to play. The people quiet down. It's one of those rare times I feel community.

"Suddenly, there he is. A man just like me, but much more gifted. I listen, I think, and when I leave, I tell the Lord how thankful I am that He allowed me to be there. On the way home, I begin to transfer what I have seen to what happens on Sunday mornings.

"As I line up to get out of the parking lot and back on the freeway, I keep thinking about the fact that Neil Diamond does not have an opening act. I've been around musicians, and they all seem to agree that an opening act is either to wake up the audience and get the adrenaline flowing for the main act, or it is often an act chosen to make the star sound good by comparison."

Several people chuckled.

"Don't laugh; it's important for concert promoters. But Neil Diamond does not need an opening act. We have all come to hear him, his music, his message. We don't need a shot of adrenaline, or any other stuff they shoot up in the restrooms to get excited about what is ahead.

"Now the sticky part. If Neil Diamond does not need an opening act on a Saturday night at the Greek Theatre, why do we think God needs an opening act on Sunday mornings at church?"

There was a pause as some of the students looked at each other in surprise.

Howard continued, "I ask that question as a future pastor and a current Sunday morning worship leader. I'm told that every great Christian movement had its own music. Think of Martin Luther, John Wesley, Dwight Moody's Ira Sankey, to name a few. Every generation has a right to their own music. Not all agree. Not long ago, I was in one of your churches. When the service ended, the lady in front of me turned to anyone who would listen and grumbled how contemporary music ruined the service, and her whole day. I guess she felt safe unloading on a stranger. I did something embarrassing, but I'm still glad I did it. I looked her straight in the face, smiled, and said, 'Lady, when you sing "The Old Rugged Cross," I noticed you weren't moved to tears like that young man over there when he sang, *"The nail in His hands, the nail in His feet."'* She just walked away in a huff."

The students applauded and one even shouted, "Way to go!"

Howard hung his head, "I wasn't trying to make points." He swallowed hard. "Keith Green's contemporary worship song, 'Oh Lord, You're Beautiful,' was what I listened to this morning to get the strength to do this, right here. Please understand, though—worshipping with Keith Green was not an opening act.

"I have given much thought and prayer to this matter. I respect all of you very much, so let me pass my conclusions by you. You don't have to agree, but I guess as a captive audience, you will have to listen."

Looking back at Dr. Nichols, Howard added, "Isn't that right?"

Dr. Nichols nodded in the affirmative as Howard continued, "Neil Diamond does not have an opening act, but there is an 'overture.' That, by definition, is an instrumental introduction to a larger musical work. When I am sitting there waiting for Neil Diamond, and the orchestra is playing excerpts from his greatest hits, I'm remembering the words. They evoke emotions from the past. Please understand I'm talking about a secular experience, while at the same time, at least for me, spiritual as well. When the last song has been sung, the audience pleads for an encore.

"As a worship leader I see our worship time as an overture. It's the introduction to, and reminder of, great truths that we will hear from the pastor." Again he paused to let that soak in.

"Our worship team spends many hours every week rehearsing and getting the notes from the pastor's sermon in advance, so that instead of an opening act, our worship time prepares our hearts to receive, and reinforce, and live out what the pastor brings us from God's Word. When the sermon is over, the time at Jesus' feet has come to an end, our worship team leads in an encore: a plea for God's Spirit to go with us as we leave the mountaintop to walk through the valley, and live out what we've been taught."

Howard moved to the electronic keyboard. "This, by the way, is more than a piano, it's a synthesizer. This little keyboard holds an orchestra, as you will hear."

Looking again at his watch, anticipating what some were thinking, he hit a few notes on the synthesizer. It was alive.

"Now let me get more personal. And again, things may get a little sticky, but don't turn me off too soon. God uses music to bring people together. Music is a catharsis, not just personally, but collectively."

Howard turned the keyboard around so they could see the keys.

"Now you notice there are black and white keys. That's no accident. Don't laugh, but God in His wisdom gave *us* the black keys and *you* the white keys." Howard grinned. "Together they create a rainbow of sound."

Murphy, not a musician but having taken a few piano lessons under his mother's tutelage many years ago, was fascinated by the tones of the black keys' pentatonic scale.

"God is the Father of anthropology. He helps us create music to express our experiences and heritage—everything from the nasal twang of Nashville to the sophistication of the Boston Symphony.

"Let me show you something interesting. These black keys make up what's called the pentatonic scale. There are only five notes. I'll play you something on these black notes, no white notes needed. Nothing personal." He grinned again. "See if you recognize any of these songs."

He keyed the opening notes of several songs; his fellow students not only recognized them but hummed along. They were all Negro spirituals.

Howard turned the keyboard back around so he could stand behind it while facing them. He produced the sound of stringed instruments to serve as his background.

"Now let me illustrate my second point. Many years ago, Africa's black Muslims and so-called Christian profiteers discovered black gold: slaves. But these slaves were real people with names. One was my great-great granddaddy. The slave traders took thousands of my ancestors prisoner. They tied them together and dragged them to sea ports where your great-great granddaddies bought them."

The room got intensely quiet as Howard continued. "One of those slave traders, Captain John Newton, was confronted by Jesus Christ during a terrifying storm at sea, and he deeply repented. He knew he was unworthy of being forgiven, and was overwhelmed at God's love for him after the horrendous grief he had brought to fellow human beings created in the image of God. Words of awe over God's grace spilled onto paper. The amazing thing about this song, written by a former slave trader, is that slaves themselves could identify with the very same song."

Howard played a haunting melody on the black keys. "I'd like to show you how I think my ancestors could have sung this song."

His deep baritone voice sang Newton's words, enunciating each word as though he wrote them, "Ahhhhmayyyy zing grace…"

At the end of each phrase, he gasped from deep within, Howard becoming the slave in chains, one of many oarsmen, rowing to the rhythm of the captain's whip. Then, as one hand created an underlying musical fiber, the other shot straight into the air and he cried out, "Oh Lord Jesus, help us! They done shoot my daddy, my brothers, my sister."

He sang the next line, "How sweet the sound…"

Howard cried, "Oh sweet Jesus, they tied my momma and me, they led us by our necks thorough the jungle."

"That saaaaaaved a wretch like meeee."

"Oh, sweet Jesus, can you hear me? There are hundreds of us. We sit in the sun all day. They pull us to white men who want to buy. Thank You, Jesus, he wants me *and* my mama."

"I ooooonce was lost…"

"Oh, Jesus, we in a black hole. Don't have room to lay down."

"But now am found…"

"Oh, sweet Jesus, Mama's too sick to talk. I think she gonna die, then I'll be all alone. Find me, sweet Jesus, find my mama and me."

"Was blind, but now I see."

"Jesus, my mama stopped breathin'. Oh Jesus, they gonna toss her into the ocean. Oh Jesus, please catch my mama; she can't swim."

"Thru many dangers, toils, and snares..."

"Sweet Jesus, now we workin' in his fields early morning 'til late at night. They work us so hard we fall down. Look at my back, sweet Jesus. It burns so fierce I can't stop crying. Heal my back, sweet Jesus."

"I have already come..."

"Sweet Jesus, it ain't gonna get better. They work us, beat us, and forget to feed us."

"'Twas grace that brought me safe thus far..."

"Sweet Jesus, the white man fightin' the white man. Dead men all around."

"And grace will lead me home..."

"Oh Jesus, we is free but we ain't free, but I have a dream you gonna come and make us really free. Come quickly, sweet Jesus."

As Howard stood looking up and sang, "Come Lord Jesus, come and make my dream real," a young man who was unfamiliar to the students walked forward and stood beside Howard. They were a study in opposites, black and white, but their countenance was of those transported to another time, another place.

Howard said, "The white keys are yours, brother; the black are mine. Let's make some music together to the Lord."

The sounds of an orchestra joined the two voices, singing as one, filling the room.

"When we've been there ten thousand years," the music soared, "bright shining as the sun..." They looked at each other, smiles creasing their face. "We've no less days to sing God's praise." They looked up to the heavens and harmonized, "Than when we first begun."

The music faded. They lifted their hands from the keyboard, raising their arms together and singing in beautiful a cappella, "Hallelujah, what a Savior." Their voices became a whisper, "What a Savior."

They turned and embraced each other.

The room was silent, except for a few sounds of stifled weeping.

Suddenly everyone stood to applaud. Murphy heard the applause multiply. He turned and saw his were not the only tears. Students from other classes were standing three deep behind the last row of desks. They packed the doorway and overflowed into the hallway. As the applause continued, Howard and Dr. Nichols exchanged seats as Howard's friend joined the crowd in the back of the room.

As Murphy made his way out of the classroom, his mind tried to take it all in. He was sure of only one thing: his heart cried for an encore.

Twenty-three

There had been three unasked questions hanging in the air in Mugabe's hut for several weeks now. What would be the consequence of Mugabe's refusal of the summons to the capital. Where did Isaka get the guitar? And when and how would the witch doctor strike next?

The last question was answered on a Sunday morning when David was interrupted in the middle of a song by a scream. People sitting near the open window cried out as they scrambled over each other to get out of the way of the witch doctor.

His upper torso, smeared with a white substance and red markings, leaned through the window as he screamed. "You old people will get sick and die; there will be no babies in your bellies; your children will throw up blood and lay still forever, the clouds will be sealed, and the seeds will languish in the ground. You will all starve!"

As he held up two rattles made from snakes, he screamed something in a language no one understood. People moved farther away from him as they wiped his spittle from their faces. He reached back and took another of his beer bottles from one of his disciples. People ducked as he hurled it at Mugabe. It bounced off the wall and onto the floor. The people still sitting on the floor quickly moved to avoid being hit. The bottle landed at the feet of Isaka, unbroken.

Before Mugabe could respond, the village chief pushed the people aside and picked up the bottle. He strode over to the open window where the witch doctor had been and pulled out the wad of paper that stopped up the bottle's neck. With a mighty yell, he hurled the bottle out of the window. "Here, you son of the devil, give the chicken back his blood and see if he comes back to life."

The only sound outside was of men running and cursing.

The village chief leaned against the wall and silently slid to the ground, putting his head back.

The silence was broken as David started singing, enunciating each word, then adding the guitar so the song would not be mistaken for a chant: "What...can...wash...away...my...sins? Nothing...but...the...blood ...of...Jesus." He picked up the tempo.

The congregation joined him in the song.

Still sitting against the wall, the village chief raised both hands and joined in the singing.

The witch doctor had been silenced, but Mugabe knew the battle was not yet won. There would be a price to pay.

"We have a challenge as Christians," Dr. Nichols pronounced. "God has revealed Himself to us; now He calls us to make Him real to those who don't know him. How do we make an invisible God real to people?"

Murphy noticed that Dr. Nichols didn't waste much time in small talk these days. There seemed to be a growing intensity in his desire to prepare them to be teachers and preachers. Murphy, himself, was very interested in experiencing more reality in his relationship with his "invisible God." He carefully tuned in as Dr. Nichols continued.

"The secret is, of course, in the person and teaching of Jesus. As God became real to His creation by the incarnation of the Son of God, we look at *that* life because He is real, and He made God real to the people in His time.

"But how do we make an invisible God real to people here and now? We follow the teaching and example of Jesus. Jesus' Gospel walked on two legs: The Proclamation of the Truth, and the Demonstration of the Truth. To make Him real in and to this world, our Gospel must walk in the same way.

"First, let's consider His proclamation in parables as a literary teaching form. Jesus made God real to the people in time and space by telling parables. He used simple, single-point stories from everyday life and culture. By doing this, not only did he teach in an understandable way, He let the people know that God understood their world. (I have a friend who will say to me, "Way to chuck," if he hears me preach and thinks it's a good sermon. I know that is a baseball reference to a pitcher throwing well, so in a way he knows I will understand, he tells me the message was on target.)

"By teaching with parables, Jesus accomplished several things: His teaching was clear and understandable. He demonstrated that God is not distant and removed from His creation, but rather engaged in it. He communicated that God understands and identifies with us. He *is* a caring, present, loving Father. His parables are memorable—particularly in an oral culture without benefit (or handicap) of tape recorders and video cameras.

"In the Parable of the Good Samaritan, Jesus connected with the people because He used a cultural reality of the times, known and practiced by the religious people, to shock them into reality. The Jews hated Samaritans, and in the story of the wounded man, He makes a member of the hated and culturally marginalized group the hero. This slap in the face of the religious Jews caught their attention, and showed them He was aware of their racial bigotry. It also showed them the true loving heart of God because His parable demonstrated a hands-on presence of love that reveals the heart of the God who cannot now be seen. God's heart overcomes racism to demonstrate caring love in the presence of need.

"So how do we make God real and present? Make clear by our actions and words that God knows and understands the social inequities and issues of the day. Nowhere do we see a better example of making the love of God real for the people than in the story commonly known as the Parable of the Prodigal Son. The cultural realities of this story are very clear and powerful for the people.

"You know the parable, so I won't retell it. But I will highlight that by asking for his inheritance early, the younger son says to the father, 'I wish you were dead, because I'd rather have your money than you.' Obviously this was an offense of the harshest degree. Jesus' listeners would understand this. So in the story, when the father runs to the returning son and embraces him, this would be so shocking to the listeners that it would bring the radical love of God directly into their world. That's why it's important to study your culture to know the needs and assumptions of the times, and take the time to tell stories that connect the people to the timeless truth of the Gospel.

"The second leg on which the Gospel walks is demonstration of Truth. Let me tell you two stories that make God real here and now. One story is success, one is failure.

"On a trip to Uganda, I was able to visit what is called an IDP Camp—an Internally Displaced Persons Camp. These are actually not camps, but small villages of about 100 people that came about because of conflict between different tribes in central and northern Uganda. A friend of mine who is a missionary-evangelist had visited these villages a year earlier, presented the Gospel, and in one of the villages, almost the entire village came to Christ.

"An overriding problem in the camps was that the people's only source of water was from a bacteria-ridden river, and not surprisingly disease was a huge problem. So my friend returned home and raised enough money to have wells drilled in the villages.

"A year later we visited the camps with him and saw transformed lives, both in the physical and the spiritual. Rather than drunk, stooped over, sick people we found upright, sober, smiling people. The presence of the wells and good water immediately cut the disease rate in half.

"We were able to interview the pastor who shepherds these believers and asked him what effect the wells have had on his ability to teach the people about Jesus and 'living water.' He said that because of the well, the people understand that Jesus is the giver of good water; both physical and spiritual water. The well provides not only a living metaphor for a spiritual truth, it also demonstrates in a life-giving, health-giving way that God knows the people are there, God knows what they need, and God provides for them in a great, loving way. The well physically represents the love and presence of the invisible but imminent God. The pastor said that the well will always be present to remind the people of Jesus as the living water.

"Acts like drilling this well pave the way for the Gospel. The well drilling *was* the presence of God and His love and buys credibility for the telling of the Gospel. The physical drilling, presence, and ongoing ministry of good water from a well demonstrates the real-time-and-space reality of Jesus. The people in the village have an appreciation for

Jesus being the living water that we can't grasp or appreciate like they do.

"The second story involves personal failure. During a sabbatical, I visited the former soviet satellite country of Belarus in order to teach at a small Bible college. The morning I left the country, it was snowing and, of course, very cold. As I sat in the bus station waiting for my bus, I spotted a young man who was obviously making the rounds, begging. There I sat, beside my two suitcases and back pack, nibbling on the food I had purchased for my journey and writing prayers in my journal. (I was pretty self-absorbed, because I get anxious when I journey by bus or train across borders in Eastern Europe. So my heart sought God's assurance, and that occupied my thinking.)

"When the young man finally approached me, I'm not sure that I even looked at him. I had more than enough food, but I ignored him. Rather than listening to the prompting of the Spirit, I listened to the common cultural voice that said, 'Don't give to beggars.' I missed an opportunity to make God real to the young man, because if I had handed him some food, I knew enough to say to him in my pitiful Russian, '*Bog tebye lubit.*' God loves you.

"There has been divorce in the Church for too long: the divorce of Gospel preaching and direct involvement in the human condition—caring for the real-life concerns of people—sometimes called social concern, social action, or social justice. We seem to have forgotten 'in' but not 'of' the world. We seem unable or unwilling to deal with messy, unclear, ambiguities.

"How do we make an invisible God real to people here and now? We follow the teaching and example of Jesus. Why is it we flee from the hungry, the thirsty, the lonely, the needy with such force and effort? Bottom-line, stripped of exegesis, original Greek, or flowery illustrations: if we *are* followers of Jesus, then we will be *doing* what Jesus did. Any questions?"

Murphy was ashamed of wishing for some small talk.

Twenty-four

Mugabe and Diolinda were both awake early. They had each been secretly considering the same idea for some time, but it was Diolinda who first spoke of it aloud. They wanted Isaka to be their son.

At yesterday's service, when Mugabe asked the people who wanted to be identified as Christ's disciples to pray with him, Isaka was one who responded. Mugabe and Diolinda agreed that as far as man could know, he had become a true believer. He had even hinted at wanting a biblical name.

They both felt sure the Lord had given them Isaka to be their son and also believed his name should be Levi. The problem was how to approach him. They wanted it to be his decision, not theirs. They agreed to talk to him.

Mugabe gently shook Isaka's shoulder to awaken him. "Time to eat so we can get an early start at the church. Our job has just begun. Putting up the walls was the easy part."

Isaka sat up, rubbed his eyes, and reached for his breakfast. He was hungry.

After breakfast, they walked to the church together until Isaka, showing youthful impatience, said he wanted to run and see if anyone was there early. Mugabe knew he really wanted to see if the church building was still standing or if the witch doctor had been there.

When Mugabe arrived, he was relieved to see Isaka opening the church's shutters. They went inside and sat down. Mugabe told him that he and Diolinda had something to talk to him about. It concerned his desire to change his name from Isaka to a Bible name. Isaka looked at the ground while Mugabe explained how, in Scripture, people were often given names that fit their personality or their ministry. Mugabe told him he and Diolinda wanted him to come into their home, not just to put his hand in their pot, but to discuss a new name. "If we could have a son," Mugabe said, "we would call him Levi." Mugabe put his hand on Isaka's shoulder, and in a trembling voice said, "We hope you will consider being our son—our Levi."

Isaka jumped up, looking terrified, crying, "No! No, you can't!" and ran out the door, disappearing in the forest.

Mugabe pondered for hours what could have frightened him in what he said. What had made him run away?

Mugabe finally walked to where they had cut trees for the church. It was a place Isaka often went to be alone. Mugabe felt Isaka thought of it as a sacred place. It was also the place where they had sweated and prayed together—and bonded, he thought.

However, Isaka was not there. Mugabe looked for fresh tracks and could find none. He prayed, wept, then reluctantly made his way back home to tell Diolinda. When he told her, she wept, and he held her.

With a strained voice she cried out, "Oh Lord, can I never give my husband a son?"

She wept convulsively while Mugabe held her tighter. They sat there for several hours, praying, talking, and wondering what had gone wrong. "Where is he?" they cried to the Lord.

When darkness fell, they went inside. Neither of them could eat, so no effort was made to prepare food.

They finally went to bed. Several times Mugabe got up and checked outside the door, but there was no Isaka.

For three days and nights, they fasted and prayed, "Lord, please bring him back."

On the fourth day, Mugabe sat in the church, in case anyone wanted to talk about Jesus, as they sometimes did. He heard someone. Looking up, he saw a dark, distraught Isaka silhouetted in the light of the doorway.

Mugabe jumped up and started toward him, arms open wide. Isaka backed off and motioned for him to stop. Mugabe froze in his tracks. He didn't want him to run.

As they stood, neither of them moving, thoughts raced through Mugabe's mind: *Has he gone back to the rebels? Has he gone to the witch doctor? Has he given up Christ?| Lord, tell me what happened?*

Isaka stood with head and arms hanging down, unmoving.

Mugabe continued to hold out his arms with love and compassion written across his grieving face, as His Lord must have done so many times when He was here on Earth.

Slowly, Isaka lifted his head. His voice was very low; Mugabe had to strain to hear him. "I cannot be your son; I cannot be the Levi that God wanted you to have."

Mugabe made a small step toward him. Again, Isaka moved a step back. Mugabe froze.

"But why? Have we mistreated you?" Mugabe pleaded.

"No, you have not mistreated me, I've mistreated you. I'm the one who killed your son. I killed Levi. I was the one who—"

Mugabe dropped his hands to his side and cried in disbelief, "You? You—"

Isaka interrupted him. "I didn't rape your wife. I didn't touch her. We were drunk. I was the only one who'd never been with a woman. They dared me, ordered me to become a man that night."

Isaka sobbed in shame. "It was easy to break in. It was dark inside, but I saw her lying on the sleeping blanket. I was scared. I couldn't move at first. But she woke up and saw me and tried to scream. An animal sound came out. She stood up, and before I could stop her, she grabbed the wedding hoe off the wall and swung it at me. I ducked, then wrestled it away from her. Before I knew what I was doing..."

He hung his head, unable to look at Mugabe, who was paralyzed by what he was hearing.

Barely able to speak, Isaka whispered, "I swung at her with the hoe as hard as I could. She put her hands out, but I heard a horrible thud as the hoe hit her belly. I felt the hoe crack. She fell to her knees, making terrible sounds, then curled up on the floor and didn't move or cry. I thought she was dead. I dropped the hoe and ran. I ran, and ran, and ran." Isaka sobbed. "I don't know what to do except run. That's why I can never be your Levi. I cannot put my hand in your pot, because I killed your son. I must leave!"

Isaka turned to go, but Mugabe called to him. "No! No. Wait. Don't leave."

Isaka turned back and again hung his head.

Mugabe did not move as he spoke. "Is this why you have been frightened to come into our hut, to look Diolinda in the face? Why you always keep your head down when you talk to her? You were afraid she would recognize you?"

Isaka whispered, "Yes, at first I was afraid she'd remember my face, but when she didn't, I still felt dirty, unworthy of going in your hut. When you said you wanted me to be your Levi, I had to run. I wanted to kill myself, but I'm too afraid to die."

Without moving any closer to Isaka, Mugabe spoke to him as he had so many times in the past months, with love and compassion: "Isaka, both of us have done something even worse than that."

Isaka looked at Mugabe, questioning.

"We both helped to kill a father's only son. So I am also a murderer."

Isaka looked confused as Mugabe continued. "We both had a part in Jesus' death, as much as if we had been there."

Mugabe waited for Isaka to grasp what he had said. "But you know what Jesus' last words to His Father were?"

Isaka slowly said, "*Father forgive them, they don't know what they're doing.*"

"Uh-huh," replied Mugabe.

Isaka looked at the ground and then at Mugabe with a flicker of hope. "And He forgave them?"

"Yes," Mugabe replied, "He forgave them." Tears rolled down Mugabe's face. "Isaka, Levi, our Father in heaven forgives, and this father forgives." Mugabe put his hand over his heart. "You are twice forgiven."

Isaka stood motionless, letting the words sink in.

"What you have told me today is a secret between you and me and the Lord."

Isaka stared at Mugabe, who answered before he was asked. "Diolinda will never be told our secret. Besides, there is nothing to tell. Forgiveness means it is as though it never happened."

Isaka shook his head. "You mean you will let me put my hand into your pot? You still want me to be your son?"

"Yes," Mugabe replied. "Now, Levi, my son, why don't you go and tell your mother that her men's bellies are empty and need food?"

Mugabe saw the hint of a smile on his son's face. The fear was gone.

"And son."

"Yes, Father?"

"What has happened...just call it redemption."

Levi, who would never again be called Isaka by Mugabe or Diolinda, gave Mugabe his brightest smile as he replied, "Yes, Father," and ran out the door heading home, practicing, "Mother, mother, your men's bellies are empty! They need food!"

Murphy had come to believe Dr. Nichols was a prophet, as well as a teacher. He had a unique way of making God's Word practical as he merged the past with the present, showing one was dependent on the other, and to ignore one was at the peril of the other.

After the daily announcements, Dr. Nichols began the class, asking, "Who are your heroes, other than some rock musician or a supposedly mature infant making millions of dollars putting a ball through a hoop? Can you give me a name?"

Murphy thought of Mr. Maxwell and his uncle, Pastor Bjorn, but wasn't sure where Dr. Nichols was headed.

"We need heroes. We need someone to look up to, to give us reason to excel. Dostoevsky said, 'A man who bows down to nothing can never bear the burden of himself.'

"We have lost the idea of knights heroically slaying dragons. We cannot agree that knights are 'good' and dragons are 'evil,' and there really is a difference between the two. Consequently, when a knight does slay a dragon, the media talking heads cry out, 'insensitive,' 'bigot,' or 'religious fanatic' (translated *fundamentalist*). In measured tones of superiority the editorial pontificators pontificate, 'Dragons are an endangered species and must be protected.' So if dragons are not to be slain, there is no need for knights in shining armor.

"I obviously disagree. My hero is not afraid of the critics. He is a man who has slain a few dragons in his day." Dr. Nichols turned behind him to an elderly man in a wheelchair. "He's been my hero ever since I came as a freshman to Mt. Hattin. Please welcome the founder and now President-Emeritus of Mt. Hattin University, Dr. Charles Northern."

The students stood and applauded as Dr. Northern awkwardly wheeled himself to the front of the class. He lowered his head, humbled, until the applause died down. "Thank you. It's a privilege to be here with this experimental class of preacher boys, as you are affectionately called by Dr. Nichols. Every class is experimental in one way or another, I suppose. I experimented on Dr. Nichols and am quite satisfied with the results." He bowed towards Dr. Nichols with a smile.

"He and I have been discussing an article by one of our favorite political commentators, P.J. O'Rourke. It describes a society without heroes. O'Rourke says Americans figure that if we get fired, it's not failure, but a midlife reassessment period. If our marriage falls apart, we'll simply try another. There's no shame in divorce. Everybody is doing it—at least those who bother to get married. If we're convicted of a crime, we'll sheepishly confess everything, join a support group at church, and get off the hook by listening to shrinks tell us we don't like ourselves enough. These are modern times, says Mr. O'Rourke. A world without heroes."

Dr. Northern's voice was gravelly from many years of teaching and preaching. "What's wrong with this picture? When you get into the pastorate you will soon discover there is little difference between how the world lives and how Christians live. Christians actually have a higher rate of divorce than non-believers. And what is most disturbing is that these divorces take place after claiming to have made Christ Lord! The majority of American Christians agree with the secular culture that morality is relative. We're missing more than heroes. Where are the prophets? Where are those courageous souls willing to say, 'Thus says the Lord.'"

Murphy noticed a resemblance between Mr. Maxwell and Dr. Northern. They both struck him as being spiritual grandfathers, aching to pass on hard-learned lessons of life. He listened carefully, not wanting to miss an opportunity to learn from someone else's experience in hearing from God.

"I've given this much prayer because if what is learned at Mt. Hattin does not affect the world outside our walls, we have failed in our experiment and it's too late for a midlife reassessment. I'm far past midlife and deserve to be fired if our students have not been challenged to seek and to be keepers and purveyors of God's Word."

His voice trembled and his hands shook, revealing the intensity of Dr. Northern's conviction. "I ask myself, where are the Isaiahs to stand up and shout, *'The whole world is on the verge of disaster; the Lord is about to judge the nations.'* How desperately we need to hear that though *God is silent, do not be mislead. He is not asleep. You cannot continue to ignore Him, for when He rises to terrify the earth, men will enter the caves of the rocks and the lips of the cliffs.*

"Where are the prophets, young and old? Where is a Spurgeon? A Moody crying out to men, women, and children to come and be saved from themselves? We have teachers of meaningless trivia for 'spiritual success,' but where are those crying out the prophetic warning of approaching catastrophe? Who is warning us of wolves in sheep's clothing? Who should we be listening to today? God has given us prophets. Think of Billy Graham. Think of A.W. Tozer, who was little-known or listened to when he lived. Do prophets have to die before we listen to them?"

He sighed deeply and shook his head. "We have eyes to see, but we do not see, ears to hear but we do not hear."

Slowly, with trembling hands he held out his Bible and pleaded, "Where is an Amos to warn us of *pride, plenty and splendid elegance in the cities...They planted, they harvested, they ate and drank and anointed themselves with the pleasures of the rich.* There was no justice in the land; the poor were afflicted, exploited, hungry, thirsty, sick. Is it any different today?"

Northern lifted his hands and eyes heavenward. "My Lord, please, where are the men of God obsessed by divine revelations? Where are the men of God who wait on You for visions of reality? Not waiting for large attendance, but for anointing. Where are men taught by Your Spirit? Not in halls of great learning, but beside the suffering, weeping with those who weep.

"Father, where are the Miriams, the Deborahs, the Huldahs, who give themselves to the spirit of 'Thus says the Lord,' not to emotional theatrics?

"Where are Your prophets who care more about truth than eloquence? Let them stumble and stutter. But, Lord, may they get the message themselves before giving it to others. We need men with torn garments and ashes to lead us in hearing You."

Wiping his eyes, he looked at the students and with a broken voice, pleaded, "Listen to Jeremiah as he cries out through many tears, *'But who will listen when I warn them? Their ears are closed and they refuse to hear. The word of God has angered them; they don't want it at all. For all this I am full of the wrath of God against them. I am weary of holding it in. I will pour it out over Jerusalem, even upon the children playing in the streets, upon the gathering of young men, and on husbands and wives and grandparents. Their enemies shall live in their homes and take their fields and their wives. For I will punish the people of this land, the Lord has said.'*

Dr. Northern slumped wearily. "You are probably thinking, *But Jeremiah lived a long time ago. Our world has changed since then. We don't need prophets. We are a kinder, gentler civilization today. We believe all people are to be treated equal. We prove it in our 'diversity.'*

"If you are thinking that, you are right, and you are wrong. Right in that Jeremiah did live more than 2500 years ago. But you are wrong about our being a gentler, civilized, sophisticated society. All we've done is trade bows and arrows for laser-guided missiles, and catapults for smart bombs. Sophistication does not eliminate killing; it just makes it less personal...back to Jeremiah. Chapter 37."

Murphy took his eyes off Dr. Northern long enough to find Jeremiah.

"Let me set the scene. King Zedekiah had killed or imprisoned all the prophets. Jeremiah was first thrown into the sewer with the refuge, then held in prison.

"Zedekiah was in big trouble. He was losing the war. In a moment of desperation at the front line, he sent for Jeremiah. Upon his arrival, the king asked with fear mingled with hope, 'Is there a word from the Lord?' Jeremiah replied, 'King, I have good news and bad news. You are not going to die.' The king smiled with relief, and asked, 'And the bad news?' Zedekiah's moment of relief was over when Jeremiah answered, 'You are going to be captured by the Babylonians.'"

Dr. Northern closed his Bible. "And we know that's exactly what happened. King Zedekiah's army was overrun by the Babylonians, and they took the king prisoner. Jeremiah was right; they did not kill him. He probably wished they had when they used hot pokers to blind him so he couldn't escape. But Zedekiah was blind spiritually long before he lost his sight physically. How different things might have been had he called for Jeremiah earlier, instead of locking him up for telling a truth the king did not want to hear.

"There's another lesson we can learn from this event. Enemies can 'destruct' a man's body but only God can 'restruct' a man's mind."

Dr. Northern appeared to have difficulty finding a comfortable position. Dr. Nichols handed him a glass of water. "So the question is still on the table. Where are the prophets today? And by the way, let me say that God never called a prophet with a three-page multiple-choice questionnaire. Nor did He train His prophets at seminars on Finding Your Spiritual Gift."

There were glances among the students. Murphy had taken the tests, but they hadn't helped him.

"So where are the prophets? I can hear Jesus sobbing over Jerusalem, crying out, *'Jerusalem, O Jerusalem, murdering and stoning the prophets sent to you.'* That's one of the saddest scenes in the New Testament. Jesus' cry would soon be silenced."

Sighing deeply, he continued: "But of course we think things are different today. But are they? We still stone our prophets, only we don't use rocks." He raised his weary voice slightly and articulated distinctly. "We stone them with silence. That's right, silence. Allow me to give you an example. I believe one of our modern-day prophets is Alexsandr Solzhenitsyn. How many have heard of him?"

Several students raised their hands.

"How many have ever read his writings?"

No hands went up.

"Solzhenitsyn spent years in prison in the Gulag Archipelago in the Soviet Union. He was first stoned by the KGB. As Jesus said, a prophet is without honor is his own country. But then he was stoned by the

American intelligentsia and press in the good old USA. The Soviet Union attempted to silence this prophet by forbidding any of his works to be published. Still, he won the Nobel Prize for literature in 1970. Because of the world-wide publicity, he was exiled from the Soviet Union. You have to understand how painful and shameful it is for a patriot to be exiled. He lives for the day he can return.

"Solzhenitsyn was admitted to the United States as a political refugee. His welcome by fellow writers in America, and the great American centers of learning, was as limited as it was cowardly. He was treated with respect by the opinion makers only as long as he remained a 'non-person.'

"He could not go to Stockholm to receive his Nobel Prize because he feared the Swedish government, in their convoluted concept of neutralism, would succumb to the pressure of the Soviet Union to return him to the Gulags as a prisoner. Later, however, he gave his Nobel speech at the very center of the stone throwers, Harvard University."

Dr. Northern took a sheet of paper from his pocket. "You judge. Is Solzhenitsyn a prophet? Was he stoned by silence? Let me read part of his four-hour speech to you. Remember this was 1970.

> "'Violence, less and less embarrassed by the limits imposed by centuries of lawfulness, is brazenly and victoriously striding across the whole world, unconcerned that its infertility has been demonstrated and proved many times in history. The world is being inundated by the brazen conviction that power can do anything, justice nothing. Dostoevsky's devils...by means of hijackings, kidnappings, explosions and fires of recent years are announcing their determination to shake and destroy civilization! And they may well prevail."

Dr. Northern looked at the students, making sure they heard it correctly, then repeated the sentence, enunciating every word, "'And... they...may...prevail.'

"Solzhenitsyn continued:

'The spirit of Munich...prevails in the twentieth century. The timid civilized world has found nothing with which to oppose the onslaught of a sudden revival of bare-face barbarity, other than concessions and smiles."

Dr. Northern stopped, looked again at the students, and gravely continued: "It gets more convicting, and prophetic. Listen.

'The spirit of Munich is a sickness of the will of successful people who have given themselves up to thirst after prosperity at any price...so that their accustomed life might drag on a bit longer...and tomorrow you'll see, it will be all right. But it will never be all right.

"Listen to his conclusion. Don't forget it. It carries a lot of the Old Testament prophets' thinking:

'The price of cowardice will only be evil. We shall reap courage and victory only when we dare to make sacrifices."[1]

The room was very quiet as Dr. Northern took another sip of water. "So, where are the prophets? They are being stoned with silence. Silence imposed by the intelligentsia and their minions, the censors of what we hear and do not hear, the mass media."

Dr. Northern breathed another deep sigh, almost a moan. "In 1983, Solzhenitsyn said:

'The entire 20th century is being sucked into the vortex of atheism and self-destruction.' These words did not make it past the clever reporters who decide what goes on the teleprompters of the talking heads giving us the evening news. 'We can only reach with determination for the warm hand of God, which we have so rashly and self-confidently pushed away...There is nothing else to cling to in the landslide.'

---

[1] See Nobel Lectures published by Farrar, Strauss, and Giroux, 1976.

"So what does this warm hand of God feel like? Listen to Jeremiah and see if you feel the warmth. *'For I know the thoughts that I think toward you, says the Lord, thoughts of peace and not of evil, to give you a future and a hope.'*

"Grip tightly. We should not feel secure until we feel scar tissue against our soft hands and hear Him say, *'Come unto me all you that are heavy laden and I will give you rest...take my yoke upon you and learn from me, for I am gentle and lowly in heart, and you will find rest for your soul.'*

"Where are the prophets?[2] Hiding out, waiting to be listened to, waiting for faith and courage to speak, knowing they will never be popular and may end up in the sewer, considered refuge. But it is better to live in the sewer, my brothers, fulfilling God's call for your life, than to suffer the guilt of hiding in silence. Whatever else you learn at Mt. Hattin, learn to listen to God."

Dr. Northern lifted his hands to pronounce blessing. "*The Lord bless you and keep you. The Lord make his face to shine upon you and be gracious to you; the Lord lift up His countenance upon you, and give you peace.*"

As Dr. Nichols wheeled him out of the room, no one spoke. It had been a sacred experience—a sermon at the foot of Mt. Hattin. It became even more memorable when they realized they had been the privileged witnesses to the last message Dr. Northern ever gave.

---

[2] For a complete thesis on prophets see *Prophetic Ministry* by T. Austin Sparks (London: Witness and Testimony Literature Trust, 1973).

Twenty-five

Mugabe followed Brother Nehemiah's recommendation and held Saturday services for people coming from other villages. Due to the crowds, he had to add a second service. They came, ignoring the white rag on the tree outside the village.

Mugabe and Nehemiah understood this was considered "sheep-stealing" but could not turn people away. They prayed and discussed alternatives. The one they always ended up with was to open a Bible school for training new pastors so those who came on Saturday could have their own church in their home village.

Official government policy dictated that a Bible school posed a threat to their culture and must be dealt with very severely at its embryonic stage and aborted at the first signs of life. However, the two men's burden to train pastors grew and they agreed it was only a matter of when and where. A Bible school would need to be in a larger village where it might meet unnoticed or, if necessary, underground.

When Nehemiah left to visit other pastors, Mugabe dreamed of his original vision, which included starting a Bible school in Maputo. He was rudely awakened by someone calling his name.

He quickly slipped his pants and shirt on, slid into his sandals, and went to the door. Still not completely awake, he tried to identify the voice. It lacked the shrillness of the witch doctor. And where was Levi?

Mugabe mumbled, "I'm coming, I'm coming," and unlatched the door.

As he stepped outside, the moon cast enough light so he could see Levi being held back by two soldiers. Their AK-47s were pointed at Mugabe. One of the soldiers stepped forward and, attempting to sound like a man, asked, "Are you Mugabe?"

Mugabe replied that he was.

"Then you're to come with us." The two young soldiers stepped forward and grabbed Mugabe's arms.

Pulling back, he asked, "To where?"

The young soldier, still propelling Mugabe forward, replied, "To Inhambane."

Standing in the doorway, too frightened to move, Diolinda cried out, "Lord, not Inhambane!" It was the capital of the province, a place where villagers were taken and simply disappeared, never to be heard from again.

Mugabe pulled away from the two soldiers, while assuring them they were in control. "I'll come with you, but first let me say good-bye to my wife and son."

Ignoring his request, the young soldiers turned him around and thrust him forward. Mugabe then saw the witch doctor run past them and disappear into the darkness.

Levi, ignoring Diolinda's pleas, cautiously followed the soldiers, who were half-dragging, half-pushing his father down the road. He slid into the shadows. He could see some doors to other huts crack open just enough to see what was going on. Someone whispered, "Tell Pastor Mugabe we'll be praying for him."

As he got closer to the soldiers, he saw Mugabe seated in the flatbed of a truck, hands tied behind his back like a criminal. The soldiers jumped up beside him.

Levi ran toward them, shouting, "No, no!"

Mugabe called, "Take care of your mother. I'll be back!"

Levi, now only feet from the back of the old truck, froze as one of the soldiers pointed his gun directly at Levi's knees. "One more step and you'll never run again."

"Please son, go home!" Mugabe shouted. "Take care of your mother, and—"

His father's final words were drowned out by the roar of the truck, which took off, leaving Levi in a trail of dust.

Mugabe's trip should not have taken more than four or five hours in spite of the roads that had had no repairs since the Portuguese left, but the soldiers stopped in several villages, showing off their captive. They strutted about like conquering heroes, taking whatever food they wanted from the marketplace, none of which they shared with Mugabe who still sat, hands tied behind him, with the hot sun beating down on his head.

The trip finally ended in front of an old building that at one time might have been a well-manicured government office. But not any more. It was a pitiful example of post-colonial freedom gone awry.

The soldiers jumped off the back of the truck, pulling Mugabe with them. Passers-by were careful to steal only a glance at this dust-covered, bound criminal.

Fear replaced Mugabe's pain from sitting so long in one position the entire day when he saw the sign on the building: SNASP, an acronym for the feared soldiers who ran the Centers for Mental Decolonization. In Hitler's day, they would have been called the SS, Mao would have called them the Red Guard, and Pol Pot the Khmer Rouge.

They differed in name only. They were Mozambique's President Machel's private army, directed by the Soviet Union's KGB. Their job was to keep the revolution pure. They had been specially trained in East Germany in the fine art of how to expose and treat enemies of the people. Answering only to the President, they had authority to imprison for as long as they felt necessary. They could assign prisoners to re-education camps, which housed many thousands of "volunteers."

And now Mugabe was being escorted into their guesthouse.

The young soldiers who had brought Mugabe from his village had finished their job. Several older, professional uniformed men escorted him past several offices, up to a manned counter. One officer curtly told another Mugabe's name.

He took a knife from his scabbard and severed the twine that had cut off the circulation in Mugabe's hands. They waited while he got the blood circulating in his fingers, wincing with pain as he did so. With studied avoidance of any eye contact, as though Mugabe was a non-person, they photographed him and took his fingerprints.

Their East German training gave Mugabe a false hope that maybe these people were not as bad as their reputation. In a country where professionalism no longer existed, Mugabe found himself relieved at their mild efficiencies.

But not for long.

He was politely escorted out of the office and down a flight of stairs. The well-lit hallways disappeared into dank, barely lit corridors. They stopped at a window. The polite young escort handed Mugabe and a paper over to an older man and walked away.

The old man glared scornfully at Mugabe, unlocked a door, and pushed him through it. Barred cages lined the room. The smell of urine, human waste, and sweat was sickening.

The guard smiled. "Welcome home. You're just in time for dinner," he said, pointing to two men carrying a large pot with a ladle. The guard laughed viciously. "We have another guest!"

"Where'll we put him? We're already pissing on each other."

The guard unlocked a cage and pushed Mugabe inside. He was met with cursing and a hard kick across the leg as he accidentally stepped on a man's hand. The Portuguese had designed the cages for four prisoners, but now they held ten or more. They all sat on the floor.

A prisoner reluctantly slid aside and made a little space for Mugabe. He slowly sat down, his body aching from the day's ride. The men with the pot and ladle arrived at the door.

The prisoners got up, all with a metal cup in their hands, and reached through a small opening in the cell while food was ladled into their cup. Some cursed at the food, some stared at it, but they all ate it. They knew it was all they were going to get.

The prisoner next to Mugabe emptied his cup and informed him that if he was lucky, maybe they would bring him a cup tomorrow.

"Until then," he told Mugabe with a laugh, "it looks like you go hungry. Better try to get some sleep. These people here do their best work at night."

Mugabe leaned his head against the wall. The cursing seemed to fade quietly away, along with the aching hunger in his belly. Jesus' words soothed him like warm water. *"If they persecuted me, they will persecute you. How blessed are those who are persecuted for My sake. If you are insulted because of the name of Christ you are blessed. If you suffer as a Christian because of your faith in Jesus Christ, do not be ashamed but praise God that you bear His name."*

Somewhere between consciousness and unconsciousness he quietly prayed, "Thank You, Lord, that You allow me to suffer on your behalf.

No matter what they do to me, let my only response be *'Father, forgive them, for they don't know what they're doing.'*"

Mugabe's body relaxed and sleep overtook him....

He was startled awake by a guard shouting in his ear, "You're next!"

The guard led Mugabe through several doors. He was passed to a young man who said, "Follow me" and walked down the hall.

Again Mugabe prayed, "Lord, let my only thoughts be, *'Father, forgive them.'*" The officious young man opened the door to a well-lit room with a couple of chairs in front of a desk. Behind it sat a man reading some papers.

Mugabe stood in front of the desk. The man stood up and stared at him. "So you are Mugabe," he said in clipped tones.

Mugabe nodded and the interrogator leaned across his desk into Mugabe's face and held a letter, which Mugabe saw was addressed to him in his village. The interrogator shouted, "How long have you been working with the CIA?"

Mugabe backed up in disbelief. "CIA?...Never."

"Then can you explain the purpose of this letter from Dr. James Graham in a place called Springfield, Missouri?"

The interrogator took the letter from the envelope. "He says he enclosed money: 'I am looking forward to the day when you work in Maputo. I will return to South Africa next week, after a short trip to the U.S. I hope we may meet one day at the border to discuss further plans.'"

Mugabe knew it would be useless to explain that building a Bible school in Maputo was part of a vision the Lord had given him, and that Dr. James agreed.

The interrogator stepped back and took a paper from his top desk drawer. He sat down, leaned back, and arrogantly asked, "Don't you know the law? Let me read it to you: 'All religious buildings and their contents are the property of the people, and the people will decide how they are to be used. Pastors are permitted to preserve them for government use. They are *never* to be used for religious meetings.'"

The interrogator smiled at Mugabe. "We've already turned many buildings into granaries."

Mugabe was tempted to ask him why they needed granaries when all grain was shipped to Russia. But he knew it was pointless.

The interrogator continued, "And as for a Bible school, you know that children under eighteen are forbidden to attend church, and anyone older must get permission from local cadre leaders." He stood up. "And you want them to attend a Bible school? How dare you!"

He paused as though fumbling for words. Then he reached over the desk, took the letter, and shook it in Mugabe's face. "You didn't want to start a Bible school, you wanted to spread the slime from your CIA. How much did they pay you?"

Mugabe wanted to answer, "How should I know? I've never seen the letter, or the money." But again, the silent prayer, *"Father, forgive them,"* rescued him.

The interrogator came around the desk, fist raised in anger. He threw the letter on the desk. "This is the proof you are not a pastor. You are a traitor; you work for the CIA." His spittle hit Mugabe in the face. "This letter is the rope that will hang you." With rehearsed theatrical disgust, he stomped out of the room and slammed the door behind him.

Mugabe was afraid to move. An older man with a smile came in, walked around the desk, and sat down. He quietly said, "Sit down, Mr. Mugabe, you must be tired, having been awakened in the middle of the night. We are, too, but we have so much work to do we cannot get it all done in the daytime."

He spoke as a father to his wayward son: "Mr. Sosa is a bit high-tempered. He must have picked that up from the Portuguese. I apologize on his behalf. But you do understand that this letter is indeed very incriminating."

Mugabe somehow felt this was not the time to relax as the seemingly gentle old man continued. "All we want from you are the facts of this case. You might be innocent, and we never want to convict an innocent person."

For the first time, Mugabe spoke and explained to him who Dr. James was, and that he had never seen the letter. The older man leaned back and listened, nodding that he understood. "Perhaps it would be easier if you just told us what you were actually doing in South Africa—you were there illegally, you know—and if there are other agents here in Mozambique. Perhaps then we can let you go back to your village, to your wife, Diolinda." He picked up a folder. "By the way, I don't see here that you have a son, but you told Mr. Sosa that you did."

Mugabe couldn't remember mentioning it to the other interrogator. He wondered who had been giving these people information. Everyone from his village knew that Levi was now their son. It had been announced in church. Even the witch doctor knew that.

The older man got up and went to the door, motioning for the guard. "Take him back to his cell, and Mr. Mugabe, we know all about you. We are honorable men. We know how hard it is to make a living during these difficult times. Think about it and we will talk again, maybe tomorrow night?"

On the way back, Mugabe heard animal-like sounds from cells with doors and peepholes. Back in his cage, he prayed again, "Thank You, Lord, that I'm considered worthy to suffer for you and also..."

Before he could finish, someone ran a tin cup across the bars outside the cell. The men all picked up their cups and reached through the bars for their breakfast.

The man sitting beside him handed him a cup. "Here—the guy this belonged to won't be coming back."

Mugabe, though shaken, was too hungry not to accept the cup. He had not eaten for a day and half. As he ate the unidentifiable gruel, the man beside him asked, between slurps, how the interrogation went. Mugabe relayed his story.

"Well, don't worry, next time you will get both working on you at the same time. The devil will spit in your face, and the saint will wipe the spit away. Only this time, you'll be in a private room—with only a peephole."

They had hardly finished their gruel when the guard called out Mugabe's name. This time the young man stopped in front of one of the rooms with a peephole. The guard unlocked the door and motioned Mugabe to go inside. There was a naked light bulb hanging from the ceiling and a small table with two chairs.

The interrogator walked in, nodded a greeting, and smiled, asking

Mugabe if he had enjoyed his time alone to think about their previous discussion. Before Mugabe could reply, the feigned gentleness disappeared. He pushed Mugabe onto the chair, walked to the door, turned again, and a little out of spittle range, shouted, "You have plenty to say, and you will say it, by God, or you will die or wish you could."

As he left, he slammed the door behind him.

Mugabe prayed silently, *Father, forgive him, he doesn't know what he is doing.*

The door opened and two men, looking more like prisoners than interrogators, entered the room.

Several hours later, a bloodied Mugabe was carried into his cage and tossed onto the floor. He lifted his head as he felt water run along his leg. A young man, sitting against the wall, was urinating on the floor. He lifted himself up on his bottom. Pain gripped his body. He slid over to his open space against the wall and began to murmur, "Thank You, Jesus, for the privilege of being beaten for You."

He knew he had won this round as he repeated from his heart, *"Father, forgive them, they don't know what they're doing.* They, like Judas, are under the devil's control."

For two nights, the torture was repeated. First the devil and then the angel, taking their turns, and then the two escapees from hell applied their trade with diabolical expertise.

Others from the cell were also taken away. One did not return. Mugabe found it difficult to stand up and get to the small bucket in the corner that had not been emptied since he had been there.

He had been there a week when the guard called out the name of the youngest of the prisoners, who had been taken out several times and always came back covered with blood, crying for mercy.

Hearing his name, he jumped up screaming, "No, no. Kill me, just kill me!" he yelled, attacking the guard. The guard made a quick exit and soon came back with two more guards. As they picked him up, he screamed, grabbing onto other prisoners, "Please! Someone help me! They're going to destroy my manhood. They'll make me a woman."

The guards dragged him down the hall as he continued yelling out graphic details of what they were going to do to him.

He never came back.

On the seventh and eighth day they came for others, but never for Mugabe. He reached a point that whenever the guard came to fetch one for interrogation, he wished they would call his name so he could get it over with.

On the tenth day, he had just finished emptying his tin cup of evening swill when his wish came true. His name was called.

The guard took him down the hallway, past the cells with the peepholes and the room where he was first interrogated. He found himself wanting to thank the guard. They entered a courtyard. Several men were standing around with guns. There were three poles at the other end of the courtyard. He almost stumbled as he realized he was walking across the execution yard.

He looked up. "Lord, thank You that I don't have to hang on a cross."

They walked him past the three poles and down the side of the yard. Suddenly the guard opened a gate. He gave Mugabe a hard shove and slammed the door behind him.

Where was he? It took him awhile to realize that he was outside the prison walls. Was this a setup? Were they going to shoot him, pretending he was escaping? "Lord, here I am," he prayed as he held his head high and limped onto a street. Several people walked by and stared at him, but no one stopped.

Two guards walking by in well-pressed uniforms ignored him.

One of them he recognized. It was the young man who had been screaming for mercy as he was pulled from the cell. Mugabe got angry as he thought how he had lain there, praying for the young man, thinking they were destroying his manhood. So it was all part of the game to get men to confess....

Three days later, Mugabe was lying on his stomach while Diolinda rubbed his body with herbs. He told little of what had happened, and neither Diolinda nor Levi asked. The wounds spoke for themselves.

As he dozed off, he thought of the soldiers who had arrested him, as well as those who had interrogated and beaten him, as he quietly said, *"Father, please forgive them; they have no idea what they are doing."*

Dr. Nichols held the door open for a well-dressed middle aged man on a mission. He went to the lectern but omitted his usual opening remarks. He looked at his guest and began: "We have a special speaker here this morning. He is a long-time friend of mine, whose friendship I value very highly. For several years now, I have tried to get him to speak in one of my classes. Jacob Benowitz has been traveling the world for several years with a group of Jewish scholars studying religious persecution."

He smiled as he looked at his guest. "I finally told him our friendship would cease if he wouldn't come and share his profound wisdom with a group of young men who will be filling some of the most important pulpits in America. Perhaps both statements are slightly exaggerated, but..."

The guest moved confidently to the lectern. "Because of my good friend's prodding," Benowitz began, "and because of my great respect for him, I will share with you what I have found as my colleagues and I have charted religious persecution in our world. It is not only disturbing, but frightening. Today I speak to you on behalf of my people and believers who have suffered for their love of the Lord God.

"I am a Jew in the most deeply rooted sense, worshipping Yeshua, the Messiah. And I am here today to warn you that I see a frightening parallel between the self-appointed elite of the world and how they deal with Christian believers, with how Hitler dealt with the Jews."

"The intelligentsia, immoral politicians, and sadistic dictators totally ignore the torture and murder of believers. I agree wholeheartedly with some of my wiser colleagues, both Jews and Gentiles, that anti-Christian persecution must be described as a global spiritual plague of massacre, rape, torture, slavery, mutilation, and imprisonment. As many as 200 million fellow believers are at this very hour being persecuted, and another 400 million suffer discrimination and second-class legal status because they profess to be genuine followers of Yeshua. I must tell you with a very heavy heart, still weighed down by the Holocaust, that tens of thousands of believers are being martyred each year.

"In countries like Sudan and India, Hindus and Muslims have declared war against Christians." There was anger in his voice. "The world is not only ignoring this modern-day Holocaust, but is encouraging it through new laws that make conversion to Christianity a death-penalty offense, or in more civilized societies, they relegate those they call right-wing fundamentalists to the garbage heap of irrelevance.

"Dr. Nichols asked me to define persecution and discuss whether believers in the United States are persecuted. Persecution is a denial of basic human rights and the infliction of suffering—mental, physical, and spiritual—because of one's commitment to their God.

"Suffering for ethnic, cultural and economic reasons has no promise of blessing. Persecution in itself does not carry any redemptive value. So don't go out and look for persecution. But at the same time, if you live under the Lordship of Yeshua, know that you will be persecuted, but you may not realize it is happening. You will simply see it as part of the privilege of being His follower.

"Now let's look at some Scriptures that shed light on why Yeshua expected His followers to experience persecution. First, John 15:20, *'If they persecuted Me, that is your Messiah, they will persecute you...'* However Matthew 5:10 promises a blessing for those persecuted. *'Blessed are those who are persecuted,'* but notice the reason: *'for righteousness' sake.'*

"In Acts 5:41, the apostles rejoiced after being persecuted *because they had been counted worthy of suffering disgrace for the name of their Lord Jesus Christ.* "1 Peter 4:16 says, *If you suffer as a Christian because of your faith in Jesus Christ, do not be ashamed but praise God that you bear that name.* That is, the name *Christian.*

"Now here's the thing. The places where the body of believers is growing are in areas of the world where there is persecution. So does this mean persecution is necessary for the body of believers to grow?"

He moved to the side of the lectern. "I have a thesis I want to give you. I want to suggest that you, believers in Yeshua, are being persecuted."

Most of the students put down their pens and listened with rapt attention.

"Stick with me now. You don't have to agree with me; just listen. Let me begin with this premise: In our continuous battle between good and evil, Satan attacks us at our strongest point. You may be saying to yourself, wrong! He attacks me at my weakest point. I agree. But remember, it was not always your weakest point. The attack came when it was your strongest and because you lost the battle, now it is your weakest.

"Let me repeat that: I contend that the area of your life where you now find sin a real and perhaps continuing problem was once your strongest attribute. Satan knew where you excelled in being a follower of Yeshua, so he attacked you in that area. What has happened? What was once your stronghold has become a desecrated battlefield. That talent, that personality, that natural giftedness you enjoyed as your strong point is now distorted and maimed; it is now your weakness. Satan no longer has to attack you there. He has won in that arena of life.

"So, perhaps disagreeing but understanding what I said, the next step is to look at what believers in the United States consider to be their strongest point. Ask yourself this question: What is it that Western missionaries contributed to pagan societies such as China, Africa, and India, which today have large communities of believers in Christ? What have missionaries brought to these countries that made a difference and caused people to know and love Yeshua? Go ahead, give me some suggestions. See if we are thinking on the same wavelength. Are we resonating?"

Several students said, "The Bible...modern medicine...education...."

"You've got it. They translated the story of Yeshua into people's own tongue, into their heart language, so that He spoke to their spirit. People were dying of diseases that had been brought into check or even conquered in this nation. Missionaries built hospitals that ministered to the body. And they ministered to the mind, the soul. They built schools and universities.

"Look at China and Africa. Many of their leaders were products of missionary schools. To further prove my point, I must, with a heavy hear, tell you that many of those leaders went on to higher education in London, Moscow, and Boston, where their minds were filled with

Humanism and Marxism. Consequently, they returned to their countries and became the leaders that led the carnage and war, like in the Congo, against those very missionaries. It's ironic that the nations sending out the missionaries also helped educate those who later fought against everything the missionaries taught. These young men were deceived into rejecting what they learned in missionary schools and in many cases created chaos in their own countries.

"So then, what is America's greatest gift to mankind? It is as you said: Education, hospitals, translations of the Bible."

He paused and eyed the students. "These are cerebral activities. They are all cerebral activities. Is all this beginning to make sense?"

There was unanimous assent from the students as Benowitz smiled. "You are ahead of me, aren't you? Good! That's what a teacher hopes for. Thank you, you compliment me. Now I am indeed pleased that I accepted Dr. Nichols' kind invitation.

"You get my point. Americans are a cerebral people. Go anywhere around the world, and you see how American minds positively affected large parts of the world. Understand my point is this: America's strongest asset and contribution to mankind is cerebral. Why else would so much of our cerebral giftedness have become perverted, and come under attack, from our great halls of learning to our living room couches? From the talking heads who inform our opinions in important matters, to the sexually saturated situation comedies and daytime soaps that make the sacred profane. This too is affecting large parts of the world.

"Our enemy, the devil, is slowly desensitizing us to what is right and wrong. We have reached the point where 'truth' no longer exists. All truth is relative; there are no absolutes, and thus, no Satan. What we know and think depends not on what a great man of God wrote when he came down from a mountaintop, but what some infidel wrote from atop a multi-storied building in New York City.

"The devil is the master of desensitizing. I want to suggest to you that the intelligentsia, the mass media, Hollywood, immoral politicians, are, unknowingly perhaps, the devils. By the time he gets through using them, our minds are often stuffed with lies, perversion, distortion, lust, greed, and hate. So what do we have? A society that cannot tell right from wrong. A society with no absolutes that holds economic determinism as its guru.

"Our great heroes won the first revolution for freedom in the 1700s, and we became a beacon, a cerebral beacon for the world. I must tell you my veins run cold when I say that the present revolution, which might be called the Prozac Revolution, is one we are losing.

"Our wounds are not seen on our bodies, but in our minds. Our bones are not broken or our faces bloodied. No, our enemy rapes our mind. Depression, despair, hate, and confusion are covered up with cosmetic smiles.

"My mission today, as a Jew, is to identify with you as a persecuted people. My people were gassed, but you are being forced to breathe lies. My people were forced to perform for their persecutors. You must cover your depression and despair with a phony smile.

"When I visited China, India, Africa, where persecution is rampant, I saw joy that doesn't exist here. We are not a joyful people, but we can be if we realize we are being persecuted. Just make sure your depression is because of hungering and thirsting for righteousness, for then you will be blessed. There is no blessing in being depressed because the stock market fell or your health collapsed.

"Your response to cerebral persecution—to depression and despair, to confusion and to being scorned for your beliefs—can make Satan's plan to pervert and distort actually backfire. He'll continue to bombard you with temptation, but many who have been physically persecuted testify to persecution being the blessing that brought them close to God's heart. Ultimately, that is God's desire, and ours. No believer is going to escape experiencing Satan's persecution, be it physical or cerebral. My challenge to you is to recognize the promised blessing."

Jacob Benowitz then proceeded to shake hands with the students, giving each one a personalized Jewish blessing.

Twenty-six

As Mugabe had approached his village on the way home from Inhambane, he'd determined to consider his experiences there as a ten-day seminar on church growth and discipleship. During his walk home, his mind had kept slipping into wondering how a letter addressed to him had ended up in the hands of the SNASP. It had to have been through someone in his village with access to the mail system. He'd decided not to explore the possibilities and had deliberately handed the question over to God, again reminding himself he had chosen forgiveness. The betrayer knew and God knew, and that was all that mattered.

The first person he'd encountered on entering his village was the witch doctor, who had appeared surprised to see him coming home. Mugabe was surprised by the witch doctor's lack of hostility.

On his return, Mugabe preached to both the Saturday night crowds and his Sunday congregation the message written on his heart, and the prayer on Jesus' lips when he hung on the cross: *"Father, forgive them, for they don't know what they're doing."*

There was murmuring across the church when the witch doctor's head was seen through an open window. Mugabe kept on preaching, not about persecution, but about the power of forgiveness.

After the services, the people told Mugabe that when they had come for service the week before, Diolinda and Levi had told them what had happened. They had prayed for him during the time he would have been preaching to them. Mugabe realized those were the two days he was not beaten or interrogated.

One night the village was awakened by cries of "Fire! Fire!"

Mugabe and Diolinda looked outside and watched smoke rising above a glowing horizon in the direction of the church. Levi took off running. It was too late to do anything by the time he reached the church. Mugabe put his arm around Levi and prayed, *"Father, forgive them, for they don't know what they're doing."*

Long after Diolinda was sleeping again, Mugabe watched the glow disappear, along with the work he and Levi had put into building the church. He did not pretend to understand, but believed with all his heart that God was in control and knew what He was doing. He was sure the Lord had plans for good and a future for him. Not even fire could destroy the plan that Via Mahondra had proposed, the plan which gave comfort while suspended under a railcar, in Bible school, in a crowded church, and a prison cell. The plan was to follow Jesus.

He had heard Jesus call him, "Mugabe, I'm in control, I know where I'm going. Do you want to go along?" They were the words that resonated with his soul and filled his heart. He also recalled the words that had been fulfilled in his life so often: *Man's ways are not God's ways,* and *What man may have meant for evil, God meant for good—that many might come to know Him.*

Mugabe was startled by the sound of someone approaching. In the darkness he hardly recognized his visitor. The witch doctor's hair had been cut, and he was fully clothed. Pointing in the direction of the afterglow of what had been the church, he said, without a trace of shrillness, "The demons did that, but not my demons."

Mugabe was again taken completely by surprise. "If you aren't responsible for the fire, then who is?"

"The devils who reported you to SNASP," the witch doctor replied. "The jealous Christians from other villages accuse you of stealing their sheep."

Mugabe had trouble taking in what he was seeing and hearing.

"It was not my people or those priests who wear the black gowns, with the great cross hanging around their neck, but those who dress and speak like you. When you were taken away to the capital, I thought you would not come back. I wanted to warn you about the pastors who say they think like you but were really plotting to kill you. Their messengers said they'd give me one cow if I would burn down your church. I told them, 'No, if I did that, I would have no place to hear about Jesus.' What I said even shocked me. They left angry with me, calling me many names and threatening to tell my dead ancestors about me.

"When you first walked into this village I hated you, I wanted to kill you. This is my territory. I am the power here. I intended to burn you out before you built the church. I planned to set your hut on fire at night. But always sitting in front was that boy, the one you now call Levi. He guarded like an angel, sitting there with a machete waiting for me, so I had to wait. Once he was gone for several days and I thought the time had come. I waited for the night to fall, ready to take care of you once and for all, but there he sat. He had come back.

"But I am not the only one who hates. The powerful men in villages with churches are jealous because their villagers come here to your church. Your Jesus is what the people want."

"But He's not *my* Jesus," Mugabe cried. "He gave His blood for anyone who will come to Him for forgiveness. No one has to come through me to have Jesus!"

"You are naïve," the witch doctor said. "Telling people that God loves them makes us hate you. Your message of love robs us of power. But it was the jealous teachers who sent their demons to burn your church."

The next day villagers from near and far came. They sat in their usual places, ignoring the ashes from the burned-out roof that now lay on the dirt floor. The crowd extended beyond the stubs of the blackened poles that supported the walls, giving truth to a simple message: *This is our place of worship, and no one can frighten us away. We will not be moved.*

The cross that Levi had made and mounted in the front of the church had been resurrected out of the ashes. Though scorched, it stood as a powerful symbol of who had won the victory in this continuing battle between good and evil.

Mugabe sat beneath the cross, as always. Sitting next to him was David, whose gnarled hands were a witness to the Lord's power to overcome.

David brought music from his five strings that revealed an invisible presence as he sang one of the hymns he had learned from Via Mahondra. Most had never heard it before, but the message stirred their hearts as he articulated each word, "Beneath the cross of Jesus I gladly take my stand..."

The singing blended with spontaneous prayers that were more full of praise to the Lord than ever before. The fire was never mentioned.

Mugabe looked at the charred framework, then at the villagers. "We have been caught between the two most powerful forces in history. Two forces are at work right here, now, in the hearts of every one of us."

There was a slight movement throughout the crowd as he continued. "God has brought us here today to choose which of these forces we will invite into our hearts and into our village and our huts. The Lord has given us this opportunity so that we might seize it."

Sounds of praise and "amens" resounded as people stirred in the ashes. Quiet ascended once again as Mugabe continued.

"These forces are opposites, like light and darkness, hot and cold, life and death, good and evil, happiness and disaster." He paused, moving his eyes from one side of the crowd to the other, then with a steady voice, said, "The Lord has brought us into this open sanctuary today to get our attention so we may make a choice."

He raised his voice, shouting, "One of these two forces is controlling you right now, at this very moment." He paused. "They are love and hate. There are no other choices."

Mugabe described incidents in other villages, as well as their own, where the devil took the truth, the love of God, and twisted it, distorted it, and perverted it into hate. He then explained how their civil war was not motivated simply by a power struggle between the United States and Russia, or Mozambique and South Africa, or the rebel groups Frelimo and Renamo.

"No," he cried, "nor is it simply a battle for control of your hearts and minds between witch doctors and Christians."

Now he really had their attention. Some looked anxiously at the window where the witch doctor was regularly seen.

Mugabe shouted, "No, it is worse than that." Mugabe's voice choked as he grieved over the facts the witch doctor had revealed that would forever be a secret kept within his household. "It can be brother against brother, Christian against Christian."

Mugabe paused long enough for the people to grasp what they

heard. He held up his Bible and said, "But we should not be surprised. Listen to God's Word, First John, chapter three, verses 11and 12, *For this is the message that you heard from the beginning, that we should love one another, not as Cain who was of the wicked one and murdered his own brother."*

After telling the story of Cain and Abel, he asked, "But why did he murder his own brother, Abel? Because Cain's works were evil and his brother Abel's were righteous. Cain was filled with hate, while Abel loved God. See the difference?"

There were shouts of "Yes, Yes, Cain hates! Abel loves!"

"Good and evil—an obedient brother murdered by a jealous brother." Mugabe pleaded as he admonished them, saying, "My brothers and sisters, do you hate anyone here? Are you jealous of their power in the community, their success, their abilities, or their popularity? I'm talking about that person sitting beside you right now. Those you can reach out and touch." He then asked, "If any of them had a tragedy in their life, would you say to yourself, 'They deserve it'?"

He held up his Bible and declared, "Then God's Word says you are a murderer. The devil controls your heart. Maybe you never visited the hut of a witch doctor and had one of your chickens sacrificed, wishing your brother dead. But if you saw one of your Christian brothers or sisters lying on the dirt road sick or wounded, would you go to the other side of the road and walk around them?

"Listen to the Word of Love, the Word of our Lord Jesus Christ: *'If anyone has the world's goods and sees his brother in need, yet closes his heart against him, how does God's love abide in him*? If we can see our brothers and sisters in need, physically, emotionally, spiritually, and walk around them murmuring, 'they deserve it,' that is camouflaged hate. If that is us, our Christianity is just a pile of ashes."

He paused for the crowd to have time to think. "Love and hate—two forces that bring internal peace, or internal war, spiritual life or spiritual death. If these two most powerful forces known to man originate not from the inside but the outside of man, who gives them to us?"

The people answered, "Jesus...The devil . . ."

Mugabe picked up their shouts. "That's right: Jesus and the devil!

The dividing line is clear. We obey the devil or we obey Jesus. God lets us choose. So choose this day whom you will serve. Jesus? Or the devil?"

The sun reached its apex over the church. No one moved. Sweat poured down Mugabe's face. He understood the moving of the Spirit. He stopped and motioned to David, who picked up his guitar and began to play. They had hardly started singing when there was a stir in the crowd.

The witch doctor walked through the door, stepped around the people, and approached Mugabe. The people held their breaths. His face was blank. Everyone anxiously watched, as they thought, *Is he about to put a spell on Mugabe and us?*

Within seconds, the fear dissipated as he knelt and asked Mugabe if God would forgive him. He wanted to choose Jesus.

Mugabe kneeled beside him and put his arms around the former witch doctor and prayed for him.

Some of the people gasped. They had never seen anything like this before.

Mugabe's new brother turned and spoke to the people. "A month ago, I wanted to kill this brother. I also wanted to kill many of you. I was filled with hate. This man is right; it came from the devil. But as I watched the sky become red from the burning flames of this building, Jesus set a fire in my heart. The words of life I had heard as I listened outside blazed with truth. Jesus' blood *is* more powerful than the blood of any chicken or goat if it can wash away my hate."

Mugabe and the people were in awe of what they were seeing and hearing. No one had ever seen the witch doctor calm and peaceful before.

"The fire in my heart tells me I must set fire to where I have worshipped the devil. I will put all my tools of worship, the statues, the animal heads, the bracelets and amulets, the necklaces, and the white cloth into my hut, and set them afire. I want to follow Jesus."

There were shouts of "Hallelujah, praise the Lord!"

Like a wave from the ocean coming in to the beach to sweep it clean of debris, a flood of weeping started at the rear of the congregation and swept forward. As David played his guitar and sang, there were shouts of joy. On the periphery of the burned-out building, people began to dance and kick the black ashes into the air, shouting as they did so. Revival had come to a small village in Mozambique.

The atmosphere at the church crackled like an approaching electrical storm over the midwestern plains. As the minutes passed, it was getting too late to do anything but run for cover or hunker down and sit it out, praying that the damage would be minimal.

It was almost with a collective sigh of relief when the head elder made an announcement at the end of the Sunday morning service. Pastor Bjorn stood back, making an attempt to show no emotion, as the elder spoke: "We know that some of you who have ears for such things are aware that our organ is getting very tired. Like some of us, it seems to do more wheezing of unpredictable sounds than exhaling those beautiful tones we have come to appreciate through the years. We have had two committees looking at the problem, at least from a financial point of view. The question before us is, would the money for repairing the organ be better spent replacing it with something a little more up-to-date?"

He paused and considered the congregation. "On Wednesday night at 7:00 we will have an open meeting here in the sanctuary. We will listen to the reports and hopefully make a decision. We encourage all of you who are interested to attend."

No translation was needed. It was time for the organ to make room for something more up-to-date. The unspoken word was *synthesizer.*

The first signs of victory were distinguishable by the suppressed smile on the young music director's face as he nudged his wife and looked victoriously at the Associate Pastor—an action the always-observant janitor did not miss.

Pastor Bjorn gave the benediction. Most of the older people left while the younger ones gathered in small groups. They were certain that victory was only three days away.

Mr. Maxwell avoided talking to anyone, hoping that maybe

Wednesday would never come and he and others would not have to face reality.

It came anyway.

On Wednesday, an hour before the meeting, Mr. Maxwell turned on the lights for those who had to set up the sanctuary for the meeting.

With some effort, Maxwell slowly made his way up to the back row in the balcony. He wanted to get away from the storm. As he headed toward a seat, he asked himself the question he had been asking often lately: *If I sit down, will I have the strength to get up again?*

He decided to take a chance. With obvious pain, he unceremoniously unloaded himself onto the seat. He put his head back, fighting the nausea that had come and gone at will during these past weeks. He closed his eyes.

His solitude was short-lived.

"I saw you coming up here. I came to see if you're OK."

Murphy's concerned voice was a welcome sound that always brought comfort to Mr. Maxwell. It made him feel that there were those who saw him as more than a broom pusher, even though most of the church was carpeted and he actually followed a vacuum sweeper around.

Maxwell motioned for his young friend to have a seat. Murphy sat, draping his leg over the arm of the chair, and faced Mr. Maxwell.

Murphy's apprehension, real or imagined, could not be hidden. But he got an *A* for effort as he attempted to casually talk about never having seen this many people at a business meeting before and especially on a Wednesday night. Mr. Maxwell made a noble effort to smile, but it was strained as he said, "Well, you know how it is out west. A hangin' always draws more people than a good old revival meetin'."

He leaned back in his seat, and with a voice laden with tiredness, he sighed. "Or a crucifixion. That drew a pretty good crowd as well."

Murphy put his head down. Over the last two years, they had grown to almost read each other's minds.

Just to make certain that Murphy was on the right page, Mr. Maxwell asked, "You don't really believe this is about replacing the organ, do you?'

Murphy replied, "No, I guess not."

The sound people finished their task as Mr. Maxwell continued. "No, Brother Murphy, this is not about getting a new organ. It's about getting rid of an old preacher who does do a bit more wheezing than he used to, but I didn't think that was a capital offense."

Murphy looked up at Mr. Maxwell. "Do you think he knows?"

"Of course he knows." Mr. Maxwell flinched with pain. "Oh Lord, one might wish he didn't; it would make it much less cruel."

Mr. Maxwell counted the chairs on the platform. There was one less than usual. Pastor Bjorn had sent his regrets that he was not feeling well and could not attend.

Maxwell stared at the ceiling as Murphy folded his arms on the back of his seat and cradled his head. After several moments of silence, Mr. Maxwell asked a question. It was not necessarily directed at Murphy personally, but to the church—theirs and others all over the hemisphere. "Do you think people realize the pain, the agony, that is about to be loosed and how it will cruelly lacerate the heart of a man who for forty years, almost all of his adult life, has lived and died for these people? Perhaps Moses had it coming. He tried to outdo God. But Pastor Bjorn has led these people through the wilderness many times, collectively and individually. He's laughed with them and cried with them. He's kept his eyes on the light and spent hours gathering manna to nourish them."

Mr. Maxwell angrily continued. "This meeting's agenda is not about instruments, it's about a man, and his life's mate, who sits at home tonight, silently suffering with him."

Murphy looked up at him. He had never heard Mr. Maxwell speak with such anger.

"This is probably the first Wednesday night in forty years that Pastor Bjorn is not up there in that pulpit. Seven nights in a week, and they pick this of all nights. And it is also probably the first night in as many years that some of those men and women down there have made it to the church for a midweek meeting." Tears gathered in Maxwell's eyes. "And when it's all over, they will go home as if they had just changed the course of Christianity."

He looked over the congregation and sadly said, "Some will leave here burdened, some terribly sad, but I suspect most will have the taste of victory in their mouths, if not in their hearts. Remember, my young friend, there is a vast difference between promised and practiced loyalty."

"So, we know how the vote is going to go," Murphy said. "What will happen next?"

Mr. Maxwell put his head back, clutched his midsection, and grimaced for a second. "On some evening, which many will call special, probably a Saturday night, the new synthesizer will sit quietly on the platform near the organ that will never be played again, while we all gather in the social hall."

Tears came to his eyes; his pain was obvious. "There will be tears—some genuine, some manufactured for the occasion. There'll be a gift, probably a trip to someplace Pastor and his wife have always wanted to go. Food will be eaten, empty words quickly forgotten, and it will be one of those nights when everyone has to get home early. Pastor Bjorn and his wife will sneak out (Norwegian men do not cry in public). They'll hear a click behind them, and the locks will have already been changed.

"On Sunday morning, both will seem to have caught a cold from staying out so late. As they get ready to read the Sunday morning paper, something that they have not done, nor wanted to do, for forty years, a man of God will realize that he is now a has-been who apparently never really was.

"As Sunday turns into Monday, there will be that realization that he has been, as so many others like him, unceremoniously taken out and dumped in the desert to pick flowers, which don't grow, and watch Gila monsters mate, which do."

Murphy asked, "If you could go down there and stand in front of that microphone and say something more than 'testing, testing,' or 'Lord, thank You for this night,' what would you say to them?"

Mr. Maxwell didn't have to think about it. "I would tell them what I just told you." He eased himself out of his chair. "Go on down and vote."

Murphy watched as Maxwell, in obvious pain, stood up and moved into the aisle. "What about you?" Murphy asked.

"My vote has never counted around here, except to recommend what kind of toilet paper to use, so there's no reason it would count tonight—after all, I'm only the janitor. But right now, I think I'll go home for awhile and rest. I'll come back when it's all over. I'll clean up the garbage. In the meantime, I want to get out of here."

Murphy watched as Mr. Maxwell slowly made his way through the door. As he did, he turned to Murphy and feigned a smile. "Remember, I was raised on a farm in Canada, and I always hated to hear the rooster crow."

Murphy fell back into the chair and prayed.

The meeting progressed as Murphy slowly made his way down to the sanctuary and took a seat near the back, where it was unlit. The head elder announced, "It would seem that all minds are clear, all have spoken, so if the ladies will come forth with the ballots, we can now vote."

A voice was heard from the back of the church. The elder squinted as if he couldn't quite make out who it was in the dark.

"It's me, Associate Pastor Murphy. May I speak?"

People turned around to look at Murphy as the elder stumbled on his words, "Well, I have declared the discussion period closed, but being you are part of the staff here, I think we can make an exception."

Murphy thanked him, cleared his throat, and ignoring the glowering staff, he began, "You don't really believe this is about replacing an organ, do you? This isn't about getting a synthesizer; it's about getting rid of an old pastor…"

Twenty-seven

Mugabe stirred in his new bed. He missed his old sleeping mat and his little village. The cacophony of Maputo did not compare to the cadence of crickets and frogs.

As Diolinda slept at his side, his mind struggled to sort through the rush of major changes in his church and his family's life in the past week. There had been the timing of Brother Nehemiah appearing in the village the week the church was burned....

Brother Nehemiah grabbed Mugabe's arm, with unbridled excitement, saying, "All things work together for good for those who love our Lord and are called by him. I've heard you preach on that very subject! Remember your vision of baptizing many people and teaching in your own Bible school?"

"Yes." Mugabe nodded, hesitantly.

"Well," exclaimed Nehemiah, "now's the time to take the big step." He raised both hands heavenward. "It's time to move to Maputo!"

"What?" exclaimed Mugabe.

Levi had been listening and moved closer, unable to hide his excitement at what he was overhearing.

"I've already found a pastor to replace you."

"Well, thanks for telling me!" Mugabe said, not yet in tune with Nehemiah's enthusiasm.

As they entered Mugabe's hut, Nehemiah never missed a beat. "He'll be here next week."

"Well, don't stop now," Mugabe said with undisguised vexation. "When and how is all this going to happen?"

Nehemiah, unfazed by his reaction, announced, "I've found a house for you and your family to live in—a real house, with a toilet, three rooms, and a tin roof."

Mugabe had shot a displeased look at Levi when he exploded with glee. He noted Diolinda busying herself preparing food for their guest.

Accepting a glass of water from Diolinda, Nehemiah slowed down. "Tell me, Brother Mugabe, what have you said you've missed the most since being here in this village? The thing you've written to Dr. James about more than once?"

"Fellowship with other pastors and Christian leaders," Mugabe said without hesitating.

"There are other pastors in Maputo," Brother Nehemiah said. "They may only meet secretly, but they do meet. The owner of the house is a government official, but a secret believer. He also yearns for fellowship."

Mugabe looked at Diolinda, then Levi. He sensed no resistance from Diolinda.

Brother Nehemiah stood. "If you agree, this secret believer can supply a Land Rover to transport the three of you to Maputo."

"When?"

Brother Nehemiah smiled. "The Land Rover will be here at 9:30 Saturday morning."

"Saturday morning! That's only five days from now!"

Brother Nehemiah gave Mugabe his famous grin. "Yes, two days less than it took God to make the world. But I'm sure you can make it...."

Now Mugabe twisted and turned on his new bed, his back aching as he attempted to get comfortable without falling off. T*he church here in Maputo has been kept from being desecrated and turned into a government meeting house,* he thought, *but no services are allowed there. What now, Lord?*

As he lay there, fighting depression, words from Deuteronomy were brought to his memory: *"If you should say in your heart, 'these nations are greater,' then how can I dispossess them? You shall not be afraid of them, but you shall remember well what the Lord your God did to Pharaoh and to all of Egypt."*

"Lord, forgive me. I'm weak, but You are strong. This is Your battle, not mine. I will remember what You did to Pharaoh."

God's admonition to "remember well" strengthened Mugabe's soul.

He remembered the help God provided to rebuild the church

building in fifty-two days. He remembered the joy and thanksgiving during the first worship service in their new church.

Ironically, the memories of the service held in the ashes of that very building were the most encouraging. The transformed witch doctor, true to his word, had burned his hut to the ground, along with all his tricks of his former trade.

Mugabe's mind went back to last Saturday morning....

At 9:30 sharp the Land Rover pulled up in front of their village hut. Men from the crowd of believers that had gathered to say good-bye helped pile their meager belongings onto the vehicle. He remembered Levi's glee as he crawled on top of the stack, while Diolinda, peacefully smiling, climbed into her reserved corner of the back seat.

Mugabe also remembered David leading them all in singing "Amazing Grace," and the wink and grin that passed between Levi and Nehemiah with their shared secret of Nehemiah's gift of the guitar for David.

He remembered Nehemiah's invitation to the former witch doctor, and his thoughtful acceptance, to travel with Nehemiah and be discipled.

Tears came to Mugabe's eyes as he remembered that the Land Rover had to slow down while going past the marketplace because of the large crowd of shoppers and merchants who had come to wave good-bye. Diolinda was especially touched as the merchant who would not sell to her stepped forward with a large basket of fresh fruit and laid it at her feet.

Mugabe remembered when they had first been dropped off by the truck in the village; they had not only been strangers, but a white scarf tied around a tree had warned them they were considered enemies of the village.

As they left, less than a year later, their new brother, the former witch doctor, stood by the tree that marked the entrance to the village. He waved to them while a small wisp of smoke wound its way up from the ground. The white scarf was no longer wrapped around the tree trunk.

Mugabe's comfort was not to be found in his new bed or the tin roof over his head but in the Lord's admonition to remember and to not be afraid. God had brought him to this place.

Maxwell and Murphy settled into their chairs in Maxwell's office. Both were consciously aware that the final curtain was about to fall on a drama they were writing as they went along. As Murphy faced Maxwell, he was very conscious of a measurable decline in his mentor's health.

Maxwell sensed that, though Pastor Bjorn had made it known that he wanted his nephew to stay on as a full-fledged staff member, Murphy knew there were murmurs of nepotism, not an unknown practice in Christian circles but strongly opposed by Murphy.

"So, you are soon to be a bona fide preacher boy," Mr. Maxwell said, while appearing to look for a comfortable position. Tuning into Murphy's a lack of enthusiasm, he asked, "What're your plans?"

Murphy sighed. "Well, my mom and dad are pretty insistent that I accept as a graduation gift joining their church group for their semi-annual trip to the Holy Land."

Maxwell nodded.

"Mom says I should now be the theologian-in-residence," Murphy said wryly.

"Nothing wrong with going to the Holy Land. I've thought I'd like to sit at the foot of Mt. Hattin to read the Beatitudes."

Murphy raised his eyebrows. "But...?"

Grimacing, Maxwell leaned back, telegraphing to Murphy that what he was going to say was important but also lengthy. Murphy recognized the signs, so relaxed and waited with an amused smile.

"Behind you, on the third shelf up, is a book I recommend you read after graduation. It's Tolstoy's *Tales of Courage and Conflict.* There's a short story called "Two Old Men" that takes place in Russia. It's about two friends, one rich and one poor. They'd talked about making a pilgrimage to the Holy Land for years, to walk where Jesus walked as their final righteous deed. It would elevate their reputation as godly men and also ensure their eternal resting place.

"One day the rich man suggested it was time. They both knew the year-long pilgrimage would be costly and strenuous, involving much walking and numerous modes of transportation.

"The poor man sold several of his prized bee swarms and took all the money he and his wife had saved. He had very little money to spare since he had a worthless son who drank and gambled, causing much heartache.

"The rich man simply went to the bank and took out enough money to cover his expenses.

"They left for Jerusalem with the village's blessing and as much food and water as they could carry.

"While journeying through a land suffering from drought, they ran short of water. The poor man suggested returning to the last farm they had passed in order to buy water. The rich man disagreed and said he would go on; the poor man could catch up to him later.

"The poor man walked back to the farm. As he approached, the house he saw an older man lying in the sun, apparently sleeping. He knocked at the door but got no answer. He tried the door and it was unlocked. He hesitantly opened it, calling out that he was coming in the name of Jesus Christ.

"On entering, he saw a listless large family, barely able to move or speak. The poor man's dismayed, questioning look was answered by the mother's whispered cry that they were starving to death."

Maxwell cleared his throat. "You really need to read it to get the full impact, but to make a long story short, the poor man was appalled and reached in his sack and brought out bread he'd purchased early that morning and fed it to them and to the old man outside who was not sleeping, but dying of starvation.

"The rich man never looked back. He was on his way to the Holy Land and nothing would stop him. His friend could catch up with him or go it alone.

"The poor man bought food and water for the starving family and over several months nursed them back to life. Finally it rained and the drought ended, but the family had no seed; they had eaten it all. The poor man bought seed and enough bread to hold them over until the seed could be harvested. It took all his money, so he returned home.

"The year passed and the rich man returned from his pilgrimage only to find that his son had taken to drinking vodka and gambling and had wasted away all the rich man's money. The poor man's son had a complete change of heart and during the months that his father was gone, he'd quit drinking and gambling and improved his father's beehive business. The poor man was now rich and the rich man was now poor.

"The former rich man came to visit the former poor man. He said, 'My legs took me to Jerusalem but whether my soul was there—'

"'That is God's affair,' his friend interjected.

"'I stopped at the farm where I thought you went to get water and asked about you, but they said an angel had fed them and given them water and seeds and new life.'

"'That is God's affair,' his friend said again and offered him some honey.

"The former rich man had also brought a gift—a bottle of water from the river Jordan where the Lord was baptized."

Murphy wasn't sure about Maxwell's point, and his face showed it.

"Please understand that I'm not opposed to visiting the Holy Land, but there are certain times in our lives when we need to walk where Jesus is walking right now. Let me explain. After my wife died, I went on a pilgrimage myself, to what I found to be a 'holy land.'"

"I'd like to hear about it," Murphy said.

Maxwell appeared to be drawing deep from the memory. His lips quivered as he began his story. "Late one evening, with only my sleeping bag, I made my way downtown to a space under a freeway overpass. I found an unclaimed spot, crawled in my bag, and pretended to be asleep. But I was really watching for what the norm was in that place. A young man came and unzipped his sleeping bag, draping it over his shoulders against the night air. I was close enough to notice it was dirty and smelly. He sat upright with his head in his hands. A girl, maybe all of sixteen, walked by, holding a bundle close to her chest. Seeing a vacant corner, she headed for it. She sat on the ground and unwrapped from the light shawl what turned out to be a very young baby. She held it close to her breast, using the shawl to cover the baby as it nursed. Then she tried to spread the shawl over her and the baby as she curled on her side on the ground. The young man watched her. He walked towards her and her eyes darted around as though looking for a route of escape. But he gently said, 'Don't be afraid. You need this more than me,' and dropped the sleeping bag beside her.

"She hesitantly accepted it, then handed him her shawl, saying, 'You'll need something to keep you warm. Take this.'

"He took it and went back to his spot; put the shawl over his head and shoulders and sat down, rocking back and forth, hands over his face, quietly talking to himself.

Maxwell shook his head. "When I woke up, I was alone. The police start clearing the area early. Later that day I sat on a bench near the county hospital, just watching people come and go. Some in wheelchairs, some being escorted, some arriving by ambulance. I saw a young man, a little older than you, come out of the building wearing medical garb. He looked around and spotted a teenage kid sitting alone on a bench. He sat down beside him, took a sandwich and drink out of his bag, opened the drink and bit into the sandwich. The kid looked at him, but before he said anything the guy offered him a sandwich. The kid eagerly took it and started eating. The young man pulled out another drink. It, like the sandwich, was accepted without comment.

"As the kid devoured the sandwich and the drink, the guy nodded toward the hospital. 'I used to be in and out of there, just like you.'

"'In drug rehab?'

"'Yeah, but one day I met someone who told me I could break the habit. I thought he was crazy. I'd tried everything but always ended up stoned and hating myself within hours of getting out. Suicide seemed the only escape.'

"The kid said, 'I got out last week, but it didn't even last a day. But I'm not going back. Rehab doesn't work.'

"The young man reached in his bag and pulled out another sandwich and handed it to the kid. After the third sandwich and an apple, the kid asked, "You got a deli in there? You just keep pulling out sandwiches like someone is inside making more.'

"'Not exactly, but close,' the young man said.

"'You got another drink?' the kid asked.

"'No, but I've got something to help the thirst.'

"The kid looked at him quizzically.

"I heard him tell the kid that the man who told him he could break the habit took him to another kind of meeting. A couple hours later, when he was offered a hit, he did something he'd never been able to do before. He said, 'No thanks.'

"'You quit just like that?' the kid asked skeptically.

"'Well, not quite that easy,' the young man said. 'The temptations were there, my body reacted, but my inside was different. I didn't want it anymore and that gave me the strength to say no. I started working in a fast-food place, went back to JC, and ended up back here as a lab tech.'

"'You mean that's not one of those gowns they put on you to keep you from running away?' the kid asked.

"'No.' The young man laughed and said he had to get back to work, then told the kid he'd be off duty in four hours. "If you want to stick around, I'll take you to the man who can help you break the habit.'

"'You got another one of those bags that never runs out of food, then I'll be here,' the kid said.

"The young man shook the kid's hand. 'It's a deal.' He handed the kid the paper bag and grinned. 'In case you're still hungry, there's more in there. See you at five.'

"A few days later I saw the girl carrying the baby and the sleeping bag walking through a downtown park. I watched her from a distance. She turned as someone called; it must have been her name. A woman ran towards her, calling out and dodging traffic. They embraced, both weeping. The woman stroked the baby and kissed it. I heard her ask, 'Where did you go?'

"The girl said, 'You'd done so much for me. When I held my baby in my arms I knew I could never repay you folks for talking me into not having an abortion, but I wanted to keep her. I was afraid you'd take her away.'

"The woman hugged her. 'We wouldn't have taken the baby away if you wanted her. We even made arrangements for you to stay in a home for unwed mothers.'

"The girl held the baby close to her and the woman carried the sleeping bag draped over her shoulder as they walked away, arms around each other."

Maxwell pressed hard on his abdomen. "Yes, I walked where Jesus walked. My feet were on holy ground."

Murphy quietly rose and stood beside Maxwell. He put his hand on his shoulder. Maxwell reached up and put his hand on top of Murphy's. They were silent for a few moments, then Murphy walked to the door. "I'm going to call my mom and dad." His wry smile softened as he said, "I'm going to tell them to send me my sleeping bag."

As the door closed behind Murphy, Maxwell painfully opened a drawer and pulled out the brown wrapping paper and string. Slowly smoothing it out on the desk, he laid the velvet-framed picture on it and carefully wrapped and tied it. He gritted his teeth as he slowly stood up, holding the package tightly against his abdomen. He walked carefully to the door, opened it, and turned to take one long last look at his office as tears gathered in his eyes. As he closed the door behind him he whispered firmly, "It's time."

Twenty-eight

The fellowship that Brother Nehemiah promised Mugabe when he arrived in Maputo never materialized. Its absence only increased his desire for what he had left behind in South Africa, but never received, even in his village.

There were other pastors in Maputo, but the problem was they were so closely associated with the government that they did not want to be seen with Mugabe. The "secret believer" Brother Nehemiah mentioned also never materialized. He could understand that if the local pastors did not want to be in his company, it would be even more important that the secret believer keep his distance.

Mugabe was not prepared for the restrictions on his movements. He knew he was being followed. Whenever he visited a fellow believer whom Brother Nehemiah had recommended as a needy contact, Levi watched from a distance. Mugabe would be in the believer's house for only a few minutes when Levi would spot one or two men who would suddenly appear on one of the side street, loitering there until Mugabe finished his visit.

Watching became a game for Levi until one day when he turned to leave and ran into an agent directly behind him. It was then he realized that Mugabe was not the only one being followed.

Levi then began to go with Mugabe on his visits. He rather enjoyed the excitement of it all. The problem was that almost all of those visited wanted help, not fellowship. Mugabe didn't complain but continued to faithfully visit all who were on Brother Nehemiah's list, as well as names given him by those he visited.

The father of one family he visited worked for the railway, making runs to the border three times a week. When Mugabe told him about how his mail from Dr. James had been censored before it was confiscated as supposed evidence of his being part of the CIA, the father volunteered to hand-carry a letter to the border to give it to another believer who would hand-deliver it to Dr. James.

Mugabe went home and wrote Dr. James a letter. He was careful to avoid anything political, but rather dwelt on the isolation that he felt, and his despondency over lack of fellowship now that he no longer had a congregation.

Several days later, the believer who worked for the railroad sent Mugabe a message saying the letter had been delivered to his friend, and his friend would deliver it personally to Dr. James that same day. He also assured Mugabe that if Dr. James sent a reply, he would deliver it to his house. It was dangerous, but the believer sensed his need for a response and insisted on doing it in spite of the police surveillance.

Mugabe waited in anticipation for Dr. James' reply. The days passed with no response. He began questioning if this was where he was supposed to be.

He got his answer one early morning when he was awakened by a quiet knock at the door. Levi whispered, "It's the police!"

Mugabe got up, trying to reassure Levi although he was certain it was the police. Through the closed door he asked, "Who is it?"

To his joy, he recognized the voice of his fellow believer who worked for the railway. Mugabe's heart leapt. He must have a response from Dr. James.

As he opened the door, the believer disappeared into the darkness. In his place stood Dr. James and Luke, one of the students from the Bible school in South Africa.

In one leap, Dr. James and Mugabe were in each other's arms.

For two days and a night, no one left the house, Levi included, as they fellowshipped—praying, praising, singing, and studying the Bible.

Late the second night, the believer came to escort Dr. James and Luke to the rail yard, where they ensconced themselves in an empty ore car for a ride back to South Africa.

Dr. James had seen the importance of his visit, not only for Mugabe, but also for Diolinda and Levi. It was agreed that Dr. James and Luke would return again in five or six weeks if there were no serious consequences from their meeting.

What Mugabe never told Dr. James was that less than an hour after they left, there was a heavy knock on the door. The three were still up, still too excited to go to bed.

Mugabe motioned for Diolinda and Levi to go to the bedroom. Just as he got to the door, an even louder knock was heard, along with the words, "This is the police. Open up!"

He unlocked the door. Three police officers, with guns pointing at Mugabe, pushed the door open, knocking him to the floor.

The police, still pointing their weapons, shouted, "Get up, Mr. CIA; there are people downtown who want to talk to you."

Mugabe got up and was dragged out of the house. Diolinda and Levi could hear the sound of a motor vehicle as it gunned its engine and raced off into the darkness.

Three days later, again in the middle of the night, there was another knock. Diolinda and Levi quickly opened the door. Mugabe collapsed into their arms and passed out.

Later, as Mugabe came around, Diolinda and Levi bathed his wounds. There were no marks on his face. It was the only part of his body not visibly wounded. His privates were swollen. His groin and buttocks were covered with cigarette burns. Several ribs had been broken. The police had learned their trade well from their mentors in East Germany.

Mugabe lay on the bed as Levi held up his head and Diolinda poured warm food down his throat. He had not eaten since he had been taken away.

The next day, as he began the recovery process, his first words were, "This must heal before Dr. James and Brother Luke visit us again." He then added, "And this must be our secret. No one else—not Dr. James, Luke, Brother Nehemiah, or anyone else must ever know."

"Father, aren't you going to tell them not to come?" Levi put his hand on his father's head and plaintively cried, "Next time the police may kill you."

Mugabe took Levi's hand and said with a smile, "Son, these wounds of the flesh will soon heal, but my spirit cannot survive without fellowship."

Murphy radiated excitement as he picked up his Bible and notes and left his room. For the past two years, students from three dorms met on the third Thursday of every month for what they called "A Night of Fellowship."

It was always well attended. There was always a time of Bible teaching by one of the students, then they would go around the room, with as many students as possible answering the question: "What has the Lord done for you since our last time together?"

It was the only time they planned for sharing how the Lord had been involved in their problems. Some got very personal. It was not uncommon to stop and pray several times during the evening for someone with a serious problem, or to stop and praise the Lord for someone whose problem the Lord had solved. It never lasted less than two hours.

Tonight Murphy felt a sense of sadness and excitement. Sad in that it was the last time they would be together like this and excited because this was his night to teach. He was looking forward to sharing what Mr. Maxwell had taught him about crises. Murphy took the stairs to the second-floor meeting room two steps at a time. He was early, so he didn't expect anyone else to be there yet.

As he approached the room, he saw a sign on the door. Drawing closer, he could not believe what it said. He then read it aloud: "Tonight's Fellowship Meeting has been cancelled. We will meet in the cafeteria to join other groups to watch the NBA Regional Playoffs. Hot dogs, pizza, and drinks will be available. Go Lakers."

Murphy, usually a great basketball fan, turned and walked slowly down the stairs, one step at a time, muttering to himself in disbelief, "Cancelled, our last Fellowship Meeting ever, for a basketball game?"

Murphy woke up the next morning still dejected over the cancellation of the Fellowship Meeting. He dressed but skipped breakfast. He didn't care whether the Lakers had won or lost. He decided to go over to the church and talk to Mr. Maxwell. He had seemed more vital the last few days. Perhaps it had only been Murphy's imagination that Mr. Maxwell looked seriously ill.

Maybe his mentor and friend could alleviate some of the feelings of annoyance that were ruining what should have been one of his celebrative days, but was turning out instead to be what he called "a terrible, horrible, no good, very bad day."

It was about to get much worse.

Murphy stopped by his office on the way to Maxwell's. He noticed an envelope on his desk with Mr. Maxwell's handwriting. A sense of foreboding came over him as he started to read:

My dear young Pastor Friend

I am certain you have noticed over the past weeks that my health has deteriorated. I know you like to get to the point, so I will as well. Three months ago, I found out I had colon cancer. The doctor told me that it probably had spread to some vital organs, but could not be sure without surgery. He could not assure me, even if it had not spread, that I would not have to spend the rest of my life emptying bags and living off painkillers. I told him I was an old man and ready to go, so to give me the painkillers so I could work as long as possible.

I would have told you sooner, but I did not want our friendship to change. You see, some of the other staff also noticed my rapid deterioration. I heard one of them comment that you and I were close, and he would ask you about me. I did not want the others to start putting their arm around me, and saying, "I love you, Brother Maxwell," merely because they knew I was dying. They never did it while I was living, so why make hypocrites out of them now?

As for you, well, you didn't have to put your arm around me—I knew you loved me as I loved you, living or dead. Words cannot express what your friendship has meant. You made me feel needed, and yes, important. But even more, you became a symbol of the son that I had destroyed. You were the Lord's gift to me. You were part of the answer to my prayer, "Lord, restore to me the years the locusts have eaten." *Be assured I thank our Lord for the many times He brought you to my office to sit in your chair.*

I wrestled long and hard whether I should tell you this face-to-face. In the end, I realized that I had neither the strength of body or emotion to tell you personally what I have to say.

I have an uncompleted task. I cannot rest, either here or where I am going, until I complete that task. I must do it before the last of my strength leaves me a dying old man who failed his son one more time.

Please forgive me. I know you will.

Until we meet at our Lord's feet....

Dazed, Murphy stared at Mr. Maxwell's scrawled signature.

Suddenly he got up and ran down the hall to Mr. Maxwell's office. He opened the door, praying, "Oh Lord, let him be in his chair."

He wasn't.

Murphy's gaze fixed on Mr. Maxwell's desk in this very familiar room. It was gone: the framed picture of Jesus—the last gift his son had given him.

Murphy stared at the empty space, trying to absorb what was happening. He noticed a small note on the side of the desk. Moving closer, he read it: *Please give all my books to Pastor Murphy.*

Murphy bolted out the door and ran for the church office. The church secretary was crying. "He's gone," she said through her tears. "He was eating breakfast alone at The Horseless Carriage. When Ella went to give him a refill, she noticed his head bent over like he'd gone to sleep. She touched his shoulder and he just fell forward. Suddenly, she realized he wasn't sleeping; he was dead!"

Murphy walked slowly back to his office, closed the door, and slumped into his chair. Leaning his head against the backrest, he stared at the ceiling. Then, looking at Mr. Maxwell's letter, he whispered with a heavy sigh, "First Roger...then Mr. Maxwell...and now..."

He had never felt so alone, but a feeling of heaviness became his constant companion through the following three days.

Now, as the organ resounded with what may have been its last peal, Murphy slowly made his way to the pulpit to give the eulogy. Though the church was packed, with people standing around the walls of the sanctuary, he was still alone.

"Your pastor and my uncle, Bjorn Erik Halvorson was born in Skelrud, Norway, 64 years and 362 days ago. He left us much more than a half cup of cold coffee. He left us with a final blessing. A loving peacemaker until the end, he quietly left us three days before his suggested day of retirement…."

Twenty-nine

It had been four days since Dr. James' and his friend's last secret visit from South Africa. Mugabe and Levi had stayed close to home, praying and waiting for the police to come. They wanted to get the beating over with so the wounds would heal before the next visit. They did not want Dr. James to know the price Mugabe paid for their time of fellowship together. When the police didn't come they decided to continue their secret ministry to the people. After a day of furtively visiting homes, some friendly, some where they had to shake the dust from their feet, they walked along the shore. While watching a cargo ship from the Soviet Union being unloaded of a month's supply of food which would be part of their city's meager subsistence, Mugabe suddenly had a vision from the Lord.

On their way home, he excitedly explained it to Levi. Over supper, he told Dioliada, and they spent most of the night in prayer.

The next day they ate breakfast, no longer worrying about a visit from the police. Mugabe and Levi made their way to the office of the Director of Religious Affairs. After an hour wait they were invited into the office of one of his assistants.

They stood patiently before the young assistant while he was on the telephone. When he hung up, he abruptly asked them what they wanted, while shuffling papers on his desk.

"Sir," Mugabe began, "each month we line up with our ration card to claim our monthly food allowance when the food arrives from the Soviet Union. It is the only time we are permitted to assemble."

The young assistant nodded, while signing papers on his desk.

Mugabe continued, "Sir, if we are allowed to gather in a line each month to receive food for our bodies," he paused, breathing a silent prayer," could we not line up together to enter the water to receive spiritual food. We Christians call it—"

"Baptism?" The assistant stood to stare at Mugabe.

"Yes." Mugabe's bravado had disappeared. In a very low voice he said, "Yes, sir, baptism...our spiritual food."

With wide eyes and raised brow, the young assistant nearly shouted, "You want the people to line up at the water to be baptized?"

"Yes," replied Mugabe quietly, "yes, that is my request."

The assistant sat down, returned to his task of signing papers and without looking up, murmured, "Mr. Mugabe, I am a very busy man." He then looked up at Mugabe and Levi and loudly said, "I am a busy man; you are excused."

They left the office, neither of them speaking until they were back on the street. Sitting on a rock ledge, they attempted to control their shaking. Levi was the first to speak. "Getting out of that office in one piece is a miracle."

Seven days later, having received the permission seen in his vision, Mugabe stood on the shore, waiting and praying. Word had traveled the gossip circuit that government officials had given Mugabe permission to give "spiritual food of baptism" if those wanting it lined up single file and did not talk. The other requirements were one had to be over eighteen, unless accompanied by a parent. The line also had to be dispersed before noon.

Several spectators stood at a distance but disappeared when they saw lights coming towards them from a distance. Mugabe and Levi drew near each other for strength as two police jeeps with soldiers holding weapons pulled up beside them.

They both trembled and silently prayed as one of the policemen walked toward them. They gasped as they recognized him as the Chief of Police.

Head held high, he walked directly to Mugabe, took his weapon out of his holster, and said, "I am a friend of Nehemiah." He handed his gun and his hat, with its gold-cord-trimmed visor, to Levi. "I want to be the first man in Maputo to publicly announce I am a follower of the Lord Jesus Christ."

The Chief of Police followed Mugabe into the water. When it reached their waist, they stopped. Mugabe put one arm behind the Chief's shoulder, the other around his waist, embracing him and then easing him under the water as he said, “My brother, I baptize you in the name of *our* Lord and Savior Jesus Christ.”

As they stood upright, dripping, Mugabe placed his hand on the Chief’s head and blessed him. They walked back to shore.

The Chief took his hat and gun from Levi. As he turned to leave, he looked at Mugabe. “I have sent some men to unboard your church building. You are free to use it to worship our Lord.” He paused and added, “And to begin the Bible school Nehemiah told me about.” He turned to Levi with a knowing smile. “You’re a fine young man. I guess you’ll soon be pulling weeds from around the church.” Turning back to Mugabe, he said, “One final thing. Your friend, Dr. James, can come as often as he likes; no one will stop him.”

Mugabe and Levi watched as the Chief of Police got into his jeep and left. Before Mugabe could say anything, Levi shouted, “Look!” People started coming out of the shadows of the surrounding buildings. No one spoke as they lined up.

The sun came up, the people continued to come. At high noon, the long line of people, quiet and sweating, ignored the hot sun and any deadline as Levi dipped the people one by one, and Mugabe baptized them in the name of the Father, the Son, and the Holy Spirit.

Finally the sun and people disappeared. Only Mugabe and Levi remained, each already eager to start cleaning the church and enrolling students for their Bible school.

Another page of Mugabe’s vision had been fulfilled.

Mr. Maxwell thrashed furiously, as though his life depended on it—and it did. He wasn’t sure how he got into the water. Did he fall overboard or was it not an accident?

All he knew was he was fighting with all the strength his frail body could mobilize to keep from drowning in the wake of the passing ships. Between mouthfuls of water, his desperate cries for help went unheeded.

In those brief moments of reprieve, between surging waves, he caught sight of the great armada of vessels in whose wake he was sure to drown. There were men-of-war, bristling with antennas and guns, ready to expunge the opposition or at least bring them to their knees. There were elongated tankers barely riding above the waterline, loaded with processed oil that would fuel the great engines with power needed to fire off their battle plans. Following their wake was a vast cargo ship stacked high with containers of equipment for anticipated needs in fulfilling this great commission. And lagging far behind were two tugs, straining at their cables attached to a barge heaped high with a mountain of garbage.

With most of the armada ahead of him, Maxwell let down his guard to tread water. It was the wrong thing to do. He was thrown up in the air and down again by the largest backwash yet to hit him. Gaining his equilibrium, he saw a great luxury ship rush past him with the master of the fleet's flag flying from its mast. For a few fleeting seconds, Mr. Maxwell could see men, dressed in informal attire, sitting at computer tables, many with a cell phone at their ear, their minions standing at their elbows ready to respond to any command, large or small. Another wave hit and while gagging on the water, he saw painted on the bow: *U.S.S. Modernity.*

Catching a quick look into the distance, Maxwell could see all the ships heading for a very wide gate, silhouetted on both sides by steep mountains, through which they had to navigate on their way to conquer the world.

Mr. Maxwell's strength was nearly expended. He was close to giving up when he looked toward the shore. Silhouetted against the late afternoon sky, standing on the beach, was a young man. He was holding a book, shouting as he walked barefoot in the sand, "Honor the fathers...absorb the wisdom of our elders...bring them into our body...listen to them…"

Maxwell's strength was failing him and he began sinking into the water. He cried out to the Lord as he gulped a mouthful of water.

As his head surfaced, he saw the man on the beach set his Bible on the sand, then lean over to pick up something, a coiled rope. While holding onto one end, he threw the rest of the rope, with a mighty heave, directly towards him.

Maxwell shouted, "I'm saved!" as a fresh shot of adrenaline surged through his depleted body. He swam as hard as he could toward the rope, crying out, "I'm saved, praise God, I'm saved!" Totally exhausted, he lunged forward, grasped the end of the rope and pulled on it, waiting for it to grow taut so he could be pulled ashore to safety. He knew his strength was gone and this was his last chance to live.

Suddenly a terrible realization struck him. He let out a panicked cry as he looked at his hands. They held both ends of the rope.

He looked again toward the shore. He was close enough to make out a squiggly deep indentation in the sand from the rope, like a snake entering the water.

He lifted his eyes. Not far from the rope print, he saw the man who had thrown it standing with his book open in the midst of a circle of young people sitting next to a campfire. Darkness was falling.

Maxwell had become the victim of priority. He could not blame the man on the beach for moving his ministry from an old drowning man to a dozen young people—it was a choice between ministering to people of the past or people of the future.

Mr. Maxwell understood and let go of the rope. As it sank, he too sank into the depths.

"Sir. Sir."

Mr. Maxwell awoke, not sure where he was. All he knew was his clothes were dry, but he feared the voracious pain and nausea would pull him under again.

A young lady smiled at him as she lifted her hand from his shoulder and spoke apologetically in broken English, "Sir, we now land; you buckle seat belt and bring seat to upright position."

She spoke to the other passengers in a language he didn't understand. He closed his eyes for a moment, ran his tongue over his dry lips, and swallowed hard, holding back the nausea. He leaned his head back, breathing deeply as the nausea subsided. He held a small package wrapped in brown paper and string tightly against his abdomen.

Sitting next to him was a tall, dark-complexioned, distinguished-looking man with curly gray hair, wearing a well-tailored blue shirt and dark suit. He smiled at Mr. Maxwell. "You've had a good rest, honorable grandfather; you slept through breakfast."

He could see Maxwell was having difficulty holding onto his package and fastening his seat belt at the same time. With long, manicured fingers he reached over to help him fasten his seat belt, while quietly asking, "May I help you?"

Mr. Maxwell lifted his package and thanked him for his kindness.

That accomplished, Maxwell leaned back as much as he could with his seat in an upright position and breathed heavily. The pain continued its merciless assault on his body. He pressed the package against his body, as though it might alleviate some of the pain.

The plane bounced as it hit the ground. Mr. Maxwell nearly passed out as he prayed aloud, "Lord, help! Not yet!"

He slowly maneuvered his body out of his seat until he was standing in the aisle with the other passengers. He looked down at the small bag under his seat, his only luggage other than the brown package he still grasped firmly.

The gentleman smiled and picked up the bag. "Do not you worry, honorable grandfather. I'll help you."

Without speaking, Mr. Maxwell accepted the offer. The gentleman held tightly onto his elbow, guiding him, and holding him up as they headed toward the open door.

The stewardess wished them well just as they were hit by a blast of hot air from outside the plane. The stairs reaching to the ground looked to Maxwell like the devil's last hurdle.

"Honorable grandfather, you hold onto your package and let me help you down." The guardian angel reached one arm around Mr. Maxwell's back and with the other, took a firm grip on his arm, helped him down the stairs, and guided him to the terminal, where a policeman opened the door for them.

The blast of cold air that greeted them was as invigorating as the hot air had been debilitating. The gentleman walked Mr. Maxwell over to a long line where people stood with their hand luggage and passports. He set Mr. Maxwell's bag at his feet and asked if he had his passport. Maxwell fumbled around in his suitcoat pocket and brought it out.

He put his passport in the same hand that held the brown package, which was now pressed against his chest. He reached out with his free hand and shook the hand of the gentleman as he attempted to thank him.

Mr. Maxwell watched him walk to a short line across the room, where he spoke to a uniformed official. Both glanced at Mr. Maxwell and nodded in his direction as the gentlemen disappeared through a door marked *Exit.*

The line ahead of him was moving very slowly. Nausea and pain were fighting for a gold medal when the uniformed official appeared in front of him.

Anxiety pushed aside the nausea and pain as the officer asked for his passport. With trembling hand, he handed it to him. The official looked at it, picked up his luggage, and said, "Follow me."

The journey had been so long—so many days, so many nights—would it end without ever being finished?

The official led him to the head of the short line. His passport was stamped with a smile and a welcome to their country, then handed back to him as he was motioned on. The security officer who took Maxwell out of the longer line picked up his bag and put the strap over Mr. Maxwell's shoulder. He also welcomed him to their country and pointed to the door the gentleman had exited through.

Tears welled up in Maxwell's eyes as he thanked them and slowly headed for the door, asking the Lord to forgive him for being a man of such little faith.

As he exited, the blast of hot air hit him again, but it could not compare with the warmth of being greeted with outstretched arms and hearing, "Welcome to Mozambique, father of Via Mahondra."

"Brother Mugabe! At last!" Maxwell cried, oblivious to the stares of those watching a white man and a black man embracing each other.

Taking Maxwell's luggage, Mugabe led him across a parking lot to the Land Rover that had brought Mugabe and his family to Maputo. It still had no roof or windshield.

Mugabe asked Mr. Maxwell about his flight. Mr. Maxwell said it had been very long and told about the kindnesses of the gentleman who had helped him. "He was the one who came out the terminal door just before I did."

"But you were the first to exit," Mugabe replied.

"Are you sure? He was tall, in a very nice suit."

"No, Mr. Maxwell," Mugabe chuckled, "you were the first to come out. He must have left by another way."

Mugabe put Maxwell's bag behind the seat and helped him in. After some pleading, the Land Rover came to life. As they turned onto a dirt road, Mugabe said, "Where we are going first will only take ten minutes. Then we'll go to my house, where Diolinda has prepared a feast to welcome you to Mozambique. She and our son, Levi, have been working on it since we heard you were coming at last to honor us with your presence."

Mr. Maxwell, lost in deep thought, did not answer.

After a few miles on what passed for a road, Mugabe pulled up to at a small, whitewashed building with a cross rising over the entrance.

Mugabe helped Mr. Maxwell from the Land Rover. Maxwell firmly held his package against his body with both hands.

Mugabe pointed past the church building. "It's just around the back; you can't miss it." Mugabe was moved by Mr. Maxwell's physical and emotional frailty. "I'll wait here."

With a look of gratitude, Mr. Maxwell thanked him. As he rounded the church, he stopped to take in the view of a small, recently manicured, burial plot.

Slowly Mr. Maxwell walked to a large wooden cross and knelt. He traced the carved words with his fingertips: *Randy "Via Mahondra" Maxwell.* Below it were the words, *He loved us.*

He struggled to remove the string from the paper. His hands trembled. Finally succeeding, he slowly removed the brown wrapping, revealing the black-velvet-framed picture of Jesus' tearstained face. His lips trembled and his shoulders heaved as he put one hand on the cross and tightly clasped the picture, crying, "My son, my son. Forgive me."

Mr. Maxwell continued lovingly running his fingers over the carved letters of his son's name, whispering and weeping, "Together at last." He felt a hand on his shoulder.

"Come, Via Mahondra's father, we will return later. You are very tired and need some food and rest."

Mugabe helped him stand. Maxwell took one long last look at his son's grave, leaning the picture of Jesus against the foot of the cross.

Mugabe led Mr. Maxwell back to the Land Rover. "Our home is not far from here, not more than another ten minutes. Why don't you lean back and rest? I will drive as carefully as possible."

Mr. Maxwell acknowledged Mugabe and lay his head back. With his hands on his lap, he closed his eyes. Mugabe noticed his face relaxing into a smile, as though the pain had ceased.

Mr. Maxwell felt himself sliding effortlessly down into water. A school of thousands of tiny blue fish came toward him. Suddenly, they made a sharp turn in unison and disappeared.

He floated in slow motion, water and peace indistinguishable. Ahead he saw a bright slit of light. With no effort on his part, the current carried him directly to the opening. He reached for the light, but the opening was too narrow.

As time no longer mattered, he slipped his watch off. The current carried it away.

He reached out again, and his arm slid through the slit. Turning sideways, he attempted to slide his body through. The opening was too narrow. He took his wallet from his pocket, watching as his credit cards fell out and were carried away by the current.

He made another attempt to slide through the opening. Almost. Removing his shoes and clothes, he now had nothing. Turning sideways, he slid through, naked.

Coming out on the other side, he was enveloped by light and water and peace. Weightless, the current carried him along. There was no sound, no fear, no struggling.

Suddenly his feet touched down. He stood up and splashed toward a shore. Someone was standing there, smiling, in a dazzling white robe. His outstretched arms held another robe.

Mr. Maxwell stumbled toward the young man who looked much the same as on that terrible day Maxwell hid behind his living room curtain.

The young man put the robe around Maxwell before they fell into a tight embrace. Standing back, he placed his hands on Maxwell's shoulders, saying, "Welcome home, my father. Our Savior has prepared a feast to welcome you. Come…."

Mugabe pulled to a sudden stop in front of his house. He could smell the food Diolinda had prepared. He turned to Mr. Maxwell, who still had his head back on the seat. "Here we are. Time for some food and rest."

As Mugabe got out of the Land Rover, Levi came running to the other side. He opened the door. Mr. Maxwell's arm dropped down, his hand opened, and Levi felt something land on his foot.

Diolinda came to stand beside Mugabe. No one had to tell her; she knew.

Levi leaned over and picked up the crumpled brown paper and string. "Well, Father, I guess we can call it redemption."

"Yes, son, just call it redemption."

All of the
author's royalties
go to

Abana Bumwami Child's Foundation

for children with aids in Africa

Abana Bumwami Children's Foundation (ABC)

The Abana Bumwami Children's Foundation (ABC) was established in 2003 by Pastor Francis Mutabazi of Christ Gospel Fellowship Church in Kigali, Rwanda.

Partnering with churches in the US, ABC provides education, medical care, food, and spiritual growth for hundreds of Rwandan children.

The children and teenagers of ABC who benefit from this sponsorship include:

- Orphans from AIDS and the genocide
- Children who are infected with HIV/AIDS or whose parents are
- Children living in extreme property

For more information on the ABC program:
www.limitlessboundaries.org/africarwanda.htmlcontact

Email: ABC@calvarylahabra.org
Phone: (714) 446-6222

About the Author

Carl Lawrence is a missionary journalist whose heart burns with true stories that will only be believed if read as fiction. "This book has been burning in my heart for years," Carl says. "My purpose for writing was to demonstrate through story the truth that even when 'man means it for evil, God means it for good.' All three protagonists long to have the mind of Jesus, whatever the cost. If any of the protagonists fail to think like Jesus, they will remain comfortable, typical Christians instead of becoming genuine disciples of Christ answering the call to 'Follow Me.'

"My initial working title was *Mugabe, Murphy, and Maxwell.* However, to me, *Just Call It Redemption* is the title, the theme, the continuing thread. My hope is that readers will desire discipleship, both to be discipled and to have opportunity to disciple after reading this story. My goal is to show God revealing biblical truths within the context of one's culture. This book is about the hard realities of ministry and discipleship. It's about real people and real events told in novel form. It's about God's power to redeem situations and people in spite of the forces of evil."

Carl has 35 years' experience with Far East Broadcasting Co. He won a Gold Medallion for his best-selling *The Church In China* (Bethany; Shannon Publishers, translated in 4 languages). Other titles of his include *Majken* (Thomas Nelson); *Rwanda: A walk through darkness* (Vision House); *The Cross and the Sword* (Shannon Publishers); *Oh India, My India* (Shannon Publishers); *The Prince Still Smiled* (Tyndale; translated into 5 languages); and *The Broken Letter* (Shannon Publishers).

For more information: **www.oaktara.com**